She looked down. A dark mist rose from the valley which only a moment ago had been green. Was it a mist? Distinctly, she smelled smoke and saw flames. Then, like an exhalation from the earth itself, the darkness swirled up to engulf her. All creation was black and boiling.

What was happening was unreal, she thought frantically. It was no more real than the flash flood at the fording yesterday and the harmless gecko that had become a ravenous dragon last night.

Margal, she thought. *The man with no legs. We're getting close and he doesn't want us.*

THE EVIL

HUGH B. CAVE

CHARTER
NEW YORK

A Division of Charter Communications Inc.
A GROSSET & DUNLAP COMPANY
51 Madison Avenue
New York, New York 10010

An Ace Charter Original

First Ace Charter Printing: November, 1981
Published simultaneously in Canada
Manufactured in the United States of America

2 4 6 8 0 9 7 5 3 1

For Richard

1

High in a mountain clearing
in a red, red house
in the wilds of Haiti,
black candles burn
in a room of many colors.

The night is nearly over.

A man of middle age,
sandy beard and thinning sandy hair,
white skin,
stands unblinking before a chair like a throne.
A Haitian with no legs
sits there.

The two talk in silence,
without moving their lips.

"You are ready to depart, Dr. Bell?"
"I am ready."
"You understand your instructions?"
"Yes."
"On whom will you call?"
"I will call on Decatus Molicoeur."
"Where does he live?"
"In Port-au-Prince."

"Where in Port-au-Prince?"
"Turgeau."
"Where in Turgeau?"
"Number twenty-three Rue Coiron."
"Close your eyes."

The white man's eyes stop staring.
Those of the legless man glow red.

"I am telling you to do something, Dr. Bell.
What am I telling you to do?"
"To kneel."
"Why are you not kneeling, then?"

Dr. Bell kneels.

"Open your eyes."
The eyes open.
"Get up."
Dr. Bell rises.
"What will you tell Decatus Molicoeur
when he is kneeling before you?"
"I will tell him to kill."
"Kill whom?"
"The president."

The legless one nods.

"You seem to have learned well, my friend.
Let's hope you have also learned to obey.
Your guide is waiting outside.
Now, go."

2

Nothing much had changed.

He had been away more than two years, yet his last journey over this road from the airport to the city might have been yesterday, for all the difference he could discern. True, he had tried out his Creole on the Haitian cab driver and found it rusty, but he had expected that. To stay fluent in a language, you had to use it, and you sure couldn't use Haitian Creole in Vermont. He would have to re-learn it if the hunt for Mildred's father took them into the boonies.

He thought of Kay Gilbert. Beautiful, loving, crazy Kay Gilbert. To become fluent in Creole—he for his AID job in agriculture and she for her nursing at the Schweitzer—they had sometimes agreed to speak no English for a whole evening. Not even in bed. Was she still at the Schweitzer? He had never written. Why keep the memory alive when he would never be seeing her again?

("All you really wanted, Sam Norman, was someone to sleep with, wasn't it? Well, to hell with you. To hell with you twice over, and from now on kindly stay out of my life!")

She'd been wrong, of course. Sleeping with her was by no means all he had wanted. But who could argue with a furious Kay Gilbert?

He stopped remembering and looked at the woman beside him. She was beautiful, too. Taller than Kay, and blonde; Kay had the blackest hair in creation. But this woman was even more likely to win a beauty contest. Except that, being the daughter of a world renowned teacher of philosophy, she would of course never dream of entering one.

Unaware of his silent appraisal, she frowned through the window on her side at the massed shacks of La Saline, the city's worst slum. She hadn't been prepared for such squalor, he guessed. Being her father's daughter, she had read up on Haiti when Daddy announced his intention of spending the summer here, but reading about a La Saline and seeing one were not the same. Could reading about the smell of rotting garbage, donkey dirt, and human urine prepare you for such a bouquet—plus, all at once, the unexpected, glorious aroma of roasting coffee? This road from the airport to Port-au-Prince passed through some of the worst poverty in the Caribbean.

Slowed by outrageous potholes, the taxi crept past a black woman riding side-saddle on a donkey which was a mass of sores and wore an expression of eternal sadness. The ancient baskets bumping its washboard ribs were filled with charcoal. The woman saw Mildred staring at her and waved. From one dusty foot dangled a worn leather sandal.

Sam laughed.

Startled, Mildred turned her head to look at him.

"It's nothing. Just the sandal. Something that happened once."

If Kay were here now, would she laugh too? Why, for God's sake, hadn't he written to her at least once, if only to find out whether she really had been that furious? *Was* she still at the hospital?

What difference did it make? He wouldn't have time

to look her up, anyway. Classes had already begun back in Vermont. As soon as they located Milly's father, the three of them would be winging back there.

Mildred continued to look at him, waiting for him to say more. When conversing with this lady, you were not expected to leave things dangling; her esteemed daddy never did. Annoyed at last by his continued silence, she shrugged her shapely shoulders and went back to peering out the window.

Deciding there was nothing new to see, Sam shut his eyes. After all, he had spent two years in this West Indian land of voodoo, poverty, problems, and passion. Port-au-Prince, to his way of thinking, was the least interesting part of Haiti, anyway. Only when he felt the cab slowing to a crawl and making an acute left turn did he open his eyes again.

They had arrived.

The Pension Calman was where he had left it, he was glad to find out. As before, it was almost directly across the Champ-de-Mars from the Palais National. The big central park was brown and dusty. There was need of rain, it seemed. The palace, as always, was a shimmering white mausoleum fronted by khaki-clad soldiers on sentry duty. Home in years past of Papa Doc Duvalier, who had been president for life and had died recently, it was now the abode of Papa's son Jean Claude, who was also president for life and seemed likely to live a long time.

"What are we stopping here for?" The Calman was obviously not the sort of hostel for which Mildred had prepared herself—was, in fact, only a very old private home converted into a guest house. Gingerbread trim was everywhere. Gray paint flaking off to expose wood on which termites were having a feast. A high stone wall with stone columns flanking the driveway entrance, a rusty iron gate hanging open. The yard inside was paved with red bricks so ludicrously uneven that the house appeared to be an ancient ocean-going ferry kicking up waves.

"This is it, Milly."

"You sent Daddy *here?*"

"It's what he asked for."

("Under no circumstances, Sam, do I want to go to one of those plush tourist hotels I've been reading about. You understand? Do you know of some small pension where I won't have to waste time dressing for meals and talking to strangers?"

("I know just the place, sir. Used to go there myself every time I hit the city for a few days." Which had been about once a month, because all work and no play in the south-coast town of Jacmel, dealing with barefoot farmers and hearing only Creole spoken, could make Jack a very dull boy.)

Sliding out of the cab, he stepped around to open her door, then watched the driver lift their luggage from the trunk and paid him. Trying his Creole again with a generous tip—*"Sa sé pou ou, compère"*—he got a grin full of white teeth and a quick, *"Merci ampil, M'sieu!"* in reply. The fellow carried the bags into the pension's big front parlor and set them down. He grinned again and departed. The parlor was empty except for Sam and Mildred. They stood there, waiting.

After a while Sam called out tentatively, "Hello! Anyone home?"

From somewhere in back, a voice answered, "Coming!" and a patter of footsteps followed. Into the room bustled a short, fragile, almost bald man in black pants, white sneakers, and an immaculate white shirt with a black bow tie. Jerking to a halt, he thrust his head forward like a turtle and voiced a yell of delight. "Sam Norman!"

"Victor Vieux!"

The Calman's owner rushed forward and clapped his

hands on Sam's arms. He stood there shaking Sam in a way that surely would have loosened some roots had Sam been a tree.

"Victor, this is Miss Mildred Bell."

Vieux stepped back and looked at her. "Dr. Bell's daughter?" He put out his hand. "My pleasure, M'selle."

"What about her father?" Sam asked.

Vieux nodded gravely. "Just as soon as I have taken you to your rooms." He reached for the luggage, but was not as young and husky as the cab driver and could not handle three bags at once. Sam quickly grabbed his own, then followed Vieux and Mildred up the wide, curving staircase. The carpet was threadbare, he noticed. The wallpaper was peeling. Maybe the place had been as shabby before but he just hadn't noticed. Mildred Bell had not been with him then.

"You have other guests, Victor?"

"At the moment, no."

They went along the upstairs hall and the little proprietor stopped at a white door with a tarnished brass number 4 on it. "For you, Sam, the room you always used. Remember?"

"You bet." (Did Kay still remember?)

"The door is open. Just go in and make yourself at home, eh? I am putting Miss Bell in five. These two bags are yours, Miss Bell?"

"Yes."

Sam watched them go down the hall to the room Kay had always used when she came to town from the Schweitzer. She had come in about as often as he had from Jacmel. The American, Dr. Mellon, had built the hospital out in the country because that was where the neediest people were, but there was little out there for a nurse to do on her day off.

He stepped into his room and looked at the bed.

Above it on the wall was the same framed photograph of the sacred voodoo waterfall at Saut d'Eau, clipped from an old *Life* magazine. He put his bag down, shut the door, walked to the bed, and stretched out on it.

Kay, baby . . . remember? When he shut his eyes and put his hand out, she was right there. He could *feel* her there.

He had first met her here in the Calman. "Kay, I want you to know a good friend of mine," Victor Vieux had said. "He's a Yankee, like you, working on that agricultural thing near Jacmel. Sam, Miss Kay Gilbert. One of Dr. Mellon's nurses at the Schweitzer."

Weather permitting, you ate your meals outdoors at the Calman: out there in the backyard on that rolling red-brick sea. One of the tables stood under a tropical almond tree whose big, gaudy leaves were likely to come floating down without warning and land on your plate. A leaf had fallen between them that evening and both had reached for it, catching each other's hands. A mere beginning but a good one. He even remembered the meal: breadfruit croquettes and a fish stew that Victor lovingly called court bouillon. The Calman was not renowned for the quality of its food. Only for the warmth of its owner's friendship.

Reluctantly, he got off the bed and shucked his jacket and tie, shifting his wallet to a hip pocket of the brown slacks he wore. There came a tapping of knuckles on his door.

"Sam? Can we go downstairs now?"

"Sure." He had the door open at once. Mildred was anxious to talk to Victor, of course. He was surprised to find her still wearing the gray wool dress she had traveled in. In such an outfit she must feel herself in a sauna here. With Mildred, first things always came first.

"I don't want to rush you, Sam, but—"

"No problem. You don't want to change into something cool?"

"Later."

They found the Calman's proprietor waiting for them in the downstairs parlor. He had drawn three chairs in a triangle around a small table which held three glasses of something pink. He rose and beckoned them to join him. "Marie will have some food ready for you in a few minutes. I'm sure you want to talk first." The three of them sat and he leaned toward Mildred. "Now, Miss Bell, to answer your questions . . ."

"There's only one, really. Where is my father?"

"I can only tell you where he should be. Whether or not he actually got there, no one can say without going there."

"We can't reach him by telephone? Or send a wire?"

"There isn't even a road." Vieux turned to Sam. "You know the mountains south of Fort Liberté. The Massif du Nord. You rode in there once with that U.N. fellow and mailed me a letter from Vallière, just to see if I'd ever get it."

Sam nodded. "Ah, yes. The famous letter."

"Dr. Bell's destination was a place beyond Vallière, even more remote. Have you ever heard of a man named Margal?"

"I don't think so, Victor."

"He is a *bocor,* a sorcerer, who seems to have made quite a name for himself in the past year or so—like that fellow Fenelon you clashed with in Jacmel." Vieux shifted his gaze back to Mildred. "Your father, Miss Bell, heard about this Margal at a voodoo affair in Croix-des-Bouquets. That's in the Cul de Sac, not far from here. A man named Ti Pierre Bastien, whom he hired originally as a driver and interpreter, volunteered to take him into the Massif du Nord to visit the fellow.

I saw a good deal of Bastien. He hung around here a lot. I didn't like him. Didn't trust him, perhaps I should say. But Dr. Bell would not listen to me."

Sam said, "You mean you tried to talk him out of going?"

"I did. Those mountains are not for people who know nothing about this country and don't even speak the peasants' language."

Sam recalled the last letter Mildred had received from her father. No mention of an impending journey—perhaps he hadn't made up his mind at that time—but there had been a hint of something brewing. "I am hoping soon to meet a man whose reputation for possessing truly remarkable psychic powers is widespread. I cannot tell you more than this at the moment, but I am working on it." That letter had arrived in Vermont more than a month ago, and since then, nothing. Before the sudden silence he had written weekly; and he had planned to return for the start of classes.

"You told me on the phone, Victor, that Dr. Bell left here on the seventh of August." Today was the nineteenth of September.

"Correct."

"He and this fellow Bastien?"

"He and Bastien, in a rented jeep. Their plan was to drive to Trou and hire animals there for the rest of the journey." Turning to Mildred, Victor explained that Trou was a town on the north coast between Cap Haïtien and Fort Liberté. "When I heard nothing for what seemed too long a time, I telephoned the police at Trou. They got that far. The jeep is there. But the only way to trace them farther is to go there."

"The police will not look for them?" Mildred asked.

"I'm afraid I have to say, 'Why should they?' Miss Bell. In any case, Trou is a very small place. I doubt the police there would be able to send out a search party."

"I just can't imagine my father doing this kind of thing, Mr. Vieux." Mildred looked at Sam.

Sam knew the reason for the look. Riding off into Haiti's high-mountain wilderness was the sort of thing Sam Norman would do for kicks, and had done, in fact, more than once. But it was the kind of behavior Dr. Roger Bell had been quick to criticize. "I can't see much compatibility between you and my daughter, Norman. The two of you are poles apart in temperament. Now she tells me you want to give up teaching and take a forestry job with some paper company, which would never suit her, of course. She just isn't the outdoor type." This, when Daddy, sensing there might be something brewing between them, had decided to put a quick stop to it. "Are you laughing at me by any chance, Mr. Norman?" Nobody at the college laughed with impunity at Roger Bell.

"Not at you, sir. Just at your idea that I might be contemplating marriage." *Did I ask you for your daughter's hand, Daddy? All I've done is take her out a few times.*

"So what will you do?" Victor Vieux was asking.

Sam wrenched himself back from the campus. "Show me Margal's village on a map, will you?"

"It isn't on any map I have. But I can show you about where to find it."

The drinks on the table were still untouched, and while Victor went across the room to a bookcase, Sam handed one glass to Mildred and lifted another to his lips. It was Rhum Barbancourt with lime and grenadine, and it gave him a needed lift.

When he returned, Victor moved the third glass to the floor and spread an oil-company map marked "Carte de la République d'Haiti" on the table.

"According to Bastien, the place is called Legrun. It's a few miles south of Bois Sauvage here." The village he pointed to was surrounded by a roadless wilderness of mountains.

"And they went in from Trou, you say." Sam looked at Mildred. "Here's Trou, up near the coast, Milly."

"It must be miles." The note of hopelessness in her voice came through loud and clear.

"And very rough going, you can be sure," Victor said.

"But we have to do it, Sam. We can't just sit here and wait."

"I have to do it. Not you."

"Uh-uh." She shook her head. "I'm not helpless. I can ride, and I've actually done some mountain climbing."

"Where?"

"Well, I've climbed Marcy and Whiteface in the Adirondacks."

"Marcy and Whiteface. Ah, yes." Sam tried to keep his voice even. "Milly, those are civilized mountains for hobby hikers. If you think Haiti's Massif du Nord—"

"If Daddy did it, I can do it."

"Victor, tell her it's no trip for a woman."

"He's right, Miss Bell. Besides, climbing a mountain the way you mean is not the same as hanging onto the back of an animal while he—"

"That's enough, please, both of you." Mildred rose suddenly. "He's my father, and I came here to find him, not to sit around a hotel while someone else does. May we have something to eat, Mr. Vieux?"

Abruptly donning an expression of blank neutrality, the little man with the black bow tie obediently led them into the garden. Was it coincidence that he seated them at the same table Kay Gilbert and Sam had used the day he introduced them to each other? Sam glanced up at the almond tree with its canopy of multicolored leaves. Then as he held Mildred's chair for her, he found himself gazing at the precise center of the round table where the leaf had come looping down and he and Kay had caught each other's hands while reaching for it.

The chairs were different colors. Mildred chose a cool blue one. Sam walked around the table and took a bright yellow enameled one opposite her. Victor Vieux excused himself and returned to the house.

"Sam," Mildred said after a short stillness, "I hope you don't think I'm being unreasonable."

He shrugged. "It's strictly up to you, Milly." After all, he was here in her interest, not his own. ("I'm frightened, Sam," she had said. "He promised to write at least once a week, and it's now more than a month. He would never do that unless he couldn't help it. Will you fly down there with me to find out what's happened?" And when he had hesitated: "Sam, you've *worked* in Haiti. It would be so much easier, with you to advise me.")

In Victor Vieux's little garden Sam leaned over the table now to put his face closer to hers. "We won't make it from Trou to Legrun in a day, you know, Milly. It could take two or three."

"That long?" She looked startled. "On horseback?"

"Muleback. And we won't be on their backs too much of the time, I'm warning you. We'll be leading them up or down gullies, washouts, stream beds, all kinds of stretches where it won't be safe to ride. You'll hate the very sight of a mule before you're finished." *And what will Daddy think of his daughter's spending her nights in a wilderness with Sam Norman?*

"I'm sorry, Sam. I'm sure you know better than I do. But I have to do it."

"Okay."

"And look." She seemed genuinely contrite as she reached over the table to touch his hand. "I'm sorry I criticized this place when I first saw it. I just didn't expect—"

"It was a natural reaction. No need to apologize."

"It's really nice, Sam. I like it. If we could be here under different circumstances, I'm sure I'd like it a lot."

That was how it was with this girl. Every now and then she surprised the hell out of you.

3

After lunch Victor Vieux offered to drive Sam to a place in Lalue where he could rent a jeep. It was not an altogether altruistic gesture, Sam soon discovered. The Calman's proprietor also wanted to talk, and began doing so the moment his little Renault was out of the yard.

"Tell me about this Dr. Bell, Sam. What kind of man is he?"

"That's a big order."

"He has several faces, you mean?"

"More than one, for sure. First, he's head of the philosophy department at the college where I teach agriculture. The highly respected head, I should add. He has a number of well-regarded books to his credit. But he's deeply into all kinds of psychic research now, as well. ESP. Telekinesis. Possession. Telepathy. Thought-healing. You name it and if it's even a little off the beaten track, he's chasing it. At the moment it's voodoo, and that's partly my fault."

"In what way is it your fault?"

"As soon as he found out I'd spent a couple of years in Haiti, he began pumping me. And believe me, Victor, he's a real quiz whiz. By the time I'd called on his daughter half a dozen times, he knew all I knew about voodoo, zombiism, witchcraft, the whole Haitian bit. Even a lot that I didn't know but had only heard about and repeated to him because he sort of sucked it out of me."

"I see."

"Next thing I knew, he'd decided to spend his summer vacation here doing research, and I was writing to you, asking you to put him up and do what you could to help him." Sam gave his companion a quizzical look. "I take it you found him interesting too, or you wouldn't be asking me these questions."

Victor was silent while waiting for a break in traffic on the Petionville road. It was always fast and thick here. He made his right-hand turn and said, "Dr. Bell seems to be a strange man, Sam. He returned from one trip into the country with a drum. A petro. Would you believe he played it by the hour in his room, even late at night?"

"Sounds like him," Sam said drily.

"I had to ask him to stop. Other guests were complaining."

"Did he stop?"

"The drumming, yes. Not everything."

"What do you mean, not everything?"

Victor had to brake sharply at that moment to avoid a wild-eyed taxi driver trying to pass a camion. By the time the Renault was free of the ensuing confusion, he had reached the side road he wanted and turned onto it. Then before they could resume the conversation, they had arrived at their destination.

It was not a rental agency or a garage; it was simply the hillside home of a friend who owned a jeep and occasionally lent it out. His name was Blanchet. After talking to Victor, he turned with a frown of concern to Sam.

"You have driven one of these things before, M'sieu?"

"All over Haiti. I worked with AID for two years."

"Good. You know what to expect, then, of both the machine and our magnificent roads."

Sam grinned. "I think so, friend."

Sam rented the vehicle for a week. "I'd better stop on the way back and buy a few things," he said to Victor Vieux.

"Such as what?"

"We'll need blankets—"

"I have some you can use."

"And, well—*things*." Sam realized he was a little tired. As he turned to climb into the jeep he suddenly remembered a question that had been on his lips half a dozen times earlier, and walked back over to the Renault. "Victor, tell me something." Laying a hand on the small man's shoulder, he gazed intently into his face, almost afraid to put the question now.

"What is it, *mon ami?* Or can I guess?"

"Kay Gilbert. Is she still here?"

"I wondered if you would ask. Yes, she is still here. I have scarcely seen her since you left Haiti, but she is here." He gave the hand on his shoulder a little pat of reassurance, and a smile played along his lips. "Now, about these items you say you must shop for. Follow me back to my place, eh? I can supply most of what you need, I am sure. Perhaps everything."

Sam only nodded. It was a little hard to speak with a tightness in your throat.

So she was still here. But how, in God's name, faced with this journey into the mountains, would he be able to see her?

He followed Victor back to the pension, getting the feel of the jeep quickly. It took him back to the Jacmel days, and he realized Dr. Bell was at least partly right: He did have a streak of the rebel in him, at least to the extent of liking to drive one of these rugged little beasts better than his more civilized car in the States. Pulling into the pension yard behind Victor, he leaped out as in the old days and strode ahead to the Renault.

"Victor, have a drink with me."

"Of course. Over there at your table?"

"You're reading my thoughts."

"You don't hide them too well."

When they were seated, Victor reached for a little bell on the table and gave it a shake. Its tinkle rang like a bird call through the yard, and a young, slim black girl came from the house. There were only eight rooms in the Calman. Victor employed only a cook, a pair of maids who doubled as waitresses, and a yard boy who solemnly swept up the almond leaves every morning. All of them lived in a building that was just barely discernible at the far end of the yard, and all looked upon Victor Vieux as someone close to God. Or, as they would have put it, *Le Bon Dieu*.

"Hello, Marie, how are you?" Sam said to the girl, and she smiled, using his name as she answered.

"Barbancourt?" Victor suggested.

"On the rocks this time."

Victor spoke to Marie and she hurried away. Sam leaned forward.

"Is Kay really here? After all this time?"

"She is."

"And still sore with me? My God, I was drunk that night. You know it. Realizing I had to go away and probably wouldn't see her again . . . I was a proper bastard."

Victor studied him. "You know something, *mon ami?* She has never discussed that night with me. Of course, I know you were not your usual self. I helped to put you to bed when you came crashing down the stairs, you may remember. Or do you? Anyway, I know nothing of what happened before that, in your room. As I said before, I have seen little of Kay since you left."

"Can I call her, Victor? Do the phones work?"

"They work sometimes. You could try."

"After we've had our drink. Because I'll have to be out of here at daybreak, and if I don't get her on the phone today—"

The girl had come with the drinks. Victor laughed softly when he saw Sam gulping.

"Go and call her, then come back. You remember the number?"

"It's still the same?"

"Still the same. And so are you, I believe, in spite of the puzzling things that happened that day. Go on."

The telephone was by the bar; there were no phones in the Calman's rooms. While waiting for the operator to put him through, Sam poured a drink to quiet the thudding in his chest. It was no easy thing to do one-handed, he discovered. You had to reach for a glass, then for a bottle, then get the cap off the bottle . . . he had never been one of those enviable characters who could prop a telephone between shoulder and ear, leaving both hands free. *Just another indication you're not the office type, Norman.*

Suddenly, the Schweitzer Hospital was talking to him. That modern hospital in the dust, the mud, the poverty of the Haitian boonies built by an American millionaire who had so admired *the* Albert Schweitzer that in his forties he had become a doctor in the U.S., then gone to Haiti and dedicated his life to helping others. Doctor and wife, both of them.

"Is Miss Gilbert there? Kay Gilbert? This is Sam Norman in Port-au-Prince."

It was a bad connection. *"Who* is calling?"

"Sam Norman. An old friend of hers, just in from Stateside."

"I'll try, Mr. Norman. Just hang on, please."

It took forever, and the phone buzzed and clicked,

and he heard people talking in both English and Creole but couldn't quite make anything out. There was a background humming noise as though someone were using a vacuum cleaner—it was probably a floor polisher—and, of all things, the faint sound of a radio playing "Yellow Bird," which of course wasn't "Yellow Bird" at all but a Haitian meringue called "Choucoune," with words by one of the country's talented poets, Oswald Durand, and melody so far back in folklore that no one remembered its origin.

"Mr. Norman?"

"Yes?" *You need another drink, Mister, or your chest is going to explode. But not now. Wait.*

"I'm sorry, but Nurse Gilbert is not here. She left about an hour ago.".

"Left for where? Port au-Prince?" If so, she might be coming here to the Calman. Glory be! Except that she didn't come here now . . . did she?

"Not to Port, Mr. Norman. She's gone north, to Cap Haitien."

"Oh, my God. I'll be passing through Le Cap tomorrow. Where can I look for her?"

"Well"—a pause—"she isn't going to Le Cap exactly, just passing through there to some village in the hills, to take a little girl home. I'm afraid, unless you want to make an expedition of it—"

"When will she be returning?" He couldn't interrupt his own mission to follow Kay into the boonies. "If it's tomorrow, I may pass her on the road."

"Not for several days, I'm afraid. Certainly not tomorrow."

"Well . . . thanks. Thank you." The tumult in his chest had subsided, and something in there felt like a blob of lead. He replaced the phone on its stand and finished his drink. Signed the chit "Norman, 1 large rum," and got up as though he weighed ten pounds more than when he had sat down. *Kay, baby, is it true you never talked to Victor about that night? Was it that bad? I'm sorry, Kay. Oh my God, I'm sorry.*

Returning to the garden table, he sank onto his chair and reached for the drink he had left there. Shook his head at Victor while downing it. "She's not there."

"Well, you could stop tomorrow. It's out of your way, of course, but—"

"She won't be there tomorrow."

"On your way back, then." Obviously, Victor wanted the two of them to get together. His face wore a look of sadness. Glancing at Sam's empty glass, he said, "Another one, *mon ami?*"

"No, thanks."

"Come with me for a minute, then, before we go to work on what you will need for your journey. I want to show you something I find very curious." Rising, he waited for Sam, then turned and walked briskly across the red-brick pavement to the house.

They climbed the rear stairs to the second floor, and the little proprietor turned to the room nearest the top of the staircase. Number 8. Opening the door with a key, he motioned Sam to enter, but Sam paused first to look down the hall at 5.

That door was closed. Evidently, Mildred was resting as she had said she would. The long flight, the heat, the discovery that her father might be in really serious trouble . . . she must be pretty tired.

She would be a lot more tired, he thought, by the time they reached that place where her father was supposed to be. *Get all the sleep you can, lady. You'll need it.* Then, walking on into 8, which overlooked the garden they had ascended from, he turned to see what Victor wanted of him.

The little man shut the door and said, "Sit down, Sam. Please."

Sam lowered himself onto a chair and looked around. The room contained two straight-backed painted chairs, a bed, a bureau with a mirror, and a closet, the door of which was open. Beside the bureau stood a drum about three feet tall made from the gouged-out trunk of a tree, its goatskin head tightened with ropes that ran crisscross to its base. There were no designs or markings on it. Petro, he thought. On the bureau stood two crudely made earthenware jars a foot high covered with intricate daubings of paint, one, mostly black and white; the other, rose, green, and red. There were clothes hanging from a wooden rod in the closet and under them a large lightweight piece of luggage with a Pan Am tag still affixed to its handle.

"His room?" Sam asked.

Victor nodded.

"If he left all these clothes here, he couldn't have taken much into the mountains."

"Only a duffle bag with the bare necessities. I advised him to buy some khaki pants and shirts, and he did that."

"You said you wanted to show me something."

"Yes." Victor sat on the edge of the bed and fixed his gaze on the drum beside the bureau. "Listen." There followed a silence that seemed to last a long while. Then he sais quietly, "You hear?"

Sam tested the stillness and shook his head, frankly puzzled.

"Listen very hard. Now. You hear it?"

I hear something. What the hell is it?—My pulse suddenly pounding? Or are invisible fingers tapping that drum, for God's sake? Sam stood, walked over to the drum and scowled down at it. If the drum were making the noise, it would have to be moving, wouldn't it? Vibrating, at least. It wasn't. He turned his head to peer at

Victor on the bed, then placed a fingertip on the goatskin drumhead.

Nothing. Nothing at all. But the sound continued, like a heartbeat in the room's silence.

"Look at the *govis*," Victor whispered.

Sam's gaze went to the bureau. *What the hell . . .*

The two jars were in motion now. Or had they been in motion all along, just as the drum could have been throbbing when he first entered the room. They trembled and swayed, only a very little, true, but it was motion all the same. He reached for them; if they became more active they might walk off the bureau and break on the floor.

"Don't bother," Victor said. "They don't get violent. I sometimes wonder if they actually move at all." He paused, then said, "Put your ear to them."

Sam drew his hand back. The jars continued to sway and tremble—if it wasn't just his imagination—but Victor was right. They seemed to be in no danger. He bent his head over the one nearest him. With his ear close to its four-inch-wide mouth, he heard a sound of singing. Both jars were singing. Chanting, rather. Time and again he had heard the same sounds, much louder, at voodoo services. *Govis* were supposed to contain spirits of the dead, or rather voodoo *mystères* removed from the psyches of persons who had died. Black and white for Guédé. Rose, green and red for Papa Legba.

Sam suddenly became aware of a feeling that someone was pulling at him. Not someone in the room, but a long way off. Pulling so hard that he had to brace himself or be tugged off balance.

"My God, Victor, what's going on?"

"Better sit down," the man on the bed advised. "I found myself on the floor here once."

Sam hastily obeyed, and sat there gazing at the *govis*

and the drum. The chanting was real? The drumbeats were not just in his mind? "Victor . . . how long has this been going on?"

"It began about ten days after he left here. Marie came in one morning to dust the room and air it out. She heard what you're hearing now, and came flying downstairs to tell me."

"It goes on all the time?"

"I hear it nearly every time I walk in here. Sam, I think your Dr. Bell has some strange power. You say he has gone deep into a study of the occult? I can believe it. Had enough, have you?"

The sensation of being pulled at was beginning to make Sam uneasy. He rose, nodding.

As he followed Victor to the door, he wondered whether Dr. Roger Laurence Bell did indeed have some peculiar power. And whether his daughter might have inherited some of it. She was a lot like Daddy in many other ways.

4

In front of the red, red house
in the mountain clearing,
in the faint light of the false dawn,
Ti Pierre Bastien waits with two mules.
Wide-shouldered, wasp-waisted and impatient,
he keeps glancing at the door of the house
until at last
the bearded white man shuffles out of it
like one walking in sleep.

"Are you ready, Dr. Bell?"
"I think so."
"We can go now?"
"He says we can."

Bastien helps the smaller man to mount,
then swings onto his own mule
and clucks to it.
They ride from the compound slowly.
The false dawn
is followed swiftly by renewed darkness.
The trail is difficult.
The mules' hoofs clatter against unseen rocks
and strike drumbeats from the dark earth,

and the snort of their breaths
is loud in the mountain stillness.

Beyond the village of Bois Sauvage
Bastien turns from the trail
to a faintly marked side track.
Bell calls to him,
"Wait. This is not the way we came."
"We are not returning the way we came."
"What do you mean?"
"Ask Margal. He gave me my instructions."
"How can I ask him now? Talk sense."
"You can ask him, Dr. Bell. You know how."

The white man struggles against what he must do,
but listens.
Listens to what?
The mountain stillness?
The thudding of his heart?

Into his head comes a voice,
a whisper, a murmer,
then louder.
"Yes, Dr. Bell,
I told your guide not to take you out
the way you came.
I prefer to have people think
you are still here in these mountains.
Have you other questions, Dr. Bell?"

"Stop doing this to me, Margal!
Give me back my mind!"
"When I am finished with it, Dr. Bell.
Remember,
you came to me,
not I to you."

5

The youngster's family name was Sam, or she said it was, and that presented a problem. *All the whole damned way I'm going to be reminded of the guy,* Kay Gilbert thought. Then she shrugged. What was the difference? She thought of him most of the time anyway.

Sam. There were more than a few Sams in Haiti. She knew a doctor with that name in Port-au-Prince. Had heard of a lawyer and a merchant. And hadn't there been a President Guillaume Sam who was dragged from his refuge in the French legation and dismembered by a mob some years ago, during an uprising? History was not her best subject.

Now, this nine-year-old girl child on the jeep seat beside her, with the skinny body and sad, little-bird face and expressive eyes—oh, those eyes!—had dredged the name Tina Louise Christine Sam out of her impaired memory only a few days ago, along with the name of her home village. So now at last she could go home. She had been living in the Schweitzer compound for months, with nurse Kay Gilbert, her self-appointed big sister.

Big-sister Kay, of course, had volunteered to be the one to take her home. Who else would the child have agreed to go with? Kay was wearing, not a nurse's uniform, but khaki pants and shirt in anticipation of what lay ahead for the next few days.

"Are you feeling okay now, *ti-fi?* The headache gone?"

Tina had headaches often. She had been immobilized by one most of the morning, which was why the expedition had got off to a late start and now, in mid-afternoon, was only just passing through the town of Ennery at the foot of the big climb.

"Thank you, I'm fine."

"Tell me again the name of this place we're going to."

"Bois Sauvage."

"You're sure now? You didn't just hear that name somewhere?"

"No, Miss Kay. That's where I live. Honest."

"Why couldn't you remember it before?"

"Well, I don't know. If I couldn't remember my name, how could I remember where I lived? All I know is that one of the doctors was reading me names from a map, and when he read Bois Sauvage it was as if a light flashed on in my head."

Bless that doctor. They had tried for so long to cure this child's amnesia.

"Well, all right, baby, I believe you," Kay said and devoted her full attention to the climb. It certainly demanded one's attention. This ascent to the top of the world was a fantastic corkscrew paved with blocks of stone. The hairpin curves made your wrists ache.

At the crest, she stopped to let the jeep quit boiling, and sat limp behind the wheel while she took in the awesome view of northern Haiti, surely one of the most spectacular chunks of landscape in the Caribbean. "*Dèyè morne gange morne,*" went the Creole proverb: "Beyond the mountains are mountains." Looking east, she wondered which of the tortured ridges in that direction concealed the Bois Sauvage she was bound for.

How would she ever get there if it was where the map said it was?

Suddenly the view was gone, wiped out by scudding clouds that smothered the road and jeep in a sneaky swift assault. Scared, she looked at the watch on her wrist. "Baby, we shouldn't have stopped. And we can't just sit here." Gingerly, she started the motor and let the clutch in, holding the vehicle to a crawl as she first tried the headlights, then put them out when the mist reflected them back at her.

In low gear at two or three miles an hour, the jeep crept down through the clouds while she strained to see the edge of the road. Nothing but space lay beyond that curving edge in places, and after ten minutes, she was so tense, she was ready to scream. Then, slowly the mist dissolved; the road became clear again.

"Whew!" She reached out and patted the child's knee. "What a time that would have been to meet a bus!"

A little later, when she had just relaxed enough to peer down at the switchbacks awaiting her below, they did indeed encounter a camion. Crudely painted orange and red, resembling an outsize roller-coaster car, it stood by the side of the road, pointed north in the direction they were traveling. Its crazy tilt indicated wheel trouble or a broken axle. Disembarked passengers paced up and down the road's edge or stood watching two men at work under the vehicle.

As the jeep approached at a crawl and she sought a way past, a man stepped into the road and held up a hand to stop her.

"*Bon soir,* Madame. Are you going to Cap Haïtien?"

"Well . . ." The hesitation was caused by his ugliness. He was a huge man, and his face looked as hard as the paving stones she had been driving over. The whites of his eyes were as red as parts of the camion. He had almost no ears.

How did the old folk song go? "Black men with little ears are wild men." It was supposed to have a hidden meaning.

"I beg you a lift," he said, and it was more threat than entreaty, the way he glared at her and stepped closer. One heavy hand grasped the edge of the windshield. "I absolutely must get to Le Cap today!"

Oh, brother, she thought. All that way with a creature like this in the car? But she was afraid to say no to him. He looked capable of preventing the jeep from moving if she attempted to drive on without him.

"Well . . . all right. Get in."

He let go the windshield and stepped to the rear, where he climbed in over the tailgate with fluid ease. Choosing the metal bench-seat on her side of the vehicle, he said, *"Merci,* Madame," and then was silent. Key put the jeep in motion, his closeness frightening her so much that she needed a bathroom. How could she stop with a man like him there?

The road descended, and after a while she found herself negotiating the hairpin turns she had looked down on from so far above. They were in the Plaisance River valley now, with the big climb and descent behind them and the countryside now so green and pretty—so much more so than the part of Haiti she worked in—that she began to feel less tense. Presently, she heard their passenger saying, "And what is your name, little girl?"

Evidently, Tina did not think him intimidating. Without hesitation she replied brightly, "My name is Tina, M'sieu."

"Tina what?"

"Sam."

There is was again, damn it. And, as always, her mind produced a picture for her to concentrate her feelings on. This time it was a picture of him standing bareheaded in the blazing Jacmel sun, forking up a patch of red earth while a couple dozen barefoot farmers stood around watching in astonishment. It was the weekend he had persuaded her to drive out there with him and see what he was trying to accomplish.

What he'd been doing was teaching a few hundred peasant farmers some of the things he knew about agriculture that they didn't know. And, unlike some other such people she had heard about, he didn't just talk.

They loved him. "Sure, M'sieu Sam. Of course, M'sieu Sam." Lots of laughter. Many willing hands.

Afterward, at the pension where he lived and she would be staying overnight, she had been impressed again. He had warned her that the food was sometimes pretty awful. "But he does his best with what he can scrounge up, so don't blame him too much, hey?" Actually, the rice and black mushrooms—*djon-djon*, they called it—were truly tasty, and the chicken, though tough, was good too. It had been a cousin, no doubt, to the hens that wandered in and out of the dining room all through the meal. And the important thing in any case was not the food, but the way the Haitian proprietor so fondly laid a hand on Sam's shoulder when he came to ask if everything was satisfactory.

"It's great, Leon. Thanks."

"And your lady?"

"I enjoyed every mouthful, M'sieu," she had said.

"Thank you, M'selle. Thank you very much."

Afterward: "Now, look, Kay. This pension is a crazy kind of place, but the town itself is one of the most interesting in the country. Want to see some of it?"

"You bet."

So they had gone walking . . . past the open market with its iron posts and roof and mobs of people milling about; down the steep hill to the waterfront to look at ruggedly basic sailboats that carried goods and passengers around the coast; up again under all those overhanging balconies with lacy iron railings that glistened like spiderwebs in the moonlight. Then, intrigued by a sound of drumming, they had sought its source and suddenly found themselves caught up in a Saturday night street dance.

Those people knew him, too. *"Bon soir,* M'sieu Sam!" *"Woy, woy,* M'sieu Sam!" Even "Hi, M'sieu Sam, come join us with your lady!"

Your lady, Sam. I got a kick out of that. But then— everything that happened later.

The child at her side and the ugly man behind her were having quite a conversation, she suddenly realized. "So you see," Tina was saying, "I have been at the hospital a long time because I couldn't remember anything. Not my name or where I lived or anything. But I'm all right now, so I can go home."

"I'm glad."

"Now tell me your name and where *you* live."

"Well, little one, my name is Emile Polinard and I live in Cap Haïtien. I have a shop there where I make furniture."

"What kind of furniture?"

"Chairs and tables mostly. It's not a really big shop. But I use good wood, like mahogany and tavernon. That's why I went to Port-au-Prince, to buy some tavernon."

"And you were on your way home when the camion broke down, huh?"

"When it broke an axle, yes. And how that driver and his helper expect to fix it is beyond me. I'm certainly grateful to *Le Bon Dieu* for causing you to come along when you did."

Seeing something odd in the road ahead, Kay moved her foot from the gas pedal. It was a length of green bamboo stuck upright in a pothole, its slender leaves fluttering in the wind. Tapping her on the shoulder as the jeep slowed to a halt, Emile Polinard said, "The Limbé bridge has been damaged in a flash flood, Madame. It is necessary to drive through the river."

"How do I get down to the river?"

"There is a turn-off just ahead on your right, where that girl is standing." He pointed to a girl about eighteen. She was barefoot, and bore on her head a battered galvanized washpan full of laundry. She peered out from under it as the jeep approached.

When it was abreast of her she suddenly flung up a hand and cried. "Wait! Wait!"

Again, Kay stopped.

The girl came closer and peered in at her. "But, yes! It *is* Nurse Gilbert from the hospital!" She might have been greeting a dear friend not seen in years. "How are you, M'selle! You remember me?"

It happened sometimes. People Kay had taken care of at the Schweitzer remembered her much later and expected her to remember them. And sometimes she did, but not this time. The girl with the laundry laughed at her embarrassment and said cheerfully, "Of course you don't. At least, not by name. How could you, with all those people to look after?" She turned to peer down the road. "You are crossing the river, M'selle?"

"Well, yes. We're on our way to Le Cap."

"Follow me, please."

Briskly, she turned from the road and went trudging down a steep, rutted slope. The jeep crept after her. The ruts continued for a short distance across a weedy flat, and then Kay saw the stream ahead. It was wider than she remembered it. Two low islands of dark, stony sand separated channels of swift water.

"Can we make it?" she asked Polinard.

"I believe so, Madame. The bus came through yesterday on its way to the capital, though the stream was lower then. Rain must have fallen again last night."

Without even removing the pan from her head, their guide strode up along the river's edge for fifty yards, then turned and waded across the first rush of water to the nearest island. Kay followed. Gripping the wheel, she could feel the force of the current against the vehicle, and water gurgled in around her feet.

The girl trudged on, now and then turning her head to make sure the jeep was still following. Traversing the bar, she chose a zigzag route through the next channel, then went far to her right on the second bar before challenging the last swift flow of water between it and the far bank. Good Lord, Kay thought, I never would have found a way across here by myself.

When the jeep struggled up onto dry land again, the girl was waiting, the pan of clothes still balanced on her head, and a bright smile on her face. Kay stopped beside her. "What can I say? If you hadn't done that, I'd be stuck somewhere in the river right now, and if we had more rain . . ." She was trembling, she realized, reacting now that the crossing was safely behind them. Her hand refused to be steady as she reached into her bag for some money.

The girl stepped back, shaking her head. "No, M'selle!"

"But you must. After what you've done—"

"No!" She shook her head so emphatically, that for the first time she was in danger of losing her laundry.

"Then tell me your name, please."

"Celestine Cassagnol, M'selle."

"I'll never forget it again, believe me." Kay reached out to grasp and squeeze her hand. "Thank you, Celestine."

"It seems you have a lot of friends," Emile Polinard commented as they climbed to the road beyond the broken bridge and put the Limbé behind them.

She only nodded, too wrung out to be drawn into a

conversation with him. His remark stuck in her mind, though, perhaps because Sam had said almost the same thing that night in Jacmel. But was it so surprising? She had been at the Schweitzer a long time, and people from all over the country came there for treatment. In a crowd of maybe two hundred at the *bamboche* that night, three had called her by name. "Crashing my territory," Sam had said, obviously delighted. "Don't you know this is my town, woman?"

The kind of street dance called a *bamboche* was strictly a peasant romp and not a thing outsiders usually took part in, but she had enjoyed this one as an off-beat adventure, even though the night air was soon musty with body odors and the drumming gave her a headache. Sam, of course, ate it up. Yet he, not she, had been the one to call a halt.

"What's the matter?" They had been dancing face to face about a foot apart and she had stepped back to frown at him, sensing a sudden change. Then she realized the change was not in him alone; the noise level all through the crowd had dropped significantly, and the dancing had slowed to a shuffle.

She followed Sam's gaze and saw, on the sidewalk, under a street lamp, a motionless figure that seemed to be staring back at him with almost savage intensity. A man of middle age, thinner than most, wearing dark pants and a long-sleeved scarlet shirt. The crowd watched him as Sam did, as though waiting to see what he would do.

"Sam, what is it?"

"I think we'd better leave, Kay. We're spoiling the party."

"But—"

"Tell you later. Come on, but don't make it too obvious that we're running." Casually waving a hand to the dancers, he put an arm around her waist and led her away, and she sensed that he was, if not scared, at least apprehensive. Not until they were well clear of the crowd and walking down the street toward the pension did he speak again.

"That was a fellow named Fenelon, Kay. He hates my guts."

"Why?"

"He's the voodoo priest, or *bocor*—God knows which. Most of my farmers go to him. An unconscionable leech who bleeds them dry. I work like the devil teaching them how to make a little money from their farming, and he gets too much of it away from them."

"And you've been putting him down?"

"I've been telling them he's a phony and to stay clear of him. To hell with it." His arm tightened about her. "Let's just sit at Leon's little bar with a drink and decide what to do with the rest of the night."

She didn't want to remember the rest of that night now. She had other problems, chief of which was a bladder that at any moment might demonstrate its independence. How, dear God, could she go to the bathroom?

"Madame." Polinard was tapping her on the shoulder again. "I feel the car swaying. Are we getting a flat, do you think?"

She hadn't noticed, but he was right. She stopped. The road was level and straight with lush greenery on both sides. Even before she could wriggle out from under the wheel—she thought she might burst if she moved too fast—their passenger had dropped from the back.

When she reached him, he was on one knee, frowning at the left rear tire. It was not flat, but obviously it soon would be.

"I'll change it, Madame. You have a pump, I see, but it would probably only go soft again." Lifting the jack and tools from the vehicle, he went to work.

She returned gingerly to the front and crooked a finger at little Tina. *"Ti-fi,* do you need a bathroom?"

The child's head bobbed briskly up and down.

"Come on, then. This is our chance."

If Polinard guessed what they were up to, he gave no indication of it. When they returned from the greenery, his tire-changing was almost finished. He completed the task, and Kay thanked him. A little later darkness fell.

She was not used to driving Haiti's country roads at night, and cut her speed so as not to be booby-trapped by potholes. Lamps came on in scattered peasant *cailles* beside the road. Now and then, the jeep passed a pedestrian holding a lantern or a bottle-torch to light his way. Tree frogs sang a shrill symphony to fill the night with sound. Little Tina fell asleep.

Driving along that empty black road with a hulking stranger sitting just behind her was not a joyous experience. It scared her. But the miles to Cap Haïtian passed without incident, and though the girl at the river had distinctly called her "M'selle" and Polinard must have heard it, the ugly man was still politely calling her "Madame" when they reached their destination.

6

It was beginning to rain when they reached Le Cap. Having been in the city only a few times before, Kay was unsure of herself in the wet darkness.

"I have to go to the Catholic church," she said to their passenger. "Can you direct me?"

He did so, remarking that he lived not far from there himself. She stopped under a street lamp near the church entrance. The rain misted the lamp and the jeep's headlights. "For us this is the end of the line, M'sieu Polinard. Tina and I will be staying here tonight with the sisters." That had not been her intention, of course. She had expected to reach Trou. But the late start had made a stopover necessary.

Their passenger got out and thanked her. Ignoring the rain, he gravely offered his hand to Tina. "*Ti-fi*, I hope everything will be fine for you when you reach home. I will pray for you." With a bow to them both he turned away.

How in the world could she have thought him ugly?

"Where do the sisters live, Tina?"

"I don't know."

"But you stayed here almost a month!"

"I didn't know what was happening then."

Kay gazed helplessly at the church, a massive dark

pile in the rain, and suddenly saw that Emile Polinard had stopped and was looking back. He returned to the jeep.

"Something is wrong, Madame?"

"Well, I—I thought Tina would know where to find the sisters, but she doesn't seem to."

"Let me. Is there a particular sister you wish to see?"

She felt guilty, keeping him standing there with the rain falling on him. But if she did not accept his help, what would she do? The church compound was dark; she had no idea what to look for. "It was a Sister Simone who brought Tina to the hospital. If you could just ask for her, please? But if she isn't there, someone else will do, I suppose."

"Sister Simone. I know her. She should be here."

He was back in five minutes holding aloft a large black umbrella under which trotted a black-robed woman not much taller than Tina. The sister said cheerfully, "Hello, you two! Tina, move over!" She climbed into the jeep. Emile Polinard handed her the umbrella and she thanked him. "Just drive on," she said to Kay. "I'll show you where to go."

Kay, too, thanked "ugly man" Polinard. He bowed again. Driving on, she turned a corner at the sister's direction, turned again between the back of the church and another stone building.

"Come," the sister commanded, and, with much rustling of her robe, swung herself out. To hold the umbrella so it would protect them, she had to reach high, she was so tiny. They hurried into the building. Was it a convent? A nunnery? Kay did not know. How many sisters lived here, anyway? Perhaps it was just a residence for two or three. She knew little about these things.

Once inside, the sister was less brisk. Giving the umbrella a shake, she closed it and placed it in a stand near the door, then hunkered down in front of Tina and put out her arms. "How are you, little one?" She was Haitian, Kay noticed for the first time. Her face, remarkably pretty, was light brown. Take away the heavy robe, and she couldn't weigh ninety pounds.

"It's a good thing I phoned you yesterday," Kay said. Actually, she had telephoned only to say they would be passing through Le Cap on their way to Trou and would stop for a few minutes. "I'm afraid we'll have to ask you to put us up tonight. Can you?"

"Of course, Miss Gilbert. What happened? Did you have car trouble?"

"We got off to a late start. Tina had one of her headaches."

"Ah, those headaches." The sister reached for Tina's hand. "Come upstairs, both of you. First your room, then we'll see about something to eat."

She put them both in the same room, one overlooking the yard where the jeep was, then disappeared, *I hope* -ing to return. There were twin beds with a window between them, two chests of drawers, two chairs. "We'll need our gear," Kay told her charge. "I'll go get it while you wash up." But on the stairs she met Sister Simone and a second nun coming up, each with a duffel bag from the jeep.

They supped on soup and fish in a small dining room downstairs: Kay and Tina, Sister Simone, Sister Anne who had helped with the duffel bags, and Sister Ginette who at sixty or so was the oldest. There was little conversation. What there was concerned only the journey. "That road is not easy, is it? . . . It so badly needs repairing . . . And the Limbé bridge was closed? . . . Oh-oh, you had to come through the river, then . . ."

Why don't they ask about Tina—what we've been doing with her all this time, and how she's coming along? They did talk *to* the youngster, but asked no personal questions. It almost seemed a conspiracy.

But when the meal ended and Kay took Tina by the hand to walk her back upstairs, Sister Simone said quietly, "Do come down again when she is in bed, Miss Gilbert. Please? We'll be in the front room."

When she descended, she found the three waiting there on uncomfortable-looking wooden chairs. It occurred to her that perhaps Polinard had built them. An empty chair was in place for her. On a small table in the center of the circle lay a wooden tray on which were mugs, spoons, a pitcher of milk, a bowl of sugar. A battered coffee pot that might have been silver was being kept warm over an alcohol flame.

The nuns rose and waited for Kay to be seated, managing somehow—all but Simone—to sit again precisely when she did. "Coffee, Miss Gilbert?" Simone asked.

"Please."

"Milk and sugar?"

"Black, please." It was a crime to tamper with this poor country's marvelous coffee.

Simone served the others as well—perhaps this was an after-supper ritual—then seated herself. "Now, Miss Gilbert, please tell us how Tina regained her memory. All we know is the little you were able to tell me over the phone yesterday."

She told them how Dr. Robek had hit on the idea of reading map names to Tina and how, on hearing the name Bois Sauvage, the child had snapped out of her long lethargy. "Like Snow White waking up when the prince kissed her."

They smiled.

"Then she remembered her own name. If, of course, Tina Louise Christine Sam really is her name. We can't be sure until I get her to Bois Sauvage, can we? Or even if that's where she came from.

The oldest sister, frowning deeply, said, "Bois

Sauvage. Isn't that away up in the mountains near the Dominican border?''

"According to the map."

"How in the world will you get there?"

"I've been promised a guide at Trou."

"But you can't *drive* to such a place. There aren't any roads."

"I suppose we'll walk, or ride mules. I really won't know until tomorrow." She waited for them to sip their coffee. Then: "Now will you tell *me* something, please? How did Tina come into your care in the first place? All we've ever heard is that she was brought to you by a priest."

"By Father Turnier," Simone said, nodding. "Father Louis Turnier. He was stationed at Vallière then and had a number of chapels even farther back in the mountains. We have a picture of him." She put her coffee mug down and went briskly, with robe swishing, to a glass-doored bookcase at the side of the room. Returning with a large photo album that smelled strongly of mildew, she turned its pages to find what she sought, then reversed the book and held it out to Kay. "That's Father on the right, in front of the Vallière chapel. Those big cracks in the chapel were caused by an earthquake just a few days before this picture was taken. Can you imagine?"

Kay saw a husky-looking white man with a cigarette dangling from his mouth. French, she guessed. Most of the white priests in the Haitian boondocks were French. He wore no clerical garment; in fact, his shirt was neither buttoned nor tucked into his pants. The way he grinned at the camera made her instantly fond of him.

"He was coming back from some far-off chapel one day," Simone said, "and stopped at this isolated native *caille* beside a little stream. He hadn't ever stopped there before, he said. In fact, he didn't usually pass that way, but a landslide had carried away part of his usual trail and forced him to detour. He was on a mule, of course. He always made his chapel trips on muleback. And the animal was weary, so he thought he would just stop and talk with these people a while."

Kay gazed at the photo while she listened.

"Well, there was this child lying on a mat inside the *caille,* and the people asked Father to talk to her. She had wandered into the clearing a few days before, they told him, and couldn't or wouldn't say who she was or where she had come from."

"I see."

"Well, you can see from that photo what kind of a man Father Turnier is. He forgot all about returning to Vallière and simply stayed there, trying to persuade the child to talk to him. He ended up staying the night and deciding she must have been through some really traumatic experience and ought to have help. In any case, she couldn't remain there with those people because they didn't want her. So at daybreak he lifted her up in front of him on his mule and carried her to Vallière, still not knowing her name or where she came from."

"He's a wonderful man," Sister Anne said.

"And loves children," added Sister Ginette.

"Then what happened?"

"Well, he kept her at Vallière for about three weeks —he and young Father Duval who was stationed there with him—but she didn't respond as they hoped she would, so he brought her here to us." Sister Simone paused to finish her coffee, then leaned toward Kay with a frown puckering her pretty face. "You haven't found any *reason* for her lapse of memory?"

"None."

"On hearing the name of her village she just suddenly snapped out of it?"

"That's what happened. We've always thought there

was nothing much wrong with her physically. Of course, when you brought her to us she was underweight and malnourished—not your fault; you didn't have her long enough to change that," Kay hurriedly added. "But she seemed all right otherwise."

"How strange."

"I wonder if her people in Bois Sauvage have been looking for her all this time," Ginette said. "It's been how long? Father Turnier had her for three weeks. We had her a month. You've had her for nearly six months."

Simone said, "It could be longer. We don't know that she went straight from her village to that *caille* where Father found her. Maybe *that* journey covered a long time." Life was full of puzzles, her shake of the head said. "Miss Gilbert, we can only say bless you for taking her home. None of us here would be able to do it, I'm sure." The puckering frown returned. "But have you thought of leaving her here and having us send for the father in that district to come for her?"

"Father Turnier, you mean?"

"Well, no, it wouldn't be Father Turnier now. He's no longer there."

"It would be someone Tina doesn't know, then?"

"I'm afraid so. Yes."

Kay shook her head. "I'd better take her myself. And I don't mind, really. It could be fun. It'll certainly be a change from hospital routine."

All the sisters nodded and looked at her expectantly. It was close to their bedtime, Kay guessed. Time for her to go upstairs, anyway. She rose.

"I'd better make sure Tina is all right, don't you think? She has nightmares sometimes."

"And the headaches, poor thing," Simone said.

"Yes, the headaches. Like this morning. Well, then . . . until tomorrow?"

"Tomorrow," they said in chorus, and little Simone

added, "Sleep well, both of you."

Kay climbed the stairs. As she went along the corridor to their room she heard a drumming sound overhead that told her the rain was still falling. *Please, God, let it stop before morning or that road to Trou will be hell.* The room itself was a steam bath. Tina slept with her face to the wall and her arms loosely clasping an extra pillow.

Kay shut the door and began to undress, shedding her clothes without bothering to put on the light. What had the sisters thought of a nurse who came to supper in khaki pants and shirt? Or hadn't they thought anything? Anyway, she had never expected to be dining with nuns, or with anyone else who might think pants on a nurse a little unusual. In bra and panties, with one hand reaching down inside the panties to scratch her bottom because muggy weather like this always made her itch, she looked with affection at her sleeping roommate.

Tina Louise Christine Sam, she thought. Sam, Sam, Sam. There is was again, like a phone in her head that wouldn't stop ringing. She had been thinking about him all day, and about that weekend in Jacmel. Until her stubborn mind got to the end of that weekend she probably would not be able to think along to any of the other things he and she had done together.

Opening her duffel bag, she took out the pajamas she had brought. Flannel ones because the mountains were likely to be cold, or at least cool. Here it wasn't cool, though. God, no. Deciding against the pajamas after all, she stuffed them back and got into bed the way she was, pulling the sheet up over her because it seemed to help a little against the dampness. There was something about this room she didn't like. Something that made her edgy. What was it?

She turned to look at the window between the beds. Light from a street lamp or yard lamp somewhere close by shone through the wet glass to create small yellow flickerings on one of the bureaus. Jacmel again, she thought, frowning. There had been a street lamp outside her window there too, and rain had begun to fall that night soon after Sam and she had left the pension's little bar and gone up to their rooms.

In Jacmel, though, the light from outside had illuminated the door, not a piece of furniture.

She looked at the door here and suddenly was not sticky hot anymore, but cold enough to shiver. If it opened here as it had there, she was sure she would scream.

True, she had not screamed that night. Hadn't known what to do when the creaking of the unoiled hinges had wakened her and she had found herself sitting up in bed like a wooden doll, staring at him in total disbelief.

If he had just opened the door and come to her in his pajamas, she might have understood, though they actually had not slept together at that time. They had killed a good half bottle of rum down there at the bar, he drinking most of it, she not wanting to hold him back because he was so obviously upset by his encounter with the voodoo fellow at the street dance. Maybe she had even wanted him to come to her room. Otherwise why hadn't she protested on discovering there was no key to her door?

But he hadn't come in pajamas to talk her into letting him into her bed. When the door finished its ghastly creaking and was fully open, he was standing there like some weird visitant from another world, naked as Adam in the light from the window, his arms dangling like an ape's and a completely unalive look on his face. Drunk? No man had a right to be that drunk . . .

From the other bed came Tina's sleepy voice. "Miss Kay, is something wrong?"

She dragged herself back from that ghastly Jacmel room. "No, baby. Why?"

"You were making funny noises. You woke me up."

"I woke you up? Gee, I'm sorry. It's been kind of a long day and I guess I wasn't sleeping too well. I must have been dreaming."

"Oh. That's okay then. Good night."

"Good night, *ti-fi.*"

Only I wasn't asleep and it wasn't a dream, baby. I wish to God it were.

7

Wearing a much-patched carpenter's apron this morning, Emile Polinard stepped back to look at the table he was working on. It was a large one of Haitian mahogany, crafted to order for a wealthy Cap Haïtien merchant. Emile switched on his electric sander but turned it off again and removed his wristwatch, lest wood dust get into the watch and do some damage.

The time, he noted, was twenty past eight. The rain had stopped just before daybreak and now the sun shone brightly on the street outside the open door of his little shop.

His helper, 17-year-old Armand Cator, came from the back room and said, "I've finished the staining, M'sieu Polinard. Should I start on Madame Jourdan's chairs now?" Armand was a good boy, a hard worker, always respectful. Polinard sometimes wished his own two sons might be a little like him.

"Do that, please, Armand."

"Yes, sir."

Glancing out the door at the welcome sunshine while turning the sander on again, Polinard saw a familiar vehicle coming down the street and voiced a small "Ha!" of satisfaction. He had been expecting to see it. To get from the church to the main north-coast highway, it

49

would have to pass his shop. He shut off the sander a
second time and placed it on a bench. Hurrying out onto
the cracked sidewalk, he fixed his gaze on the approaching jeep and waited.

Just before it reached him, he waved both arms vigor-
ously and called out, *"Bon jour,* good friends! Be safe on
your journey!"

"Why, that's Mr. Polinard!" said little Tina Sam to
Kay Gilbert. "That must be the furniture shop he told
us about." And she returned Polinard's wave.

Kay waved, too, but did not stop. They had got off to
a late start again, at least later than she had hoped for;
the sisters had insisted on giving them a big breakfast.

The jeep sped on and Polinard stood on the sidewalk
smiling after it.

"You know those people, sir?" Armand asked from
the doorway.

"Indeed, I do. They gave me a lift yesterday when the
camion broke down. She's a charming woman. And the
little girl . . . well, Armand, that's a curious story. You
know what it means to lose your memory?"

"Huh?"

The jeep had disappeared from sight, and Polinard
came back into the shop, where he walked over to the
bench and retrieved his sander. Without turning it on,
he leaned against the bench and gazed at his helper.

"The little girl you just saw in the jeep has been at that
hospital in the Artibonite for a long time—months—
because she could not remember her name or where she
came from. Very sad. And she is such a bright child, too,
Armand. But she has at last remembered and is going
home."

"That's good."

"Yes, good. Provided, of course, that what she told
them is a fact and not just her mind playing tricks again.
By the way, don't you have a pal who came from a place

called Bois Sauvage not long ago?"

"Yes, sir, I do. Luc Etienne."

"You see him often?"

"Two or three times a week."

"Ask him, then—because I am curious—if he knows of a girl about eight or nine years old who used to live there until, say, six or seven months ago. Her name is Tina Sam."

"Of course, sir. I'd better write it down."

"Do that. You might forget."

Armand stepped to the bench and reached for paper and a carpenter's pencil. "Tina is T-i-n-a, sir?"

"Correct."

"And Sam is S-a-m?"

Polinard nodded.

"I may see him tomorrow at the cockfights."

"You spend your Saturdays at the fights, risking your hard-earned wages on chickens?"

"Only a few cobs now and then. But Luc—now there's a fellow who bets big and almost never loses. Everybody wonders how he does it. Why, the last time I was there, he—"

"I don't approve of cockfights and wagering," Polinard said sternly. "But ask him about the little girl, please." And he switched the sander on to fill the shop with noise.

The cockfights which Armand Cator attended were held near the coastal village of Petite Anse, just east of the city. Approaching the crowd, he searched its outer edge for his pal's familiar face but failed to find it.

It was not good to fail when his employer asked him to do something. M'sieu Polinard, though strict, was a kind and decent man. Worried, Armand sought an opening in the crowd and worked his way into the pit to look at the circle of faces there.

A fight was in progress. A white bird and a black and red one made the gray sand of the enclosure fly like rain as they tried to kill each other. Spectators leaned over the wall of knee-high bamboo stakes, yelling encouragement.

The white was getting the worst of it. Even as Armand located his friend across the pit, the battle suddenly ended in a spurt of blood. There was a rush to collect bets.

Armand worked his way around to his friend and was not surprised to find Luc Etienne clutching a fistful of gourde notes. Luc must have a sixth sense, he so seldom lost a wager. "Hi," Armand said, grinning. "You've done it again, hey?"

The tall young man chuckled and stuffed the notes into a pocket of his shirt. It was an expensive multicolored shirt; not another in the place could be compared with it. He offered Armand a cigarette—another expensive item these days—and the two stood side by side just back from the bamboo barrier, smoking and talking.

This was not a good time to ask about the little girl, Armand decided; as preparations got underway for the next fight, the crowd was too noisy. He would wait until Luc was leaving and then leave with him. They usually went back to the city together, anyway.

"Look at Gri-Gri," Armand said.

The man called Gri-Gri, a middle-aged fat fellow known to be the owner of some of the most courageous cocks in the district, had produced a bird which the crowd knew well. He was seated under a bayahonde bush with it, giving it a final grooming. Quite a following had gathered to watch.

"That's the bird he refers to as his little terror," Armand. "I'll bet on it any time. It's won six straight."

Luc scowled at Gri-Gri in silence.

"You agree?" Armand anxiously pressed. He almost never placed a wager unless Luc pronounced it a wise one.

"No. That's not the cock you think it is."

"What? Of course it is!"

"Wait here," Luc said and walked over to join the crowd watching Gri-Gri rub the dun-colored bird with rum and half a sour orange. Some in the circle glanced at him and nodded, but he ignored them. After gazing at Gri-Gri intently for a while, he returned to Armand. "You're planning to bet on that bird?"

"Well . . ." By the contemptuous look on his friend's usually good-humored face Armand could see something was wrong.

"Don't. It's a ringer, supposed to lose. Gri-Gri's pals will bet against it for him and themselves, and go home rich."

"Luc, you're crazy. I would know that cock anywhere. How many of that color do we see around here?"

"I didn't look at the cock. I was studying him."

"What?"

"Behind that solemn look on his treacherous face, Gri-Gri is laughing his head off. If you want to bet, bet the other way on that one." Luc glanced toward a man who sat on the other side of the pit in a patch of shade cast by tall cactus, readying a small brown-red bird that looked no more ferocious than a common yard fowl. "As a matter of fact, here," he said, plucking the wad of gourde notes from his shirt pocket. "Bet this for me at the same time. If I do it, they'll suspect what's up. They know I usually win."

Armand went through the crowd, calling out that he had money to wager on the favored dun's opponent. After finding takers he returned to Luc, and they watched the combat. The dun and the brown-red were placed in the pit and went at each other at once—say this for Gri-

Gri's ringer, he was willing enough—but the outcome was soon apparent. The dun knew what it ought to be doing but couldn't do it and was repeatedly bloodied, while the crowd groaned in anguish. All too soon, the fight was over.

Armand went about collecting his money and was aware that people watched him as he returned to Luc Etienne. "We ought to leave, I think," he said. "If they see me handing all this over to you . . ."

"I agree. Keep it for now and come on."

They made a point of strolling about for a time, pretending to be interested in the next match, then quietly departed. As they trudged out to the road, Armand handed over the other's winnings, and Luc, having won big, returned ten gourdes to him for his help. Soon after they had boarded a tap-tap to the city, Armand remembered to speak about the little girl. He consulted the paper on which he had written her name, to be sure he was remembering it right.

"Did you know her when you lived in Bois Sauvage?" he asked. "Was there really a Tina Sam in your village?"

The little bus clattered along the highway through shimmering waves that rose from the macadam in a swelter of midday heat, and Luc gazed at him with an expression of incredulity.

"What's the matter?" Armand said. "All I asked was if you knew such a girl when—"

"No, I didn't!"

"Well, don't get sore with me. What's wrong with you, anyway? I only asked because my boss told me to."

Luc Etienne got over whatever it was that had caused him to become so suddenly and strangely tense. "You say this girl is on her way to Bois Sauvage now?"

"That's right. With a nurse from the hospital where her memory came back. If it really did come back. I guess it didn't if you never knew her."

"When do they expect they'll get there?"

"How would I know? They left here yesterday morning in a jeep. Can a jeep get to where they're going?"

"No. From Trou they will have to use animals."

"Well, all I want to know for M'sieu Polinard is, was there really a Tina Sam in your village or is she going there for nothing?"

"She is going there for nothing," Luc said and then was silent. And since he was peculiar anyway at times, Armand contended himself with looking out the window as the tap-tap took them to town.

Luc was the first to get off. "Be seeing you," he said, and jumped out the back. For a moment he stood there, hands in pockets, frowning after the tap-tap as it went on down the street. Then he turned and walked slowly up a cobbled lane to a gate and opened the gate and entered a yard. The yard was of hard-packed brown earth that bore the scratch marks of a twig broom. He crossed it to a small wooden house at the rear. This was where he had lived since coming to Cap Haïtien about eight months ago.

When he opened the door and walked in, the girl he lived with was on her knees, rubbing the wooden floor with the flat surface of half a coconut husk. She looked up in surprise. "Well, hi, you're home early, aren't you?" She was about sixteen. The dress she wore, made from flour bags with the printing still on them, was both old and too small. Luc had picked her up at a small backyard dance one night about a month ago and brought her here to live with him. Now there were times he wished he hadn't, for though she was willing enough in bed and looked after the house as well as could be expected, her being around all the time interfered with his freedom.

He walked on into the bedroom without speaking to

her. Kicking off his shoes, he first sat on the edge of the bed, then swung his legs up and lay on his back with his fingers twined under his head and his gaze fixed on the underside of the zinc-sheet roof above.

Going back there, he thought. *Tina Louise Sam going back there? That's bad.*

His girl appeared in the doorway. "Don't you intend to speak to me? What's the matter?"

He ignored her.

She came into the room. Standing beside the bed, she looked down at him in silence for a moment and then smiled. She was an attractive girl. Her long-fingered hands, moving swiftly, unzipped the tight flour-bag dress and she shrugged herself out of it. It slithered down her thighs to the floor, leaving her naked. With the swift grace of a mongoose gliding through grass, she slid to a position on top of him.

"Not now," Luc said. "I have to think about something."

"You can think afterward."

"No!"

Laughing, she tried to put her mouth on his, but he jerked his head aside. Then she realized he was in earnest and, sliding off him, lay there at his side and frowned at him. It was the first time anything like this has happened.

"You didn't go to the cockfights, did you? You've been with some other girl!"

Gazing at the roof again, he shook his head.

"Well then, what's wrong? *You* took my dress off me yesterday. Have I changed since then?"

He stopped roof-gazing and turned himself to face her. His arm went around her and his hand clasped her small, firm bottom for a moment while he rubbed his nose against hers as though they were puppies at play.

Then he said, "Go on now, clear out for a while. I have to do something."

"What must you do?"

"Stop acting as if you own me, damn it, and do as I say! Put your dress on and get out of here! Come back—" he hesitated, wondering how long it would take, if indeed he could do it all—"Come back in an hour."

She looked at him in silence, waiting for him to say more. When he did not, she shrugged and got up. Putting the dress back on took longer than discarding it had—or was she deliberately taking her time! At last, with a final angry look at him, she left the room.

He heard the outside door slam. Leaving the bed, he went and turned the key so she could not return before he wished her to, and so he would not be interrupted by unexpected callers. Back on the bed, he assumed a sitting position with his back against the headboard and his arms looped about his knees, then closed his eyes and fixed his thoughts on a face.

Only twice before had he attempted this, and on both occasions he had only partially succeeded. The second time had been better than the first, though, so maybe he was learning, as Margal had predicted. Aware that he was sweating, he peeled off his expensive sport shirt and tossed it to the foot of the bed, then resumed the position and closed his eyes again. After a while the sweat ran down his chest in rivers.

The face was beginning to come, and there was a difference.

Before, the image had appeared only inside his head, in his mind. But not this time. No, man. This time it was out in front of him, in space, floating over the lower part of the bed just out of reach. It was more than just a face this time, too. Below it a pair of shoulders had appeared, and below the shoulders a chest was forming.

Something really unexpected took shape then: *legs*.
He was startled and confused. How could legs appear
when Margal didn't have any? True, they didn't look
solid like the rest of him. Only an outline of them was
there, and that seemed to consist of a kind of glow, like
the phosphorescence you sometimes saw in the sea at
night. But how could there by *any* kind of legs on the
image of a man who had been legless for two years?

He concentrated on the face in an effort to give it
more substance, while his own face felt as though someone were painting it with warm oil. But fixing his
thoughts on one part of the image made the whole thing
more real. It even summoned up the chair Margal was
sitting on.

Could he be imagining this? Dreaming it? Leaning
forward, he stretched out a hand to try touching the
thing that floated there over the bed and found he could
not. But that didn't prove anything, did it? You didn't
summon the man himself, only a vision of him, and the
vision was now complete: Margal sitting there legless—
but for some strange reason not so legless as he was in
real life—in the chair he always used, and now even the
room was partly visible. That many-hued room in which
he, Luc Etienne, had so often assisted the *bocor* in his
work.

"Margal, you've come," Luc whispered.

The eyes stared back at him. No one but Margal had
eyes as terribly piercing as those.

"Can you hear me, Margal?"

The head slowly moved up and down. Or did he imagine that?

"I have something to tell you," Luc whispered. "You
remember that little girl, Tina Louise Sam?"

This time the floating head did move up and down, he
was certain.

"Well, she is on her way back to Bois Sauvage right

now. After she disappeared from Dijo Qualon's house
she could not remember her name or where she came
from, but now she *has* remembered, Margal. A nurse
from the Schweitzer hospital is bringing her home."

The eyes returned his stare with such force that he felt
they would stop his breathing. Ah, those eyes! The face
might be just an ordinary middle-aged peasant face if
you didn't know how special it was, but no one else in all
Haiti had such eyes, no. He heard a question and replied, "Yes, I am sure." Then another question and he
said, wagging his head, "No, there is nothing I can do.
It's too late. They left here yesterday morning."

The floating image slowly faded and was gone. He
waited for something more to happen, but nothing did.
After a while, so drained of energy that he felt he must
be as crippled as the man he had been communicating
with, he sank down on the bed and lay there shivering in
his own sweat until he fell asleep.

8

The tortured mountains
of the Massif du Nord
behind them at last,
the bearded white man and Ti Pierre Bastien,
now ride over flat, dusty
cactus land.
The sun's heat
presses down on them,
a smothering blanket.

"Margal, I will not do it!
I will not follow this man of yours
a step farther!"

Such a childish challenge,
the mind of Margal
will not even honor
with an answer.

The distance between master and servant
increases.
There comes a change.
Subtle, yes,
but a change.

* * *

Feeling free for a moment,
Dr. Bell reins in his mule
and defiantly thinks—
or even says aloud—
"No, Margal, you cannot command me!"
Then, the struggle
of mind against mind,
will against will.
The white man's body writhes
in agony
and his face oozes sweat.

Ti Pierre Bastien,
his companion,
watches and waits
without expression:
There can be but one outcome.

In the beginning
Dr. Bell's revolts are brief,
but as time passes—
the distance between master and servant increases—
they endure longer.

Until, one day, the man from Vermont
is even able to free himself long enough
to speak to his daughter Mildred,
though afterward he cannot quite remember
what he said to her.

9

"Tell me something, Milly," Sam Norman said. "Have you ever carried out any ESP experiments with your father?"

Ever since the start of their journey at six that morning, his thoughts had been returning to the drum and *govis* in her father's room at the pension. Now, speeding along in the rented jeep on the north-coast road between flat fields of sisal, they were only a few miles from their destination.

Mildred hesitated rather obviously, he thought, before shaking her head. "No. Not really."

"What do you mean, not really?"

"Well, Daddy has played around with things like telepathy and ESP for years, of course. But I don't call it 'experimenting'—to write something down and then say, 'Tell me what you're thinking about,' just to see if he's guessed right. Why do you ask?"

"No particular reason. Just wondering." And Sam let the silence return.

They had not talked much on the journey. He had, of course, told her what he knew of the towns they passed through—St. Marc, Gonaïves, Cap Haïtien—and the names of the plants that she was not familiar with. But the ride had been hot and dusty until rain began to fall soon after their fording of the Limbé where the bridge was damaged. An alert entrepreneur no more than eight years old had shown him how to cross the river.

The only bad moment for him had been when, soon after leaving the coastal town of St. Marc, they had passed the junction of the road that led to the Schweitzer. It was on that road one afternoon a long time ago—such a long time ago, it now seemed—that Operation Sandal had taken place.

He had been driving Kay Gilbert home that day because she had ridden into town with one of the doctors instead of using her own car. He had the AID jeep in which he had driven to the city from his job in Jacmel. They hadn't known each other a long time then.

You could drive that road to the Schweitzer without being too vigilant. Relatively speaking, of course. At any rate, it was reasonably flat and fairly wide, and along most of its length any oncoming traffic could be seen before it got too close. Taking advantage of that, he had elected to remove one hand from the wheel and put an arm around the girl at his side, pulling her over against him or at least applying enough pressure to convey a desire to do so.

They had stopped for a swim before St. Marc—not at a proper beach but at a bit of shore where you could park just off the road and walk in through the sea-grapes. Magic water, crystal clear, with white pebbles lining the bottom . . . the place was little known but very special. Having planned on it, they had donned swimsuits under their clothes at the Calman.

After swimming, they had walked the shore to dry off, then put their clothes back on over the swim suits. No hanky-panky at that stage of their relationship. But, driving along the hospital road, Kay was still barefoot.

"Hey, you're a nurse. Don't you know you're not supposed to go barefoot in this country? You could get hookworm."

"In a jeep?" She wriggled as pretty a set of toes as he had ever seen, and definitely turned him on by doing so.

"Lady, all kinds of people ride in this jeep. *All* kinds."

"Okay, if you insist, sir." Reaching for her sneaks, she banged them against the side of the vehicle to get the sand out, then peered into them and dropped them back on the floor. "No, to hell with it. They're still yucky."

Responding to the pull of his arm, she slid over closer to him, so that his right hand came to rest on her right breast. "Mm," she said, surprising him. There hadn't been much contact between them up to then. Their dates had consisted of dinner at a couple of Port-au-Prince restaurants and dancing at a well-known thatch-roofed nightclub in Petionville.

He slowed the jeep and bent to kiss her, and she squirmed into a position that would make the kiss mean something. Without actually intending to, he was sure, she managed to get one bare foot outside the vehicle. Not dangling outside but thrust out, like a driver's arm signaling a turn.

That kiss was one that would have made any man of spirit neglect the fine points of his driving. He *saw* the donkey approaching, all right; saw the peasant woman on its back and the sandal dangling from her foot as she rode along with a leg outthrust. A more disciplined man would have stopped, of course. But he was too busy discovering things about his companion to think about putting a foot on the brake and freeing his right hand to wrestle with a shift stick. Not fast, but still moving at maybe five miles an hour, the jeep continued on its course.

The woman was riding side-saddle as nearly all of them did, along the footpath at the side of the road. All these roads had such paths, worn smooth by the feet of animals and pedestrians. They were still kissing when they passed her. She let out a yell. And so did Kay, blasting her outcry right into his face as she broke from his embrace.

He brought the vehicle to a jolting halt and looked back to see if he had hit the woman. Apparently, he hadn't. She had reined her donkey in, though, and was staring at her outthrust foot.

Kay was gazing in astonishment at her own foot, still stuck horizontally out of the jeep. Her mouth fell open and a look of incredulity came over her face. Then she began to laugh.

She laughed until tears came, and it was contagious. The woman on the donkey began to laugh with her and soon was nearly hysterical. Sam looked in amazement at the sandal.

It had been dangling from the black woman's foot before. Now it dangled from Kay's. "You know something?" he said in awe. "If we tried a thousand times to do that again, I'll bet we couldn't do it."

The woman slid from her donkey and came to the jeep, not at first touching the captured sandal but simply standing there, gazing at it. When she did remove it, she carefully examined Kay's foot. "You are not hurt, M'selle?"

"Not at all."

"Nor am I. You are from the hospital, no?"

"That's right, I am."

"You people make miracles all the time. This was another one." She began laughing again, softly now; chuckling, really. "Imagine, my shoe on your foot. The things that can happen in this world!"

Kay got her leg back into the jeep and reached to the floor for the sandy sneakers. They were nearly new ones, expensive in Haiti. "Would you like these, so you can put a shoe of mine on your foot?"

As she held them out the woman looked at them, then lifted her gaze to Kay's face. "Thank you, M'selle." No laughter now. Pure dignity. "You are kind."

"Operation Sandal," Kay said as Sam put the jeep in motion again.

They had never called it anything else.

The voice of Mildred Bell cut into Sam's thoughts. "Sam, what made you think I might have researched ESP with Daddy?" Mildred hated unfinished business.

He shrugged. He had not told her, of course, of the drum that whispered drumbeats and the painted jars that exhaled voodoo voices. He had no intention of telling her, at least not now. She would have enough to worry about on this journey they were attempting.

She looked at him, awaiting an answer. When none came, she, too, shrugged, though not physically.

Hers was a mental gesture.

Strange, she thought, that Sam should have asked such a question. She was sure she had never told him about having helped Daddy with that part of his research. For one thing, she had believed for a time that Sam Norman might be a man she could love and marry, and she had a feeling he was not one to approve of such research. He was just too down to earth. After all, her own mother had never stopped trying to persuade Daddy to abandon it. Even as a little girl, she remembered . . .

What, exactly, did she remember?

Not much, and yet a lot. Impressions, mostly. A twelve-year-old girl walking home from school in Warwick, Rhode Island, with a crowd of schoolmates. Clowning. Giggling. Having a time. Suddenly, not hearing what the others were saying but stabbed in the head by Daddy's voice, though Daddy was half a mile away. Not feeling good that morning, he had announced he would be staying home from his teaching job at the high school.

"Milly, you hear me?"

"Yes, Daddy. But it hurts."

"Never mind that. Where are you?"

"By the diner, Daddy. Just crossing over to Gorton's Pond."

"All right, listen. I want you to do something for me. Go back to Apponaug. Go to Morin's drugstore. Tell Mr. Ambrose you want the medicine he has for me. Hear?"

"Yes, Daddy."

"Good girl. Go on now."

Telling her schoolmates there was something she had forgotten to do, she hurriedly crossed over to the bank, ran down the road to the fire station and cut through the city hall yard to Post Road. Morin's drugstore was empty when she burst in. Why was her head aching? She'd been okay before Daddy talked to her.

"Hi, Milly." Mr. Ambrose was nice; she had always liked him. "You on your way home from school?"

"Uh-huh."

"Good thing you stopped. I've got something for you."

"Medicine. I know."

"You do? How? Your father only called me a few minutes ago." As he took the bottle off the shelf, he looked at her in a funny way, and she wished she hadn't said anything. Because if he asked her to explain, she wouldn't know how to tell him.

When she reached home, Daddy was working at the typewriter in his study. Without getting up he said, "Come here, sweetheart," and put his arm around her. "You and I," he said then, "we really can do it, can't we?"

That had been the first indisputable proof of the

power they both had, though they had exchanged thoughts before in some of the games they played. It pleased him immensely, and she was glad. But her headache lasted for hours and frightened her. As for Mama . . . well, Mama just didn't understand at all.

"How did you know to stop at Morin's, Milly?"

"Well, I didn't. I just stopped."

"For what?"

"*I* don't know, Mama. Nothing, I guess. Us kids go in there a lot for ice cream and stuff."

Mama was suspicious, sensing there was something going on. She came from a religious background. Her father had been a Presbyterian minister and she just didn't approve of some of the things Daddy did.

They were the devil's things, she said.

10

In the village of Trou, Sam Norman stopped the jeep in front of a shop. They had made good time. At quarter to six there was still some daylight left.

Stepping out of the vehicle, he said, "This shouldn't take long, Milly. I stayed overnight at this man's house when I was here before, and he was able to find some mules. Here's hoping he can repeat."

He walked in and found a muscular man of thirty or so, but not the right one, standing behind the shop counter, weighing out flour. Sam waited. The fellow glanced at him in silence, displaying a face the texture and nearly the color of cantaloupe rind. He placed a piece of newspaper on the hanging scale in front of him. He scooped flour onto it from a large sack on the floor, peering at the dial as he did so. When he had the right amount of flour on the paper, he dropped the scoop into the sack.

Sam said then, "Good evening. Is M'sieu Lafontant here?"

A nod.

"Will you call him for me, please? I'm an old friend."

Another nod. But with the flour weighed, he still took time to fold the paper and tuck its ends in and place the package with others already completed before interrupting himself. Turning then to scowl at the open door of a

back room, he called loudly, "M'sieu Lafontant! Someone here says he is a friend of yours!"

"Coming, Alfred." A short, frail-looking man of sixty
or so came limping through the doorway and cocked his
head to squint at Sam. A smile changed his anxious expression, and he hurried around the end of the counter
with a hand outthrust. "M'sieu Norman! What a surprise!"

Sam grasped the hand and shook it. "How are you,
friend? When I saw someone else behind your counter,
I was scared."

"My assistant. As you see, I limp now, the result of
breaking an ankle in a camion accident. I don't get
around as well as I did." Looking Sam over, he nodded
his approval. "You haven't changed as much as I. And
what this time? Another journey into the mountains?"

"This time with a woman."

"A woman, eh?" The eyes twinkled. "That should be
interesting, to escort a woman to Vallière."

"Don't jump to conclusions so fast. She's the daughter of an associate of mine, a man named Dr. Roger Bell
who came through here some weeks ago on his way to a
place called Legrun. You may have met him."

"You told him to look me up?"

"No, I didn't know he was coming here."

"I have not heard of him." Lafontant wagged his
head.

"Well, his daughter and I are going to Legrun to look
for him. Something seems to have happened." Sam
paused, aware that the man behind the counter had
stopped measuring flour and was listening, apparently
with all antennae extended. "Do you suppose you can
put us up tonight, M'sieu, and help me find a couple of
mules again?"

"Of course, *mon ami.*"

"Good. Now I can start relaxing."

Lafontant's house was next door to his shop, and after introducing him to Mildred, Sam drove the jeep into the yard there. The man's wife was a tiny woman with a whispery voice. Like her husband, she remembered him.

"I was just going to call Paul to supper," she said happily. "Now you two can join us. You must be hungry."

Mildred seemed embarrassed. "Really, I don't think we ought—"

"We're starved," Sam corrected. "All we've had since leaving Port is a couple of sandwiches Victor Vieux gave us. You know how these trips are. Even if you can find an eating place to stop at, you've wasted an hour of precious time."

Mrs. Lafontant's supper consisted of roast pork, rice and peas, and tender green shoots of the mirliton vine. ("It tastes like spinach," Kay had once remarked, "and I still say to hell with it.") Over the meal, Sam explained the reason for their journey into the mountains.

"So your Dr. Bell went in there to see Margal, eh?" the shopkeeper said. "A wicked man, that one."

"Is he?"

"Well . . . so they say. I know nothing about him at first hand, never having met him. As I understand it, he only came to these parts about two years ago."

"But his reputation is bad," Mrs. Lafontant added with a sympathetic look at Mildred. "I do hope your father is not in trouble with such a person."

Sam said, "What does he look like?" It might help to be prepared.

"He has no legs and is said to have strange eyes. Hypnotic eyes."

"No legs? How come?"

The shopkeeper shrugged. "The story most told is that he was sent for by some important politician in the capital—someone who required his services—and he re-

fused to go. Then he was visited by men who beat him
nearly to death to punish him. This supposedly happened just before he came here and was the reason for
his coming. In other words, Legrun was a good place for
him to hide."

"Where did he come from?"

"Again, no one seems to know. I have heard Léogane
mentioned—perhaps because voodoo is so strong there.
Also Aux Cayes and Jacmel."

"He didn't come from Jacmel," Sam said. "The big
man in that business when I worked there was a fellow
named Fenelon. Well, never mind. Can you locate two
mules for us, friend?"

"I believe so. What else will you need?"

"Not much else. A few supplies from your shop, I
suppose. Mostly your advice on how to find this Legrun.
It isn't on any map I've seen."

"You will need a guide. I had better lend you my
helper, Alfred Oriol. I can get along without him for a
few days."

*Your man who finished weighing and packaging a
pound of flour before he would give me the time of day,*
Sam thought. "Why him?"

"He comes from near there. Do you know Sylvestre?"

It was a name on the part of the map Sam had so
carefully studied at the Pension Calman. He nodded.

"His home is there. Suppose we have a talk with him,
eh? We should call at the police station, too, I think, to
find out if they have anything to tell you. And we can see
Alcibiade about the mules at the same time." Supper
was over and Lafontant stood up. "You ladies will excuse us? We'll have coffee with you when we return."

They walked across the front yard and through a gap
in a hedge of candelabre, only to find the shop door
closed and locked. Obviously annoyed, the proprietor
rattled the latch and called out, "Alfred!" but received

no response. "Now, where can he have gone? He has never done a thing like this before!"

"He'll be back soon, no doubt. Let's see about the mules, shall we?"

The man who had supplied Sam with mules before, Alcibiade Fombrun, lived only a five-minute walk away. Sam remembered him only vaguely until he was face to face with him; then it came back. He was an aging peasant farmer who resembled most other such men except that his bare feet were perhaps a little more knobby, and without nails.

He remembered Sam, though not by name. "The man who took two of my animals to Vallière," he said, gravely nodding as they shook hands, "and was good enough to look after one with compassion when it fell and gashed a foreleg on the way back. I am happy to meet you again, M'sieu."

"Can I rent that big gray again?" Sam asked. It had a mild disposition and would be fine for Mildred. An ordinary Haitian mule, it was said, would serve you faithfully for ten years just for the chance to kick your brains in once.

"M'sieu, I am sorry. I rented that animal just yesterday to Corporal Larus."

"Damn. Who's he?"

"At the Poste Police," Lafontant said. "Why would Larus want to rent a mule from you, Alci? The police have animals."

"It was for an American woman, a nurse, who had to take a child into the mountains to Bois Sauvage."

Inside Sam, something stirred, as though chemicals had combined and begun to boil. "An American nurse? What's her name?"

A shrug. *"M' pas connais,* M'sieu." That maddening Haitian phrase: "I don't know." Always to be expected when you wanted to know something badly enough.

It couldn't be, though. Of course it couldn't. Yet, where but at the Schweitzer would there be an American nurse in this country? And hadn't the girl there said on the telephone that Kay was going into the hills?

"Something is wrong, M'sieu?" Lafontant asked, anxiously peering at him.

"No. It's just that I may know this nurse."

"Anyway, she has the mule you would like," Alcibiade said. "But I can give you another one just as good."

"Two others. I need two."

"He needs three," Lafontant corrected. "He must have a guide."

"No problem."

They went from there to the police post, but the man on duty, the same Corporal Larus who had rented the mule, could tell Sam nothing about Dr. Bell. "I obtained animals for him and his companion and they went off into the mountains," Larus said. "As yet they have not returned. His jeep, as you can see, is still here in the yard. He left the key with us and we start it up every few days to keep the battery alive." The corporal was a tall, slim, handsome man who had apparently never learned to smile. Of course, this was not exactly an occasion for smiling.

"It hasn't occurred to you to send someone in there to look for them?" Sam said.

"I have given it some thought, M'sieu. But Dr. Bell did not say how long he planned to be in there, so we don't know whether to be alarmed or not."

"One thing more, please. The American woman for whom you rented the mule from Alcibiade yesterday. I believe I know her. Is her name Miss Gilbert?"

"It is. Her jeep is in the yard here, too."

"And she's going to Bois Sauvage?"

"Correct."

We'll be passing through there and may meet her, Sam thought. *May even overtake her on the way, by God.*

Returning to the shop, he and Lafontant found it open, with the muscular fellow whose face resembled cantaloupe rind once more behind the counter. "If you please," Lafontant said with the exaggerated politeness of an angry man of his class, "where have you been and why did you leave my shop without telling me?"

The fellow had not expected to be found out, Sam guessed, or an answer would have been ready on his tongue. It wasn't. "M'sieu Lafontant, I . . . well, you see, something happened . . ." Obviously he was stalling for time to put his wits to work.

"What something happened?"

"Well, I . . . this friend of mine came and told me there was a fellow in my yard who shouldn't be there. One I had told to keep away from my wife and—"

"You are not married."

"My woman, then. And he was there talking to her, my friend said. Which was a thing I had to see for myself, naturally, so that I would know what to do about it. I was not gone long."

"And this man who shouldn't have been there was there?"

"Well, no. He had left."

Lafontant let some silence take over to convey his displeasure. Then he said, "Tell me something, Alfred. Do you know where the village of Legrun is?"

"Certainly. It is not far from Sylvestre, where I am from."

"You have a job, then—probably at better wages than I can afford to pay you. Not for long, unfortunately. Just long enough to serve this man as a guide, for Legrun is where he wishes to go."

Oriol looked at Sam. "May I ask why you wish to go to that place, M'sieu?"

You already know, buster. You were listening with all your might when I told your boss here. "We hope to find someone."

"And you wish to leave when?"

"At daybreak."

"Very well. I will see about mules tonight."

"They are already arranged for with Alcibiade," the shopkeeper told him. "We attended to that while you were checking on the faithlessness of your woman. Just bring them to my house in the morning." He stepped behind the counter. "Now then, M'sieu Norman, tell me what you need from my poor shop and we can complete the preparations for your journey."

11

As the gray mule climbed doggedly through an eerily quiet mountain wilderness, Kay Gilbert found herself thinking of Sam Norman again.

"You must have one hell of an effect on me, Kay. So help me, I have never in my life done anything like that before.".

Those were the words he had spoken that night in Jacmel after walking naked into her room.

Naked and intoxicated? She would never know. He *had* drunk a lot at Leon's bar before they climbed the stairs to their rooms, but she hadn't been dating him long enough then to know his capacity.

You still don't know his capacity, Gilbert. Face it, there are lots of things you don't know about Sam Norman.

She had not panicked when her door opened that night and the light from the street lamp revealed him standing there. Sliding out of bed on the side away from the door, putting the bed between him and her, she had grabbed a heavy glass ashtray from the night table and taken aim with it as he came stumbling over the threshold.

"Hold it right there, Mister. Don't come one step closer!"

He had stopped then. Whether the threat or the mere

sound of her voice had stopped him, she couldn't know.
Like an aroused sleep-walker struggling to orient himself, he stared at her, first vacantly and then with growing comprehension. Then he looked down at himself—
right down at the parts of him that emphasized his nakedness—and said in a hoarse whisper, "Oh, my God!"

Lurching about, he fled from the room, reaching out
to slam the door behind him as he went.

Badly shaken, she had switched on the light and got
dressed, then sat on the bed and tried to think. Were
there things about Sam Norman she had never sus-
pected? Mental things? Character flaws? Did he need
help?

How would she get back to the capital in the morning? By camion?

For ten minutes she had sat there with her thoughts,
first angry, then full of compassion, certain one minute
he had been drunk, then just as certain he had not been.
Hearing footsteps outside her door, she took in a quick
breath and reached again for the ashtray.

The footsteps ceased and hesitant knuckles rapped on
the door. A voice full of contrition said, "Kay? May I
come in?"

She did not know how to answer.

"Kay? I'm all right now. Can I talk to you?"

"Well . . . I suppose so."

The door opened and he came slowly into the room,
leaving it open behind him. That was to reassure her, of
course, because he knew he had frightened her. He was
dressed now. Not just in pajamas, but dressed. Halting
at the foot of the bed, he looked at her with misery in his
eyes and seemed to have trouble finding his voice.

"Kay . . . I must have been walking in my sleep. I
swear to God, I don't remember leaving my room. I
wasn't aware of a thing until you spoke to me and
snapped me out of it."

It was the truth, she decided. Not just an alibi. He hadn't *looked* right when he was standing there naked in the doorway. "Sam," she said, "sit down." She had risen but now sat on the bed again.

He went to a chair and sank onto it, staring at her and slowly shaking his head. He looked tired, she thought. He looked old. He looked ill.

Above all, he looked scared.

"Sam, has anything like this ever happened to you before?" It was Nurse Gilbert speaking now, as coolly detached as she could be with her emotions so rampant.

He shook his head.

"Was it the rum?"

"I didn't drink that much rum."

"None in your room after we came upstairs?"

Again, his head moved from side to side. "Not a drop."

"Sam, does it have anything to do with that man— what's his name?—at the *bamboche?*"

"Fenelon? How could he be responsible?"

"Well, you said he's big in voodoo. We've had patients at the hospital who claimed—" She let it drop; she could see no point in going that route. After all, who could prove anything where voodoo was concerned? Rising, she went to him and put her hands on his shoulders and bent to peer into his face. "Are you all right now, Sam?"

"I feel like hell. As though I've been drugged."

"That's how you look, too. Why don't you lie down?"

"Here?"

"Yes. I don't think you ought to be alone right now." She took his hands and helped him to his feet, then put an arm around him and led him to the bed, knelt and took off his shoes while he sat there. Helped him off with his pants and shirt, leaving him in shorts. Then swung his legs up and drew the sheet over him.

When she walked around the bed and lay down on its other side—still fully dressed and on top of the sheet, not under it as he was—he turned to face her.

"Kay . . ."

"Yes?"

That was when he said, "You must have one hell of an effect on me, Kay. So help me, I have never in my life done anything like that before."

"Well, if you ever get a notion to do it again," she said, trying to help by keeping it light, "just give me a little advance notice, will you? I mean I mightn't object to it if I'm not scared half to death. The truth is, Sam Norman—"

The sound of swiftly moving water interrupted her recollection of that Jacmel night and brought her back to the Massif du Sud, where she now gave her full attention to the trail. If they were coming to a stream, maybe their guide, Joseph, would stop to let the mules drink. She hoped so. They must be thirsty after so many miles of hard climbing. She knew she was. She was tired and sore, too.

The saddle on this big gray animal had never been designed for a person with a bottom and thighs shaped like hers. The insides of her thighs felt as though they had been massaged with coarse sandpaper. Tina must need a break, too, although the child was so excited about going home, so happy to be riding with Joseph on his mule, that she had not once complained.

Joseph. Thank God for Joseph. She saw him looking back to check on her now, and she waved to let him know she was okay. He returned the wave, and while she was not close enough to see his good-looking young face, she was sure he was smiling. He was about nineteen, a good boy. She had encountered enough Haitian young men at the hospital to know the good ones. Clean, intelligent, mild of speech and manner, he was exactly the sort of guide she had hoped for. The corporal at the police post in Trou had produced him.

They had left Trou about one o'clock and it was now after five by her watch. When planning this trip, she had counted on reaching Vallière the first night. It was only a village, but there was a church, and the priest would put them up, she was sure. But the various delays— getting away from the hospital yesterday hours later than her schedule called for, the late start from Cap Haïtien this morning—had put Vallière out of reach, she knew now. Perhaps the hard rains of the past few days would have thwarted them, anyway, for time and again they had had to walk the mules over portions of the trails which, Joseph said, would normally have present- ed no great problem.

And since they couldn't reach Vallière, where *would* they sleep tonight, the three of them? On the early part of the journey they had passed a few peasant huts, some in clusters, some standing alone in remote forest clear- ings, and Joseph had spoken to some of those people. Whether he actually knew them or not, she had no idea. But in the past hour or so they had seen no houses any- way. So would they spend the night out in the open, beside the trail? But what if Joseph, like most country people, young or old, feared the *loup-garou* and evil spir- its?

The sound of running water was louder and, ahead, Joseph's mule had disappeared around a bend of the trail. It was dark here, she noticed. A spooky kind of place, unlike anything they had encountered before. The trail had entered a steep-sided ravine and the small amount of late-afternoon light from above was filtered through great feathery tree-ferns growing high up on both walls. Riding into it was like venturing into a lush, tropical greenhouse, with the stream saturating the warm air with moisture. Such an unusual place . . . at another time she might have been really interested, wanting to stop and explore it. But now she was tired and saddle-sore and hungry and anxious about Tina.

Swollen by the rains, the stream raced through the gorge in a torrent, a good thirty feet wide and full of boulders. The trail wound along beside it, so wet that it seemed to disappear in places. The noise was deafening and disconcerting. With the other mule ahead and out of sight now, her feeling of apprehension deepened. *I don't like this place! I don't like it at all!* Then, rounding a sharp bend, she saw that Joseph had stopped where the trail seemed to run straight into the stream. Having dismounted, he was lifting little Tina from the saddle.

Kay dismounted too, and looked with consternation at the rushing water, which was swift enough to be white but appeared dark green in the strangely filtered light here. "My God, Joseph, do we have to ford this?"

"It won't be so bad, M'selle. People do it all the time."

"With the river this high?"

He shrugged. "In these mountains if one waited for low water all the time, one wouldn't do much traveling." He gave her his outrageously handsome smile. "Look, I'll show you while the animals rest a little."

At the stream's edge he studied the flow for a minute or two, then knelt to take off his shoes and roll his pants up over his knees. Rising, he entered the swift water and slowly, calmly felt his way through it to the opposite bank, then turned and retraced his steps. It really wasn't all that deep, she realized, noting that his pants were not wet.

"You see, M'selle?"

"Well . . . all right, after we've rested." She hunkered down before Tina Sam—*Ah, Sam Norman, I wish you were here now in spite of everything!*—and took hold of the youngster's arms. "How are you feeling, baby?"

"Fine."

"Your legs sore?"

"A little. Not so much."

It was different, no doubt, being perched up there on Joseph's mule and knowing Joseph would not let her fall. Quite a bit different from having to grip the saddle hour after hour with both legs to be sure of staying on board. Giving the child a pat on the bottom, Kay rose and faced their guide. "Have you any idea where we can sleep tonight, Joseph?"

"I know a place, M'selle."

"Where? It will be dark soon, won't it?"

"We will be there in time. Don't worry."

She worried anyway, not for herself but for the child. After all, this little girl had only just recovered—if indeed she had recovered—from some mysterious malady that for months had deprived her of her memory. Even with all the care she had been given by a concerned staff at the hospital, and by the doting Cap Haïtien nuns before that, she was still not physically what a nine-year-old ought to be.

I wonder if we should be letting her go home this early, especially to such a remote village. Should we have made her wait a while longer?

Joseph had watered the animals. Now he said, "When you are ready, M'selle, we can continue."

She looked at the racing green water. Ready? Even if she were not, what could she do about it? *Gilbert, you get yourself into the damnedest situations sometimes . . .*

"All right, Joseph. Let's go."

He watched her mount the big gray, then swung himself onto his own mule and reached down for Tina. He was careful to seat the child securely in front of him. Would Tina be scared? *He* had walked across there and back, but it was still fast water foaming among huge boulders. There could be deep holes.

Beckoning her to follow, Joseph coaxed his animal into the river. "Don't try to guide your mule, M'selle!" he yelled back above the river-roar. "Just let him follow mine!"

She did, and it seemed to be sound advice. She respected this big gray animal; he had already earned her trust time and again. Slowly, with no sign of nervousness, he splashed toward midstream, his hoofs turning up some of the smaller stones with a hollow cloppy sound that echoed through the gorge.

But what was happening to the light?

Kay rubbed her eyes and turned her head right and left. The gorge had been dim from the beginning, of course. With these high walls and so little room at the top for light to seep down, it was almost like a cave. But there had been light, even though it was subdued and spooky green. Now, for no apparent reason, the light was fading.

In a moment, the gorge was almost night-dark and the sound of the river had become an earsplitting roar, deep and menacing.

She felt the gray mule stumble, then hesitate, then come to a halt and begin to tremble. It scared her that this powerful animal trembled just as she did. The flow of water against his quivering legs was now furious. It was a Niagara rapids kind of thing. As it crashed against the bigger boulders and exploded, she felt the spray sting her face and arms and hands, inflicting real pain. The whole gorge was sound and fury.

Why? Had there been a flash flood higher up in the mountains? She had heard of such things. One of the hospital doctors had lost a car once when it stalled at a supposedly safe fording and was caught in such a rush of water. But if this was only a swiftly rising river, why the *darkness?* Had something happened to her eyes?

She leaned over the mule's neck, straining to see what

Joseph was doing. It was no use. Even that eerie green light was gone now, swallowed up by the swooping gloom. On the verge of panic, she drove her sneakered feet into the gray mule's flanks and slapped his neck to urge him forward. Whatever was happening, she could not just sit here in midstream waiting for it to engulf her.

Unused to such treatment from her, the mule voiced a snort she could hear even above the river's roar and lurched to one side. She had braced herself for a forward motion and was taken by surprise. She tumbled sideways from the saddle. The river boiled over her as she screamed. Then the current sucked her under and her mouth filled with water.

She struggled. A stream that Joseph had walked through only a few minutes ago should not have the strength to make her struggle so desperately, but it did. She felt herself slammed against boulders, scrubbed along the bottom, ripped against submerged tree branches. Felt herself flung back up to fresh air from time to time, and had sense enough left, no matter how mad the nightmare, to fill her lungs. Some relenting current swept her into a quiet eddy and she staggered to her feet, grabbing at an overhanging branch to steady herself. "Joseph . . . Joseph . . . where are you?"

It was a feeble cry. She hadn't enough strength left for an honest yell. On the other hand, the roar of the river was subsiding. The canyon walls no longer hurled thunder at each other. It was as though someone who had been amplifying all the normal sound effects was at last turning the volume back down.

Hauling on the branch, she pulled herself up out of the stream and called again, this time with more strength. "Joseph!"

"M'selle, where are you?"

"Here!" Where was here? Downstream from the fording, of course, but how far down? And what had happened to Joseph and Tina? And to her mule?

Strange. As the din diminished, the darkness began to subside, as though a thick sheet of dark glass in front of her eyes were dissolving. She could see the stream again, the cliffs, even the strip of sky above.

"M'selle, please! Where are you?"

"Here, Joseph." It was going to be all right. If Joseph had come through it, Tina must have, too. But come through what? Something real or just imagined? Was there such a thing as unreal reality?

Never underestimate this country, one of the hospital doctors had warned her once. Listen carefully to everything a patient tells you, and don't weigh it on the scales of your own experience. Things happen here that don't lend themselves to rational analysis.

She heard someone crashing through the streamside jungle nearby and called out again. "Joseph! Over here!" Suddenly, he burst through a tangle of hanging vines not six feet away, and stopped. With obvious relief, he stood there looking at her while getting his breath back. Then, quietly: "M'selle, are you all right?"

She nodded, realizing for the first time that she must appear to be half drowned. "Tina?" she whispered.

"She is only frightened. I told her to wait with the mules while I found you."

"Mules? Both of them?"

"When it happened, I was almost through the river. Your animal followed without you. M'selle"—as he came toward her, his bulging eyes were something to behold in the restored green light of the gorge—"what in God's name did happen? The darkness, the river going mad that way . . ."

Feeling she was strong enough to walk now, she let go the tree limb to which she had clung since her crawl from the river. "Joseph, I don't know," she said. "But I think we ought to get away from here. Fast."

12

The outskirts of Port-au-Prince.
Ti Pierre Bastien
faces the weary white man
he has led across half of Haiti.

"This is where we part company, Dr. Bell.
You have your street map of the city?"
"I have it."
"To reach Turgeau from here, you—"
"I cannot go directly to Turgeau.
I must go to the Pension Calman first."
"No, Dr. Bell. Margal said—"
"Don't be foolish!
Can I call on a university professor
looking like this?
I must have a bath
and a change of clothes.
Also I need a rest."
"Margal is not a patient man, Dr. Bell."
"Nor am I indefatigable.
Good-bye."
Dr. Bell trudges away
from the man
who for many days

and many weary miles
has been his constant companion.
An hour later
he arrives at the Pension Calman.
Finding no one about,
slowly climbs the stairs to his room.
Collapsing on the bed,
he lies there
gazing at the ceiling.
With the slow passing of time,
he at last feels able to attempt
another challenge.

"Margal, I will not do it!
Do you hear me, Margal?
I will not do it!"

Silence.
But only for a moment.
Then, becoming aware of a faint sound
in the room,
he turns his head
to gaze at the voodoo drum
beside the bureau.

It is a drum
he acquired weeks ago
at a service in Léogane
to which he was taken by the man
who later took him to Margal.
He bought it,
he paid for it,
but it is a genuine petro drum
used in genuine voodoo ceremonies.

Now it is filling the room with

a whispered throbbing
while on the bureau the two painted jars
acquired at the same ceremony
are faintly chanting
in a way
that fills him with terror.

It is happening.
He cannot be mistaken.
He leaps to his feet,
staring first at the drum,
then at the *govis,*
while the voice of Margal
takes possession of his mind.

"You may rest an hour, Dr. Bell.
Then you will do as you were instructed.

"Yes . . ."
"As Bastien told you but an hour ago,
I am not a patient man."

13

Standing alone in a clearing, the house was a small one of wattle and clay, roofed with banana-leaf thatch. Only moments before, Kay had wondered if Joseph really had a stopping place in mind or was merely hoping to chance upon one. Glad to have reached any kind of destination after so many hours of riding, she gratefully swung an aching leg over the saddle and dropped to the ground.

Stumbled.

Sat down hard on her bottom.

Then just sat there with her arms looped about her knees, laughing partly from sheer relief, partly from embarrassment at having made herself look foolish in the eyes of the man and woman who had just emerged from the house.

Lowering Tina to the ground, Joseph slid smoothly from his animal and ran to help her.

She wagged her head at him. "Let me enjoy this minute. It's the first soft thing I've sat on since we left." She flapped a hand in salute at the two old people hurrying anxiously toward her. "I'm all right," she assured them. "Just weary."

It was no lie. After the incident at the river, Joseph had set a wicked pace, either to get away from there as

fast as possible or to get here to this *caille* before dark.
Climbing steeply from the gorge, the trail had become a
God-awful roller-coaster that made every mile a misery.
Steady climbing was not so bad; you got used to leaning
forward and more or less wrapping your arms around
your mule's neck. Descending was all right, too, after
you accustomed yourself to leaning back, clinging for
dear life to the pommel, and hoping to God that the
leather stirrups would not snap under the strain. But a
constant shift from one to the other was pure hell, scar-
ing the wits out of you while subjecting your poor tired
body to torture. More than once she had envied little
Tina, so confidently perched there in the crescent of
Joseph's sturdy arms without a care in the world.

Without a care? Well . . . that weird business at the
river had frightened the child, no question about it. People who said a black face couldn't pale were wrong.
Tina's had certainly been ashen when Joseph and she
reached the place where he had told the child to wait for
him. Standing there by the mules, she had been staring
back at the river as if in a trance, her soft, full lips
pressed tight but trembling.

"Tina, are you all right?" Hunkering down to her,
Kay had caught hold of her hands.

"I don't want to stay here, Miss Kay!"

"Well, we're not going to. But are you—"

"Please! I'm afraid of this place!"

The fear had faded as they had put the gorge behind
them. Had there been a chance for them to stop and
consider, they might have found an explanation for
what had happened, but with nightfall threatening, they
had pushed straight on.

Tina, thank heaven, seemed to have forgotten the
whole thing now in her pleasure at reaching this place
where they might eat and sleep. Joseph, too, though for
a time he had certainly been shaken. As she sat on the

ground now, looking up at the man and woman from the house, he said to her, "M'selle, I know these people. They will put us up for the night."

She struggled to her feet, though a number of muscles protested, and Joseph introduced the couple as Edita and Antoine, no last names. She shook their hands. They were in their late sixties, she guessed. Both were barefoot, both nearly toothless, both wore slight facial disfigurements indicating long-ago bouts with yaws. That curse was pretty well wiped out in Haiti now, thank God.

"Please go into the house," Antoine said. "I will attend to your animals."

There were two small rooms. The front one contained four homemade chairs and a table; the other, a homemade double bed. No connecting door. No kitchen. Cooking was done under a thatch-roofed shelter outside.

"You and the child will use the bed," Edita said in a manner that forbade any protest. "My man and I will sleep here in the front room, as will Joseph. Joseph is my sister's daughter's son."

"Thank you." It would not be the first time she had slept in a peasant *caille*. Nurses at the Schweitzer often did things their Stateside sisters might think extraordinary. The bed could harbor bedbugs, of course. More, likely, the swept-earth floor was a breeding ground for the little beasties called *chigres*, which were worse. Those got under your toenails and laid eggs there.

"Tina should rest before supper," she said. "I'll help you with the cooking, Edita."

The woman seemed pleased.

The child fell asleep as soon as she climbed onto the bed, and Kay joined the woman in the kitchen. Supper was to be a chicken stew: First, kill the chicken. Edita attended to that with a machete, then cleaned the severed head and put it into the pot along with the rest of the bird. Kay prepared malangas, leeks, and carrots. While working, they talked.

"Where are you going, M'selle, if I may ask?"

"Bois Sauvage. Tina lives there."

"Oh?"

Kay explained, stressing the child's loss of memory.

"Strange things happen around Bois Sauvage," Edita said, implying that a loss of memory was not the strangest. "Do you know the place?"

"No. I don't know this part of Haiti at all."

"As I say, strange things occur there. So I am not surprised at this story you tell me concerning the child."

"What do you mean by 'strange things'?"

"Well . . . unnatural things."

"Voodoo?" Any time a country person talked this way, the underlying theme was likely to be voodoo. Or associated mysteries.

"I think not voodoo, M'selle. Rather, sorcery or witchcraft."

Associated mysteries. Correct. Kay glanced at the fire where the stew was cooking in an iron pot that could well have been used in certain voodoo ceremonies. The *kanzo* service, for instance, at which those being elevated to *kanzo* were required to dip their hands into boiling oil. *Remember the time we finally got to see that one, Sam, and couldn't believe it when the girl showed us her hand afterward and it wasn't even blistered?*

Squatting by the fire and stirring the pot's aromatic contents, Edita looked up and said, "Do you know about a man named Margal in that district, M'selle?" More than yaws was responsible for the depth of her frown.

"Margal? No. Who is he?"

"A *bocor.* You know what a *bocor* is?"

"A witch doctor?" Admit you know something and you may learn more.

Edita nodded. "Margal is a big one, it is said. Perhaps the biggest of them all. Much to be feared."

"He lives in Bois Sauvage?" Kay was not happy at the thought of taking Tina to a village dominated by one of those.

"In Legrun, a few miles from there. And practically owns it, though he came there less than two years ago. But his powers are not confined to there." The frown persisted. "Perhaps you will not encounter him. I hope not."

"I hope not, too."

Night fell while the stew was cooking. The woman used a bottle lamp in the outdoor kitchen but called on her man to bring a lantern when the food was ready to be carried to the house. Kay waked Tina and the four of them sat at the table in the front room where, with the door shut, there was a strong smell of kerosene from the lantern now hanging from a soot-blackened wall peg.

Edita bowed her head and murmured a grace, then served the food. After a few moments of eating in silence, she looked across the table at her man and said, "These people are going near to where the legless one is, Antoine." The frown of concern was back on her pocked face.

"So Joseph has been telling me."

The nurse in Kay was curious. "*Legless,* you say?"

They nodded.

"Born that way, you mean?" All kinds of abnormal children were brought to the hospital, usually by mothers who pitifully begged the doctors to "make them right."

Antoine's head wagged. "No, he was not born that way."

"Then how—"

"Different tales are told. One is that he lost his legs when a camion he was riding in overturned and crushed him. Such accidents do happen, of course. Another is that he became involved in politics and was beaten up, left for dead, by assassins from the capital, and saved himself with his *bocor's* powers but was not able to save his legs. Still another tale is that his mule fell from the cliff at Saut Diable."

"Hardly likely," Edita interjected, "because most people agree he was legless when he came here. Anyway, you will be seeing Saut Diable tomorrow and can judge for yourselves whether one could survive a fall there. At any rate, he is legless but very much alive."

"And to be feared," Antoine said.

"You are convinced of that? He really has extraordinary powers?" Kay asked.

They stared her to silence without answering her, as peasants were likely to do in such a situation.

Edita pulled an old, rope-bound suitcase from under the bed in the back room and took blankets out of it while Antoine and Joseph moved the table outdoors to make room for sleeping. It was time to turn in, Kay realized. In these remote mountain districts no one stayed up much after nightfall. For one thing, kerosene for illumination had to be transported long distances and was expensive.

She was a little disappointed. She had planned on discussing that puzzling occurrence at the river with Joseph, thinking they might come up with an explanation if they pooled their thoughts. But maybe this was safer. Though apparently over it now, Joseph had been frightened, she was certain. Stirring up his latent superstitions with more talk might not be wise.

"Well, good night, Edita, Antoine."

"Good night, M'selle," they responded, and the woman hesitantly added, "M'selle?"

"Yes?"

"What you are doing for the child is a loving thing. May *Le Bon Dieu* reward you."

"Thank you." She reached for Tina's hand. "Come on, baby. Let's get some sleep before we have to climb onto those mules again."

Falling asleep on that bed was not going to be easy, she soon discovered. At least, not with all her aches. The mattress was stuffed with some kind of coarse grass that had packed itself into humps and hollows. Each time she sought a more comfortable position, the stuff crackled as though it were on fire. Tina slept, and that was something, but in the end Kay could only abandon the struggle and lie there. At least, she was resting, not struggling to stay on the back of a mule.

The *caille* was far from quiet, too. One of the three sleepers in the front room—the old man, she guessed—snored from time to time, achieving some remarkable whistling effects through his not-quite-normal nose. In the thatch overhead, geckos croaked and clicked and made rustling sounds as they moved about. Outside the house, other lizards sounded like people with sore throats trying to cough, and tree frogs whistled like toy trains. But the outside noises were muffled; the room had no windows. At this altitude, the problem was to keep warm, not cool. Especially at night.

A roachlike fire beetle, the kind the peasants called a *coucouyé,* came winging in from the front room, pulsing with green light as it flew. It made a whirring sound until it crashed into a wall, then dropped to the floor—*thunk!*—and lay there, still pulsing. A few of those in a proper container, she thought idly, might serve these people better than their crude bottle lamps of kerosene with a rag for a wick. The light from just this one was eerily bright.

Tina was asleep now, and despite the lumpiness of the bed, Kay felt herself dozing off, too. Good . . .

Awake again, she floated back up to full consciousness and looked at the luminous dial of the watch on her wrist. Eleven-thirty. So she really had slept a while. The fire beetle, if it was the same one, had recovered from its fall to the floor and climbed part way up the wall and was pulsing there. Lizards still clicked in the thatch.

She dozed off again, awoke at two-twenty, and sleepily noticed that the beetle had moved up close to the roof. Trying to sleep in the same room with it was like trying to sleep with an advertising sign that kept winking on and off. Maybe one of the lizards up there would take care of it. They were fond of bugs. Again she felt herself dropping off to sleep.

Tina, beside her, began to tremble.

Dreaming?

If so, it was quite a dream. The youngster's movements became almost violent. She had been sleeping with her hands pressed palm to palm under one cheek, and now she turned convulsively on her back and began moaning.

Damn. I don't want to wake her but I'll have to if she doesn't stop. It must be a nightmare. Propping herself on one elbow, Kay peered at the child's face, glad now for the pulsing light of the beetle above them.

Something dropped with a dull plop from the thatch onto the foot of the bed. A gecko, of course, but she glanced down to make sure. The geckos were small and harmless. Kind of cute, in fact. The bigger lizards were supposed to be equally harmless but were *not* cute. Not in her book, at least.

The nightmare was causing Tina to thrash about in a frenzy that made the whole bed shake. Kay reached for her to wake her. There was a second small plop at the foot of the bed, and Kay turned her head again.

The fire beetle had fallen from the thatch. Still glowing, it struggled on its back with its legs frantically beating the air, six inches from the gecko.

The lizard's head swiveled in the bug's direction and its beady eyes contemplated the struggle. Its front feet, looking like tiny hands, gripped the blanket. Its slender brown body moved up and down as though it were doing pushups.

Mouth agape, it suddenly lunged.

Crunch!

With the light gone, the room was suddenly dark as a pit.

The child at Kay's side sat bolt upright and began screaming in a voice to wake the mountains.

The rest of what happened was simply not believable. It was so incredible that Kay felt a massive urge to scream along with the child.

At the foot of the bed, the beetle-devouring gecko had become larger. Was now, in fact, a great black shape half as big as the bed itself. Its feet spread out to grip the blanket, and its huge reptilian head turned toward Kay and the screaming child. Its enormous dragon-body began to do pushups again.

It was about to leap, to open its awful jaws and crunch again!

"Oh, my God!"

Tina's eyes were open at last. She was seeing the thing too. Her screaming seemed likely to tear the house apart.

Scarcely aware of what she was doing, Kay grabbed the child and rolled with her off the bed, onto the swept-earth floor near the doorless doorway. Not a second too soon. As she scrabbled for the doorway, pulling the shrieking youngster along with her, she heard the thing spring and land on the old bed, which groaned in protest. Heard the jaws snap together on something. A pillow, she thought. Both pillows? Then, still on hands and knees, still hauling the child with her, she reached the front room.

The screaming had aroused the sleepers there. They were all in motion. Slow motion, it seemed. Unless that was just another part of the nightmare.

Antoine was lighting the lantern. His woman caught hold of Tina and hugged her, telling her to stop screaming, she would be all right, just stop screaming and tell what had happened.

Joseph, helping Kay to her feet, peered strangely at her, then turned to look into the back room as Antoine stepped to the doorway and held the lantern high to put some light in there.

Tina stopped screaming.

Kay stepped to the doorway to look into the room she had just frantically crawled out of.

Nothing.

But I saw it. It was there. It was huge and it leaped at us!

She walked very slowly past the two men and into the room, terrified of what might happen when she approached the bed where the monstrous thing had materialized. But she had to know. Antoine followed with the lantern. Joseph trailed him.

Nothing.

After a while Antoine said, "M'selle, what frightened you?"

"I don't know."

There was nothing on the bed. Not even the small lizard that had eaten the fire beetle. And if the huge one's jaws had really closed on the pillows, they had done so without leaving a mark.

You imagined it, Gilbert. Just as you must have imagined the flash flood at the river.

But Tina had become frightened first. Tina, not she, had done the screaming.

She looked at her watch. In an hour or so it would be daylight. Backing away from the bed, she turned and walked into the front room where Edita was seated on a chair now with Tina on her lap. The child was whimpering softly.

"Are you all right, M'selle?"

"I guess so. But I know I can't sleep anymore. Just let me sit here and wait for morning."

The woman nodded.

"I can't explain what happened. Can't even try."

"M'selle, sometimes we can't."

Kay sat. She had slept in her clothes, expecting the night to be cold, expecting to change to clean clothes in the morning and wash the slept-in ones at the first stream they reached. All that was unimportant now. She looked at Tina, then up at the woman's disfigured face. The child had stopped whimpering.

"She's asleep?"

"I think so, yes."

Joseph and Antoine were back in the room. They, too, sat. Both looked at Tina, then at Kay, no doubt waiting for an explanation.

Don't she warned herself. *You even try, and Joseph might decide to go back.*

But they were not willing to sit there in silence. "M'selle," Joseph said, "what happened, please?" He had to be answered somehow.

"Well . . . I'm ashamed, but I believe I just had a bad dream. I don't remember what it was about, even. Only that it was frightening. Then I guess I woke Tina up, poor thing, and she began yelling. Really, I'm sorry."

"That is all?" Joseph asked.

"That's all."

But she could tell by the way they looked at her that they were not buying it.

14

Nothing could occur before dark, Alfred Oriol decided. The message he had sent the legless one could hardly be delivered before then. No one walked these trails more swiftly than young Kajo or knew more short-cuts, but the distance was still great. And, of course, the lad would not have employed an animal. Not when he had to leave Trou after dark and travel all night.

So then, relax. Just let the mules clop-clop along at their own good pace. Enjoy the journey and the anticipation of action later. Not to mention Margal's undoubted gratitude.

They had been riding since daybreak and it was now close to noon, the sun blazing brightly above the narrow gorge through which they traveled. Slowing his animal with a light pull on the reins, Oriol turned in the saddle and looked back at Mildred Bell. Loudly enough for his voice to carry the fifteen feet that separated them, he said, "Are you hungry, perhaps, M'selle? Should we stop to eat something?" *He* was certainly hungry.

She shook her head. "Not yet."

"As you say." Slouching in the saddle, he gave the mule its head again.

Twenty feet behind Mildred, Sam Norman heard the exchange and frowned. I don't like that bastard, Sam thought. I didn't like him when he was measuring out his flour and giving me the finger, and I don't like him one bit better now. I wish we hadn't hired him.

There was something he did like, though, to compensate for his negative feeling about Oriol. That was the unexpected durability and good nature of Mildred Bell. Whether because of her father's warning that she was not the outdoor type, or because of too early a judgment on his own part, he had expected this journey to be an ordeal. And, true, it was taking much longer than it would have taken, had he and Oriol been alone. There had been frequent stops because she was hurting. Who, subjected to the tortures of such a trail for the first time, would not be hurting? Yet she hadn't once complained, except to remark wryly that her bottom and the insides of her thighs would surely be black and blue for the rest of her life.

Okay, Milly, you're a gutsy gal. I guess I was wrong about you.

What, he wondered, was she thinking about as they pushed deeper and deeper into this tropical mountain wilderness which to her must seem as strange as something on another planet?

She was thinking about him. About their first meeting.

"Mildred," her father had said, "do you know that new man in agriculture? That fellow Sam Norman?"

"I'm afraid not, Daddy."

"Interesting man. He worked in Haiti for a number of years before coming here. I've asked him over for dinner on Sunday."

Strange. They seldom had callers. In fact, the rundown New England cottage they lived in, so inconveniently far from the campus, had been purely and simply an investment in privacy. *Daddy's* investment in privacy. Before Mother's death he had led a reasonably normal social life—she had demanded it—but since then, he'd been a loner, content to cocoon himself in with his research.

What kind of man would Professor Norman be? She was curious, naturally. Agriculture? Daddy had no interest in agriculture. The attraction was Norman's knowledge of Haiti, obviously. There were half a dozen books about Haiti on the shelves in the den. Herskovitz, Rigaud, Rodman . . . To Daddy, Haiti meant voodoo.

What ought she to have for Sunday dinner?

"What? Oh, the food. Good heavens, child, whatever you think best. You know that's not my department."

That's right, Daddy, the meals and the house are not your concern, are they? They weren't when Mother was alive, and they're not now. And that's partly the reason for the buried way we live, isn't it? For you buying this house. Because with Mother gone and you so helpless about ordinary, everyday things, you have to have me around in order to survive. So I'm kept under wraps. Were I to get married you'd be . . . well, darling, to use a phrase that would shock you, you'd be up shit's creek, wouldn't you?

The very thought of using such language to her father had made her gasp.

A leg of lamb, she had decided. Daddy and she ate chicken every Sunday, and this Sunday ought to be different. Sam Norman was tall, handsome, and young. Not more than a year or two older than she, she was certain. It wasn't true that she didn't know him. While she hadn't actually met him, she knew who he was. Daddy might try to keep her bottled up like Stevenson's imp, but she did visit the college now and then, chiefly on errands for him. And one day, driving past the college farm and seeing a group of students and their instructor lining out a field for something which to her was totally mysterious, she had to stopped to watch. And a girl student in the car with her had said, "Isn't he refreshing in this stuffy old place?"

"Isn't who refreshing?"

"Professor Norman. The good-looking one in khaki."

No . . . not chicken for dinner. Even leg of lamb was awfully ordinary, but unless she was prepared to drive twenty miles, she couldn't do better.

Then, damn it, Daddy had gone and wasted it all.

Not intentionally, of course. Food just didn't mean anything to him. If she ever did leave him, he would probably exist on kippered herring snacks and crackers. "Perfectly adequate food, Mildred; we pamper our stomachs too much, anyway." So the roast of lamb, the mint sauce, the potatoes and cauliflower and Vermont apple pie came and went while Daddy dug for information on Haiti like a miner digging for gold and afraid his claims would run out before he reached it.

It was that kind of evening, Daddy doing his best to be relaxed and friendly but all the time entirely too tense to bring it off. At fifty-one he simply was not a relaxed and friendly man, no matter how much effort he expended. Slight of build, short of stature, he brought to mind a determined and rather *un*friendly Scottish terrier. All through the meal she felt the Scottie had backed Sam Norman into a corner and was barking at him.

Toward the end, when Daddy's bladder, thank God, had forced him to excuse himself—a thing it could be relied on to do with some frequency—she had been able to talk to Sam alone for a few minutes. To her total astonishment, he had asked if she would like to go to a basketball game with him. The school was playing Rhode Island, he said, and the game was sure to be a good one. Did she care for basketball?

Not wanting to refuse, but afraid to accept without consulting her father, she had asked if she might call him with her answer, and he jokingly said he would be sitting by the phone. All of which seemed to indicate that he found her attractive. Which was something, even though one had to remember that few women other than students were available to him there.

After his departure, Daddy had said, "Well, Mildred, what do you think of him? Like him, do you?"

Be careful, she warned herself. "I think so. I don't dislike him."

Daddy wore the expression that usually meant his mind was hard at work. With a little effort, she probably could have read his thoughts. "Fascinating, the things he told us about Haiti. I'd like to know him better, Mildred."

"Would you? He asked if I'd go to the basketball game with him Wednesday evening."

"And you said?"

"That I'd call him. I didn't want to say yes without asking you. But if you approve—"

"I certainly do."

"You're getting really keen about Haiti, aren't you?"

"Stop reading my mind."

"I don't have to. You can be pretty obvious at times, you know."

"Now, Mildred—"

Sensing he was annoyed, she had stepped forward and touched her lips to his cheek. "It's all right, Daddy," she said. "I'll cooperate."

Things kept reminding Sam Norman of the time he had ridden this same trail with Jack Ulinsky from the U.N.

There had been no special reason for that trip. They had become friends through their work—trying to help the Haitian peasant farmer produce more and better food—and both were interested in seeing as much of the country as possible before their tours of duty ended.

Getting two weeks off at the same time, with a jeep available, they had explored the Hinche area, visiting that hard-to-reach but marvelous Bassin Zim waterfall, then driven the incredible road from there to Cap Haï-tien and headed for Fort Liberté along the north-coast highway.

On inquiring at the Catholic church in Trou for a priest he had expected to find there, Ulinsky was told the man had been transferred to Vallière, back in the mountains. "Sam, let's go to Vallière!"

"Why not?"

"Gentlemen, you will need mules and a guide."

"Oh, come on, Father, we don't want a guide. We know this country."

"You don't know that part of this country." The priest smiled. "But all right, I'll draw a map and brief you. Sorry I can't put you up tonight—we're a bit crowded just now—but I'm sure my good friend Paul Lafontant will be able to, and obtain some mules for you as well."

It had been an adventure. And this trip was bringing it all back. The sound of the mules' hoofs in a deep green stillness. The sight of a mongoose streaking belly-down across the trail, turning its ratty head for a lightning look at the intruders before disappearing again. The sudden loud flutter of a big ground dove startled into flight. The haunting flute-notes of the musician bird, a creature so shy you almost never saw one. All just great.

He was remembering the stream crossings, the steep descents where high mossy walls shut out the light, the stiff climbs to heights from which the views were breath-taking. Most of all, he was recalling feelings. Especially the feeling that life was pretty damned good after all, and could properly be addressed with a yell of exultation while waving one's hat in the air. And this even without the rum Ulinsky and he had lugged along.

Feeling good, he fixed his gaze on Mildred, riding ahead of him behind their guide. Not the worst woman to be here with, he decided. But somewhere ahead was another one, bound for a village not far from the place they were headed for.

Would he overtake Kay Gilbert? Probably not, unless the youngster she was escorting slowed her down. But he might meet her in Bois Sauvage, or on her way back, if she returned at once.

Of course, she might just shake hands and say, "How are you, Sam Norman?" while looking straight through him. When you'd been monopolizing a woman for months, even sleeping with her, you were supposed to keep in touch, no? Letters, certainly. And telephone calls from Vermont to the West Indies were not earth-to-Mars, for God's sake.

When you hurt someone, you could at least apologize. *Of course, she'll look right through you, Norman. What the hell do you expect? What else do you deserve?*

Their guide had stopped. "M'selle, I think we should eat something, no?"

Mildred turned to Sam as he rode up. "What do you think, Sam?"

"He's right, I suppose. I know you're eager to get there and find out what's happened, but we have to stop for the night in Vallière, anyway." It would be nice to see Père Turnier again, he thought. Nice guy. Heart of gold and great sense of humor. And, oh, brother, those wild Chinese checker tournaments and dart games!

Seated beside the trail, with the mules tied twenty yards away so as not to flavor the food with sweat-smell, they ate Haitian breadrolls and canned corned beef from Paul Lafontant's shop in Trou and washed it down with water from canteens. You didn't drink the water in these mountain streams unless you were a Haitian peasant, immune to assorted microdemons. There were almost always people upstream, even in the most remote districts, washing themselves, their babies, their clothes, and even their animals in the same water.

"How much farther is it to Vallière, Sam?"

"My memory's not that good. Oriol? How much more?"

"We will be there before dark," Oriol said. *And then it will begin, perhaps. In any case, it will begin before morning, for the legless one won't want you coming closer than Vallière.*

"Then there's no need for us to push on as if the devil's after us, is there?"

"None at all, M'sieu." *Because the devil will wait.*

"Damn it, I should have brought some rum," Sam said.

Their guide rose and went to the mules. From a saddlebag on his own animal, he lifted a bottle of five-star Barbancourt which, on returning, he solemnly held out.

Sam opened the bottle and motioned the others to hold out their canteen cups. "Thanks, Oriol, I underestimated you."

Silently, their guide returned his grin.

15

The approach to Vallière was along a widening trail worn smooth over the years by bare feet with leather-tough bottoms. Crowds of near-naked youngsters lugged water from the river in gourds, lengths of bamboo, and such civilized containers as lard tins, most of them facing a wearying uphill walk as they struggled to supply their households before dark.

The mules found the uphill track to the church and rectory just as rugged. They used their last reserves of strength to negotiate it and were shining with sweat when at last allowed to halt.

Through the open rectory gate, which was made of tall wooden slats, paced a small woman wearing a white work dress and a red bandanna. She peered out, to see why the strangers had stopped. She was not one of the servants Sam remembered.

"*Bon soir,* Madame. Is Père Turnier here?"

"Who?"

"Père Turnier. I'm Sam Norman. He may remember me."

Frowning up at him, she wagged her head. "Père Turnier has not been here for a long time, M'sieu. The vicar is Père Remy now, but he is not here. He and his *curé* are in Grosse Roche for a week." She was the fathers' housekeeper, she added.

There was a chapel in the tiny village of Grosse Roche, some five hours' distant by mule. He and Ulinsky had ridden there with Father Turnier one day just to keep the man company. He hooked a leg over the saddle, not without wincing, and dropped to the ground. "Madame, this is embarrassing." Chin in hand, he solemnly gazed at her. "We need a place to sleep tonight and were counting on Père Turnier's hospitality. I've stayed here before."

"There is no problem, M'sieu. We have beds."

"Bless you."

"Please come in."

He helped Mildred dismount, and Oriol began removing the gear from the animals.

"You can tie them to the hedge for now," the woman said, indicating the hibiscus hedge that gave the priests' residence a little privacy. "I'll have someone show you later where to put them for the night." To Sam and Mildred: "Come, please."

Inside the house she led them through a living room to the long, narrow bedroom Sam had used with Ulinsky. It contained two cots. "This will be all right?"

"I'm afraid we need two rooms."

"Oh?" She hesitated, looking distressed. "Then we do have a problem. We have only this one guest room now. There is another at the back, but when the fathers are away I use it." To Sam's amusement, she actually wrung her long-fingered hands. "I wouldn't dare let one of you use the vicar's room or the *curé*'s. Not without their permission."

"It's all right." Sam stepped to the door and peered into the living room. Damn. There was no couch, no sofa, nothing at all he could be horizontal on. "I can sleep out here on one of these chairs," he said grudgingly.

Mildred said, "After being on a mule since daybreak, and with more of the same tomorrow? No, Sam."

"But—"

"We can both use this room," she said firmly to the woman, forgetting the housekeeper did not speak English. Getting a blank look that made her aware of her mistake, she turned impatiently to Sam. "Tell her, will you?"

"Daddy's not going to like it," Sam said.

"Daddy isn't here and needn't know. I won't have you scrunched up in a chair or sleeping on a floor all night!"

Sam said to the housekeeper, "The m'selle says we can use this room. No problem."

"Good." She was obviously much relieved. "Then I'll go and see about your man and the mules, and start supper."

"We have some food."

"No need. I bought a goat today."

Where, Sam wondered, would friend Oriol sleep? On a mat somewhere, no doubt. He didn't care enough to bother asking. *To hell with you, Jack; go measure your flour.*

He looked at Mildred. She must be dead tired, yet she looked more alive than he had ever seen her look in Vermont. "All day long you've been surprising me," he said. "Now this."

When she smiled, something altogether unexpected happened to her daughter-of-Daddy face. "You know something?" she said. "If I weren't worried about my father, I'd be having the time of my life. All this is so new."

"You're liking it?"

"Loving it."

"Why? Tell me why."

"Later," she said. "Right now I want to draw a

bath. I must smell as high as that beast I've been sitting on."

"Both of us. There used to be a shower out back. Let me check."

There still was, he discovered, but he wondered how Daddy's little Vermont girl would like it. You stood under a bucket that had holes punched in its bottom, and you pulled a chain. This allowed water to flow from a pipe into the bucket and down through the holes. Cold water, of course. Returning to the room, he found Mildred awaiting him in a black bikini.

"Don't laugh," she said when his eyes popped. "I bought it at least two years ago and have never worn it. I only brought it along because it weighs nothing."

She was a good-looking woman, Sam decided. All curves and all in the right places. But why, for God's sake, did the moment remind him of a time Kay Gilbert and he had showered together at the Calman, solemnly and silently soaping each other all over before a night in bed?

Leading Mildred to the shower, he explained how it worked, then, after she had finished, took his and returned to the room to find her dressed in clean clothes and anxious to wash out the ones she had worn all day. He himself had only just finished dressing when there was a knock on the door.

The fathers' housekeeper said, "Supper will be ready in half an hour. Would you like a drink?"

"Love one."

"Oriol says he will eat with me in the kitchen. Do you have any clothes you want washed?"

Solemn as a church, she went away with Mildred's clothes and his, to return in a few minutes with a tray bearing a bottle of rum, two glasses, an earthenware jug full of water, and some ice. The rectory had a kerosene refrigerator, Sam remembered. As he fixed the drinks, his eyes fell on the water jar, which brought to mind the singing *govis* in Dr. Bell's room at the pension.

How had Mildred's old man made the *govis* sing and the drum throb that way?

He handed Mildred a drink. Downing it, she passed it back for a refill as though the two of them had been boozing together for years. "Nice," she said. "It's been quite a day, Sam."

"Hasn't it, though?"

"I'm hungry, too. Goat, did she say? I could eat a horse."

"Never eaten goat?"

"Now, where in the world would I have eaten goat, when I've never been out of New England before?" Her laugh ran around the room, rippling over the walls, caressing the two cots. If she had never slept in the same room with a man before, Sam thought, she must be a little nervous. Daddy had kept the cage door locked until now, more than likely.

Supper was an event. Both a little high on Barbancourt plus fatigue plus relief at having found a haven for the night, they might have been slightly silly, anyway, Sam figured, but were certainly made more so by what was placed before them in the rectory's little dining-room. It was goat soup, served from a huge aluminum tureen. In it swam assorted vegetables. You knew it was goat because the animal's head was in it, too—the whole head, big as life in the middle of the dish. Its eye sockets stared at Mildred, and she stared back at them, speechless for a moment, while Sam said, "Thank you, Madame," and the housekeeper said, "I hope you are accustomed to our kind of cooking, M'sieu, and please call me Françoise."

"Françoise," Sam murmured.

She departed, smiling.

"What are these things?" Mildred asked, finding her

voice. With a spoon she lifted from the tureen a number of white objects that appeared to be nuts of some kind. The soup was filled with them. "Are they Haitian?"

"Taste one."

She did, and looked at him in astonishment while nibbling it. "Garlic?"

He grinned. "And not Haitian. At least, not so far as I know. Haitians use garlic, of course, but not like this. I suspect the *curé* here is a French *paysan,* like Père Turnier before him. Incidentally, when I was here with Jack Ulinsky, we had dishes of these garlic corms at every meal, even for breakfast. Everybody stank to high heaven and nobody gave a damn."

She ate the ones she had fished from the tureen and was just tipsy enough to be comical when she gravely nodded. "I like them."

I like you, Sam thought.

She ladled out soup for them both and tried it. "This is good, too. You know something, Sam? This trip is becoming an education."

You keep on being so unexpectedly nice, Sam thought, *and it may indeed be an education. For both of us, maybe.* Why did he keep seeing her in that black bikini?

But why, on the other hand, did he keep thinking of that shower at the Pension Calman?

Françoise came with slices of roast goat in a pepper sauce so fiery it made their eyes water. Then with two glass cups of Jello that hadn't jelled. Then with coffee. Finished, Sam went into the kitchen to tender their thanks and compliments.

"By the way, Françoise, did some other strangers pass through here yesterday?"

"Not yesterday, M'sieu. But I heard that a white woman came through this morning with a little girl and a guide. Someone said she was a nurse from that hospital in the Artibonite."

"Going where?"

"To Bois Sauvage, the guide said, but I doubt it. He rode through here again in mid-afternoon, alone, and it is certain he could not have reached Bois Sauvage and returned in that short time."

Sam felt something tighten in his chest. "He came back *alone?*"

She nodded.

"Did he say why?"

"I don't think he stopped to talk to anyone, M'sieu. In the morning when the woman and child were with him, yes. In the afternoon, no. That's what we have heard, anyway."

Why, Sam wondered, would Kay Gilbert have hired a man to guide her into these mountains and then have sent him back? Did she plan to stay in here a while, as he and Ulinsky had? If so, where would she stay?

Full of questions that made him want to do something —but what?—he returned to the dining room. He said to Mildred, "Would you like to see something of this village before we turn in? There won't be time in the morning."

Maybe—just maybe—he could find out more about Kay than the housekeeper had been able to tell him.

"I'd love to, Sam, but it's dark out there."

He glanced out a window and saw she was right. Thanks, probably, to the goat soup and his delight at her acceptance of it, he hadn't noticed. You frequently failed to notice the coming of night in this country. There was little twilight. You suddenly and unexpectedly found yourself groping in a blackout, especially if you happened to be in a country village like this where there were no street lamps. There'd been kerosene lamps on the table at supper, he realized now. Amazing, his intense preoccupation with other things.

"We have flashlights," he said. "And there's some

kind of moon. Stars, at any rate."

"All right."

He went to their room for the flashlights, and they set out through the village, Mildred casually taking his hand when the track became a series of gullies.

Past the Garde d'Haiti post with its wide flight of concrete steps flanked by tall palms.

Past wattle-and-clay houses, not a straight line in the lot, topped with roofs of rusting galvanized iron.

Past the village market, now just an empty forest of dark and spooky poles supporting roofs of thatch.

Stars and moon provided some light as Sam had predicted, though not much. The flashlight beams aroused the village dogs—gaunt, bow-legged curs that slunk snarling and barking out of dark yards but were careful not to challenge too boldly and ran with their tails between their legs when lunged at.

At a place where two paths intersected, Sam halted to examine a five-foot-high wooden cross worn smooth as glass, apparently from much stroking. Globs of old candle wax encrusted the circular concrete slab at its base.

"Voodoo?" Mildred asked.

"Baron Samedi guarding the crossroads. The candles are lit for special favors, such as protection on a journey."

"If I had one, I'd light it for us."

"Would you? Why?"

"Why not?" she said, smiling.

But soon after that, Sam sensed a change in her. She seemed to lose interest in walking about the village and paid less and less attention to what he was telling her. He had some good stories, too, he felt with a twinge of disappointment. Father Turnier, for instance, had told about a too-persistent village tax collector who, at the people's request, had been run out of town by a *bocor*. Then the *bocor* had been arrested and fined for forbidding the rain to fall because he wasn't paid for his job on the tax collector. You wouldn't hear tales like that in a Vermont college town, now would you?

But Mildred was tired. It had been a hard day, and the rum before supper had probably made her sleepy, too. Taking her by the hand again, Sam headed for home, choosing the shortest way back that he knew.

One more stop was a must, though, when his light picked out a small, weathered, blue and white sign on a humble house by the path. The sign said, "Bureau Postal."

He began laughing.

"Something?" Mildred asked vaguely as they halted.

"I mailed a letter when I was here before, just to see if such a post office could be real. I sent it to Victor Vieux at the Calman." Dropping her hand, he went a few steps closer to the railed veranda, peering at the sign and remembering.

"He never got it, I suppose," Mildred said behind him in an out-of-focus voice.

"Would you believe he did? And in less than a week. Amazing things happen in Haiti. The crazy part of it was, I never thought he *would* get it so I didn't actually write a letter, just mailed him an empty envelope, not even a return address. Then when I got back to Port I didn't happen to see him for a while to tell him what I'd done, and poor Victor spent all that time wondering who in Vallière could have mailed him an empty envelope, and why. It nearly drove him up the wall. He didn't know Ulinsky and I were going in there, remember. We ourselves didn't know." Still gazing at the sign, Sam waited for her laughter.

She didn't laugh. Didn't even answer him.

Puzzled by her silence, he swung around.

She was no longer there.

16

"Hey!"

Lurching back into the middle of the path, Sam aimed his light up the hill toward the distant rectory. Mildred hadn't gone that way. With such a stiff climb facing her, she could not have got out of sight so soon.

He swung around and stabbed his light down the hill, where the path made a turn. She could have gone that way. *Must have* gone that way, unless she had run in between houses.

He ran after her, yelling, "Milly! Milly! Where are you?"

Except for the occasional barking of a dog, the village was quiet now and his voice carried far in the stillness. It bounced off the clay-walled houses past which he raced and came back to him as more than one voice. He rounded the corner and saw a deserted stretch of road with another turn ahead. On his left a door opened, letting out a rectangle of lamplight. A man stepped out to peer at him.

"Compère, did you hear someone pass by here just now?"

The fellow pointed, and Sam ran on, the beam of his flashlight sweeping the path ahead. He was waking up half the village with his yelling, he realized. All kinds of doors were being opened. Had the hour been later, they probably would have stayed shut, but it wasn't late enough for werewolves and evil spirits.

When he called out to ask if anyone had passed, people pointed, saying that they had heard running footsteps. Following this phantom trail, he found himself on a narrow path winding down to the river. Not the main road to the fording where the kids had been drawing water, but a side path twisting away from the village. It led, he knew, to a stretch of rocks and deep pools where the women went to bathe and do their washing.

Why was Mildred following this track? How did she even know about it? How, for God's sake, could she even *see* it in the dark? For she was not using her flashlight. Not once had it even winked on. Could a total stranger run through the twisting paths of a mountain village at night without a light? Impossible!

He stumbled on down the path. It was the only path now, this one that followed the coils of the river. The stream was swift. He could hear it growling over rocks as it entered the chasm where big boulders lined its sides. The beam of his light zigzagged with the path's crazy turns, causing him to lurch into massed branches of rose-apple trees whose white pompom blossoms slapped at his face like spectral hands. In a voice now hoarse and scratchy, he kept calling her name.

Then he saw her.

She had left the path and run out onto the rocks—huge, flat-topped boulders here that ended in a sheer drop of fifteen or twenty feet to the stream racing through the casm. He knew the spot, had stumbled upon it one day when he had been out with Père Turnier's shotgun, hunting wild pigeons and guinea fowl for the rectory larder. A careless step on those rocks, and you could go plunging down into white water or deep, swirling pools.

"Milly, for God's sake stop!"

She was only walking now, not running, and, at the sound of his voice, she turned her head to look back. Looked right into his light while his yell crashed among the rocks and broke into shards like a flung bottle. If she took even two more steps . . .

"Don't, Milly! Don't do it!"

She raised an arm to her eyes as though his light were blinding her; then, as he stumbled toward her, she turned away. With the slow movements of a somnambulist, she took one of the last two steps she would ever take.

His right hand shot out and caught her by the belt.

It was not a sure thing, though. His headlong rush brought him down, and she fell with him, both so close to the edge that he found himself looking down over it at the rushing water. He could see the water only because it was white in the chasm's dark depths; his flashlight was back there among the rocks where he had dropped it so he could grab at her. Working his legs furiously, he dragged her away from the danger and struggled to his feet, hauling her up with him. He pulled her over to his flashlight and picked it up, shone it on her face.

"Sam?" she said, blinking.

He let his breath out and the fear went with it, leaving room now for anger. "Milly, what the *hell* were you doing?"

She looked around, puzzled at finding herself where she was. "What . . . ? Sam, I don't remember coming here. What is this place?"

Whatever else it might be, it was no place for a conversation, Sam decided. "Come on. Let's get out of here."

Meekly, she allowed him to grasp her wrist and lead her back to the path, then up the path toward the village. Halfway there, his light touched something shiny beside the track. It was her flash, where she had dropped it or thrown it away. He turned it on and handed it to her.

As they walked up through the village, doors opened again. One woman, peering out with her man, called, "Is she all right, M'sieu?" and Sam answered, "I think so, yes."

Was she?

At the rectory, the fathers' housekeeper opened the front door while they were still walking to it from the gate. She held a lamp high and peered into Mildred's face as they entered. Closing the door, she said, "I heard you in the village, M'sieu. Sound carries far here at night. Is something wrong?"

"Not now, Françoise. Miss Bell wandered off and I was trying to locate her in the dark." He had to tell her something.

She continued to peer at Mildred as though wondering whether to believe him. "Would the m'selle like some coffee?"

Sam translated, and Mildred shook her head. "Thank you, no."

"A little rum, then?"

Maybe that was it, Sam thought. The rum. They hadn't drunk much, but if Mildred were one of those who couldn't handle even a little . . .

Mildred said, "I'll just go to bed, I think. May I, Sam?"

"Of course." He took her arm and walked her to the room they were to share. The housekeeper had put a lamp on a table there, the wick low because they were expected to leave it burning all night. He turned it up while Mildred went to her cot and sat down. Seating himself on his own cot, at the other end of the room, he realized he could not easily talk to her across that much space and went to sit on a chair within arm's reach of her.

"Want to tell me what happened?"

"I don't know what happened."

"We were at the post office. I started to tell you about mailing a letter there, and you answered me. I finished the story—a long, stupid story—with my back to you, and when I turned around, you were gone."

She shook her head. "I remember the start of the story. You mailed a letter to Victor Vieux, to see how long it would take to reach him. After that . . . Sam, I don't know. I don't remember leaving you."

"Milly, you went down through the village without using a light. You went along that path to the pools without a light. God knows how you did it. What *do* you remember?"

"I heard you speaking to me. I looked back and there you were, shining your light in my eyes. But, Sam, I still had to do what I . . . was being told to do. I still had to go to the edge there and walk off."

"Told by whom?" Sam demanded, feeling small things with many cold legs walking over his body.

She shook her head slowly again. "It was like some kind of dream. That's the only way I can describe it. Some kind of nightmare. I just had to do it. I couldn't help myself." Leaning forward on the cot, she unlaced and removed her sneakers. "I've got to go to bed, Sam. I'm sorry. I just can't talk anymore now. Please?"

He nodded and stood. Went to his own cot and stripped down to the underwear he would sleep in. When he looked across the room again, Mildred was in bed with a blanket pulled over her.

17

The section of the capital called Turgeau.
An impressive old residence in Rue Coirin.
Dr. Roger Bell pushes open the gate.
A bell tinkles
and at once a tawny Great Dane
lopes down the wide driveway.

The front door opens at the same time.
A tall, slender Haitian,
light brown of complexion,
calls to the beast from the veranda,
then welcomes Dr. Bell.

Dr. Bell advances,
climbs the steps,
shakes the man's hand,
thanks him for consenting to see him.

They enter the house.
Dr. Bell is led into a handsome,
mahogany-paneled study.
On one of the book-lined walls
hangs framed proof
that Decatus Molicoeur

holds a degree of Doctor of Philosophy
from the University of the West Indies
in Jamaica.
There is nothing to indicate he is also
a close friend and confidant
of Haiti's president for life,
Jean Claude Duvalier.
But he is.

Dr. Molicoeur waves his caller
to a chair
and smiles at him.
"Now, Dr. Bell,
what can I do for a distinguished
doctor of philosophy
from a state
I have never had the good fortune
to visit?"
His English is flawless,
his friendliness not to be questioned.
In another part of this lovely old house
he has a charming, beautiful wife,
an equally beautiful four-year-old daughter
about whom Dr. Bell has been told
—warned—
by the legless *bocor* in Legrun.

Looking into the face of this man,
and thinking of the wife and daughter,
Dr. Bell now stiffens in his chair,
turns pale.

"Is something wrong, Dr. Bell?"
"No, no, it is nothing.
It will pass."
* * *

The voice of Margal
has re-established control.
Bell is once more
the obedient servant.

"You asked what you could do for me, Dr. Molicoeur."
"Yes."
"Begin, please, by looking at me."

That was how Margal had begun with him.
The eyes were the web
that held the victim.

18

"Miss Kay?"

"Yes, Tina?"

"Did you see that thing in our room last night?"

"I saw something, baby. What it was I'm not sure. What do you think it was?"

"I don't know."

They were naked, she and the child, having a bath in one of the prettiest mountain streams she had ever seen. A welcome bath, too, for the sweat of yesterday's ride and last night's tension was still on her, and they had ridden for another hour this morning since leaving the home of Edita and Antoine. At the house, there had been no water for bathing. At least, none she could have used without feeling guilty. Antoine and his woman would have had to walk far for it.

Soaped from head to foot, she lay back in the clear, shallow water and watched little Tina imitate her. Downstream, around a bend that hid him from sight, their guide Joseph was bathing, too. She could hear him splashing around and singing the folk song "Plotonnade" about the girl at the river who preferred making love to doing laundry: "You have water, soap, bluing, and starch. Why aren't you washing, girl?"

A minnow swam in between her legs and she said with

mock indignation, "Hey, you, where do you think you're going?" Undeterred, it kept on coming until she put a hand down and splashed it away.

"Miss Kay?" Tina stood up and solemnly frowned at her. "It *was* a lizard, wasn't it?"

"I think so, baby."

"But such a big one!"

"Well, now, that's what I'm not sure of. You were asleep, and one of those lizards in the thatch dropped onto the bed. But it was only a little one, and I don't believe it really got big. I think we just imagined that part. And you were making noises in your sleep when it fell. I'll bet you were dreaming. Do you remember what you were dreaming about?"

Tina wagged her head, mechanically lifting water in her graceful hands and letting it run down over her slender body.

"You don't remember?"

"Uh uh."

Kay, too, stood up, feeling wonderfully clean and refreshed. "Anyway, we're okay this morning, aren't we? So I guess we'd better just forget it." Wading toward the bank, she paused to watch a crayfish scoot under a stone, then skirted a pool full of minnows to reach the overhanging rose-apple limbs on which Tina and she had draped their clothes after washing them. The clothes would have to be packed in the saddlebags wet, but no matter, they were clean. "Coming, baby?" she called, turning her head. Then she gasped.

The child was calmly sitting in shallow water, having herself a bowel movement.

Oh, brother, Kay thought, wincing. Even after all those talks at the hospital about clean water . . . Would this poor, miserable, wonderful country ever change?

Donning dry clothes, she called to the child again, then went down the trail to the mules. Joseph was already there, looking scrubbed and cheerful. Tina appeared a few minutes later, and their journey continued.

Passing through the village of Vallière an hour later, she looked for the church and rectory Sam Norman had told her about two years ago, and for the bell tower he had described as "a kind of big white tombstone with a bell in the top of it." They were not hard to find, dominating the scene as they did.

So this is where he had had such a great time, she thought, and felt cheated. Why couldn't *she* have been with him when he came here, instead of that fellow from the U.N.?

In the village she had to wait several times while Joseph stopped to talk to people he knew. But not for long. Beyond Vallière, the trail continued its slow, twisting climb and the stillness returned.

The mountain stillness. No bird cry or leaf rustle could have much effect on a silence so profound, nor could the muffled thumping of the mules' hoofs over the layers of leaf mold. She felt as if she was riding through another world.

Why hadn't Sam written after returning to the States? Had she been that rotten to him their last night together?

In the stillness of the forest, her mind drifted back to that agonizing last weekend. Would things have ended differently if she had been able to get to Port-au-Prince on Saturday, as she had promised?

Sam had arrived there Saturday. She had not. Friday evening, a camion en route from Cap Haïtien to the capital had gone off the road near St. Marc, landing upside down in a ditch; many of its passengers had been injured and brought to the hospital. What was she supposed to do? Say to the doctors, "Look, I can't help with these people, I have a date in Port"?

So she had arrived at the Pension Calman Sunday afternoon, a whole day late, and found that Sam was not there and everyone else, Victor Vieux included, was acting strangely.

"Victor, where is he?"

"I don't know, Kay. He stayed around all last evening waiting for you. Then this morning he took off."

"Didn't he say where he was going?"

"No. I'm sorry."

"Oh, God, Victor, I know I should have phoned him, but I couldn't. The damned telephone out there hasn't worked for days!"

"Kay, he knows that. He tried to phone *you* and they told him."

"Then why did he get angry?"

"Kay, be patient. Come, have a drink with me and wait for him. We both know he won't spend his last night in Haiti just driving around the city feeling sorry for himself."

It was a conspiracy of silence, of course. Something had happened, but Victor was not talking. The maids were in on it. Their unnatural reticence told her so.

Had Sam got drunk when she failed to appear? She didn't know his capacity, had never seen him truly drunk—unless he had been drunk that night in Jacmel when he tried to crash her room naked. Something was wrong, but what?

Then, at ten o'clock he had returned—

Stop it, she told herself. *That was more than two years ago, and there have been other men since then, and Sam Norman is long gone and long forgotten.*

Why, then, was she thinking about him now?

But she had been thinking about him almost constantly since leaving the hospital with Tina, hadn't she? And not just because of Tina's name, or even because Sam had traveled part of this wilderness trail before her.

He could have written, damn him. He could at least have

said he was sorry for that last Godawful night.

They were climbing, she realized, and had been for a while. Without even thinking about it, she had leaned forward to grip her mule's neck as it clawed its way up an almost vertical stretch of rocky path. Now the trail was leveling off and she saw Joseph ten yards ahead, looking back and waiting for her. As usual, Tina sat snugly and smugly in front of him, fenced in by his arms.

She pulled up alongside, and he said, "For a little while it will be hard now, M'selle. Should we stop a while?"

"I'm not tired, Joseph."

"Well, all right. I was thinking you might be hungry, but maybe we should get this place behind us. Then we can stop thinking about it."

Remembering something the woman had said last night, Kay frowned. "Is this the place they call Saut Diable?" It meant, she knew, Devil's Leap.

He nodded.

She peered ahead. The sun was high and the track mottled with tree shadows, but after a short stretch where it leveled off, sloped down into a kind of trench. They had ridden through similar cuts already: places where the earth was soft and seasonal rains had scored it to a depth of eight or ten feet. Riding through such a place, you sometimes had to remove your feet from the stirrups and lift them high. Otherwise, if the mule lurched sideways, you could end up with a crushed leg.

"M'selle," Joseph said, "the defile ahead is narrow and very steep. You must make your animal descend slowly. You understand?"

She nodded, feeling apprehensive.

"But don't even start down it until I call to you from below."

"Until you call to me?"

"At the bottom, the trail turns sharply to the right,

like this." Dramatically he drew a right angle in the air. "I will be waiting there to help you."

She was not sure she understood, but watched him ride on and noticed how carefully he put his mule to the trench. Riding forward herself, she reined in at the top and watched him go on down until he disappeared beyond a curve of the cut. It seemed a long time before she heard him calling her, from far below.

Scared, she clucked her own mule forward.

It was the worst stretch they had encountered, not only steep but slippery. The red-earth walls rising sheer on both sides smelled wet and musty and were only just far enough apart to permit passage. Her mule took short, mincing steps, stumbled at times. At one twist of the trail he went to his knees, all but pitching her over his head, then was barely able to struggle up again. Her feet had to be out of the stirrups, and she marveled that she was able to stay on the animal's back.

Luckily, her feet were back in place for the last few yards. The walls of red earth were a little farther apart. At the bottom, Joseph waited for her, standing on wide-spread legs against a patch of deep blue sky. He held in his hands a dead stick about as long as a baseball bat and, in fact, looked like a batter standing at the plate awaiting a pitch.

"Come slowly," he called to her. "And hang on!"

As she came within reach of him he swung the stick. *Whap!* It caught her mule across the left side of the neck and caused him to wheel abruptly to the right. As she clung to the pommel to keep from falling, she got the full picture and promptly wet herself.

Joseph had been standing on the edge of a sheer drop, to make sure her mule didn't take one step too many before turning. Had the animal done so, both she and it —and Joseph too, no doubt—would have gone hurtling down into a valley hundreds of feet below.

Her mule stopped. A little distance ahead, Joseph's animal was waiting, with Tina aboard and looking back. The trail was a ribbon of rock no more than six feet wide, winding along the cliff face for a hundred yards or more with awesome heights above and those terrifying depths below. Joseph, still clutching his stick, caught up with her and gave her mule a pat on the shoulder, as if to apologize for clubbing it.

"You are all right, M'selle?"

"I'll never be all right again."

He chuckled. "Actually, I was not worried. This gray beast of yours has been here before and is not stupid. I only wanted to be sure he would remember that place. Just give him his head now and let him follow my animal along here. Okay?"

"Okay," she said, hoping he would not notice her wet pants.

He walked on ahead and swung himself into the saddle, saying something to Tina that made the child look at him with adoring eyes. His mule started forward, and Kay's animal clop-clopped along behind it.

Then the trail began to go dark.

Kay looked up to see what had happened to the sun. It was there but fading, and the sky began to look like a thick sheet of overexposed photographic film becoming blacker every second.

She looked down. A dark mist rose from the valley which only a moment ago had been green. Was it a mist? Distinctly, she smelled smoke and saw flames. Then, like an exhalation from the earth itself, the darkness swirled up to engulf her.

Suddenly, she could see nothing in front of her, nothing above or below, nothing behind. All creation was black and boiling.

Her mule stopped. Why? Because in her sudden terror she had jerked the reins, or because he, too, was now blind? What was happening was unreal, she thought frantically. It was no more real than the flash flood at the fording yesterday and the harmless gecko that had become a ravenous dragon last night.

Margal, she thought. *The man with no legs. We're getting close and he doesn't want us.*

19

The sky, the valley, the trail snaking along the cliffside in front of her—all had disappeared. The darkness had engulfed them and was furiously alive, shot through with flames and reeking of smoke. The smoke made her cough and she could not stop coughing, had to cling to the saddle as she struggled to breathe.

And now the thunder. Peal upon peal of thunder, filling the fiery darkness in the valley and bouncing off the cliff in front of her and behind her. So, was this just a freak mountain storm after all?

Only it wasn't thunder she was hearing, was it? No. It was a booming of drums, ever so many drums, dozens, hundreds of drums. The sound assaulted her head and she wanted to scream but knew she must not. A scream might frighten the big gray mule. He wasn't easily frightened. He had proved that more than once. But he was still standing motionless, waiting for her to urge him forward again.

Should she do that? Had his world, too, gone mad? Or did he still see the trail in front of him, Joseph and Tina on the mule ahead, and the green valley below?

Can't stay here. Can't risk it. But there is no way to turn and go back!

Should she try to dismount and walk back? No, no!

The world was so dark, she might as well be blind. If she tried to slide from the saddle on the cliff side, the mule might step away to make room for her. Might take a step too many and go plunging over the edge. And if she tried to dismount on *that* side without knowing where the edge was, she might drop straight into space.

She clucked to the gray as Joseph had taught her. Touched him, oh so gently, with her heels. "Go on, fella. But slow, go slow."

He gave his head a shake and moved forward through the stinking smoke and the drum-thunder, while she prayed he could see the trail and would not walk off its edge. Or grind her into the wall.

If he does grind me into the wall, I'll know he can't see any better than I can. Then I can pull him up and at least wait. But if he goes wrong on the outside . . .

She began to cry. The smoke had got to her eyes and was burning them. And she was still coughing.

The mule plodded on through the unreal darkness. The drums thundered. Tongues of scarlet leaped high from the valley—high enough to curl in over the trail and stab at her feet, as if to force her to lift them from the stirrups and lose her balance. Fighting back the panic, she gripped the saddle with both hands and ground her knees into the mule's sides for an added grip.

Saut Diable. The Devil's Leap. Had the legless one lost his legs in a fall from here? She didn't believe it. No one could survive such a fall.

Dear God, how much longer?

The gray could see. She was convinced of it. He trudged along as though this journey through the nightmare were all in the day's work. Not once did he brush her leg against the cliff, and so she had to assume that not once did he venture too close to the drop on the other side. Was the darkness only in her mind, then? Was Margal responsible for it?

Never mind that now, Gilbert. Just hang on. Pray.

It almost seemed that the one creating the illusion knew his grisly scheme was not working. Knew she had not panicked and spooked the gray mule into plunging over the trail's edge with her. The thunder of the drums grew louder. She thought her skull would crack under the pounding. The darkness became a gigantic whirlpool that seemed certain to suck her into its vortex. She tried shutting her eyes. It didn't help.

I'm not seeing these things. I'm thinking them.

The big gray walked on.

The whirlpool slowed and paled. The flames diminished to flickerings. The sky lightened and let the sun blur through again. Slowly the image of the other mule took shape ahead of her, with Joseph and Tina on its back.

She looked down and saw darkness leaving the valley, the smoke drifting away in wisps, the green returning. It was like the end of a storm.

Ahead, Joseph was stopping where the cliff passage ended and the trail entered a forest again. He dismounted and swung Tina down beside him. The child clung to his legs. On reaching them, Kay slid from the saddle too.

She and Joseph looked at each other. Joseph's handsome face was the hue of wood ash, drained of all shine, all sparkle, all life. Trembling against him, the child stared at Kay, too, with eyes that revealed the same kind of terror.

They rode through the nightmare, too. It wasn't just for me.

Kay felt she had to say something very commonplace. Very calming. "Well . . . we're here, aren't we? Saut Diable is behind us." *Brilliant,* she thought. *Just what we didn't need.*

"M'selle . . . what happened?"

"I'm not sure, Joseph. What do *you* think happened?" Get him talking. Get that ghastly look off his face. Off Tina's, too.

"Everything went dark, M'selle."

"Yes."

"The valley on fire."

"It seemed to be. The flames reached right up to the trail and the smoke made me cough."

"Drumming. I heard all three drums: manman, second, and bula. And I think even a fourth—even the giant assotor."

The assotor, she thought. *So big they have to stand on a ladder to play it.* Only on very special occasions was that huge drum used. She had never seen one; only heard about them.

"It was all in our minds," she insisted. "It wasn't real."

"It happened, M'selle." He turned his ashen face to look at Tina. "Didn't it, *ti-fi?*"

Tina nodded, still too frightened to speak.

"No," Kay said. "There were no real flames. There was no real smoke. There was not really a fire. Look down there."

He moved a few steps and looked, but they were too far from the end of the cliff trail, so she took him by the hand to walk him back. At that he froze.

"Just to the cliff," she said. "So we can see."

He shook his head.

"It didn't happen, Joseph. I'm telling you, it did not happen. We only imagined it. Now come!"

His head jerked again from side to side and she could not budge him.

At the hospital she was known to have a temper when one was called for. This occasion called for one. "Damn it, Joseph, don't be a child! Come and see!" Her yank on his wrist all but pulled him off his feet.

He allowed himself to be hauled far enough back along the trail so that he could look into the valley. It was fighteningly far down, to be sure, but in no way was it marked by fire.

"You see? If there had really been a fire raging down there, you would still see smoke. Still smell it. Now will you believe me?"

"I know what I saw."

"You don't. You know what you thought you saw, that's all." Oh, God, if only there were words in Creole for this kind of discussion, but there were not. It was a bare-bone language, scarcely adequate even for dealing with basics. There were words for working, eating, and sex; so few to *think* with.

Well, then, stick to basics. Stop trying to explain things.

"All right, Joseph. There was a fire but it's out now. Let's go, hey?"

He shook his head. "No, M'selle. Not me. I am turning back."

"What?"

"These things that have happened are a warning. Worse will happen if we go on."

She faced him with her hands on her hips, knowing her face was white with strain. "You can't do this to me, Joseph. You agreed to guide me to Bois Sauvage. I've already paid you half the money!"

"I will give it back."

"Joseph, stop this. Stop it right now. I have to take Tina home, and you have to help me. These crazy things that have happened don't concern us. They're meant for someone else. Who would want to stop Tina from returning home?"

"I am going back, M'selle. I am afraid."

"You can't be such a coward!"

He only shrugged.

She worked on him. There, at the end of the cliff-side trail overlooking the valley, she talked to him for twenty minutes, pleading, cajoling, begging him to consider Tina, threatening him with the wrath of the police who had hired him out to her. Long before she desisted, she knew it was hopeless. He liked her; he was fond of the child; he was gray with fear.

She walked back to the mules, and he followed. Eyes flashing with anger, she wheeled on him. "All right. If you won't go any farther, you can at least tell me how to get there. Because I'm going without you!"

"M'selle, you must not!"

"Does this trail lead to Bois Sauvage, or can I get lost?"

In a pathetic whisper, with his gaze downcast, he said, "It is the main road. You will not get lost."

"Please, rearrange the saddlebags, then, so Tina and I will have what we need."

He did so in silence, while she and Tina watched him. The child's eyes were enormous.

"Now lift Tina onto my mule, please. I know I'll have to do it myself from now on, but you can do it one more time."

He picked the child up. Before placing her on the gray mule, he brushed his lips against her cheek. His own cheeks were wet now.

Kay carefully swung herself into the saddle, then turned and looked down at him. "You won't change your mind?"

"M'selle, I will wait for you at my aunt's house, where we stayed last night."

"Don't bother," she said bitterly. "A lizard might eat you."

Then, tight-lipped and full of anger, she clucked to her mule and rode on.

20

Mildred looked at her watch, its dial faintly visible in the lamplight. Two-twenty A.M. Lifting herself on one elbow, she peered at the other cot in the rectory bedroom. Sam Norman was still asleep. He hadn't moved in the past half hour.

Why, at a time like this, was she thinking about Daddy again? Because she couldn't sleep? Because she was frightened? Because he was the one person likely to understand what had happened to her?

What *had* happened? She didn't know. What she had told Sam was the absolute truth: She didn't remember leaving him at the post office. She didn't recall a thing until hearing his voice at that terrifying place by the river.

Daddy, I need you to tell me what's happening. Please, Daddy, you can do it. Remember the time I was coming home from school and you sent me to Morin's for the medicine? And the time you had the run-in with those tough kids?

She had been a sophomore at Warwick High at that time. It was the same school Daddy taught in. There was a gang of dropouts who tore around in junk cars and wore black leather jackets with heads of Trojan warriors painted on them in silver, and thought they owned the

city. Three of the Trojans had caught little Margie
Cirillo walking home from a girlfriend's house in East
Greenwich one night and dragged her into the car they
were riding around in. Margie was fifteen. They took
her to an abandoned quahauger's shack and raped her.

Daddy had just happened to be driving home from an
adult evening class which he taught in East Greenwich
and saw them come out of the shack and pile into their
jalopy and take off. When he learned the next day that
Margie had been found there, raped and hysterical, he
went to the police.

The police rounded up the boys and grilled them for
hours. They swore they hadn't been anywhere near the
shack and that Daddy was just trying to incriminate
them because he disapproved of their lifestyle. "You're
a fucking liar, Bell!" one of them yelled in his face at the
police station. As for Margie Cirillo, the poor girl was
scared out of her wits and said she didn't know *who* had
dragged her to the shack and raped her. It was too dark
to see their faces and she didn't recognize their voices,
she said. The police couldn't make her change her story,
and it didn't come out until later that the Trojans had
threatened to beat up her young brother if she identified
them.

Daddy taught his adult class three evenings a week,
and exactly a week after the rape he did not come home
at his usual time. It was a seven-to-nine class, and he was
almost always home by ten, but eleven o'clock passed
and still no sign of him. Mildred had finished her home-
work and was watching the late news in the living room.
Mama was sitting at her sewing machine in the dining
alcove, making some of her fancy place mats. Mama
loved to sew, but that night, when the news was only
half over she said in a tense voice, "Mildred, must you
have that thing on?"

"Why, Mama? What's the matter?"

"Do you know what time it is?"

"Of course."

"Your father should have been home an hour ago!"

"Oh, Mama, he probably stopped to talk to some of the people in his class. You know how those evening classes are."

"I'm going to call the school," Mama said.

"What?"

"I'm going to call the school. Ever since Daddy got involved with those terrible boys, I've been worried."

She went to the phone and dialed the school's number. Mildred turned off the TV so she could talk without competition. But after a couple of minutes of waiting in silence, Mama put the phone down and said, "They don't answer. Mildred, do you suppose we ought to go and look for him?" The family's Olds was in the garage. Daddy always took Mama's Falcon to East Greenwich.

"Mama, wait. If we pass him on the road without seeing him, he'll get here and find the house empty and wonder where *we* are."

But that argument was only good for another half hour, and then Mama insisted.

They locked the house, leaving lights on and a note, in case Daddy did return, and Mama drove out to Post Road and through Apponaug to East Greenwich. The adult classes were held in East Greenwich High School. The school was dark, and the parking lot, empty. It was now past midnight.

"I think we ought to stop at the police station," Mama said on the way back.

"All right. If there's been an accident, they'll know."

At the station in Apponaug, the policeman at the desk told them he didn't have a report of any accident. Listening to Mama's reason for being worried, he nodded. "I don't blame you, Mrs. Bell. Those are hard characters, those kids. I'll alert our patrol cars to be on the lookout for your husband."

Mildred and Mama went home to wait.

The next two hours were bad. Mama just wouldn't sit still anywhere but kept pacing through the house. She would stop and stare at the phone as if willing it to ring, then go to a window and stare out at the dark waters of Gorton Pond, then try to sit, only to jump right up again. She made coffee in the electric perc, which was broken and didn't shut itself off as it was supposed to; then she forgot she had started it, and the machine would have gone on blub-glugging forever if Mildred had not run into the kitchen and stopped it. All of this was causing Mildred's head to ache—or, *something* was —and after a while the throbbing inside her skull grew worse. She was sure she would begin screaming at any minute if it didn't stop.

Then she heard him.

"Milly . . . Milly . . . am I reaching you?"

"Yes, yes, Daddy! Oh, yes! Where are you?"

"Listen carefully, child. I'm in bad shape. Those kids stopped my car, five of them. Two got into the Falcon and drove it off, I don't know where. And the other three, the ones who raped that girl, forced me into their car and drove me to where I am now. I'm hurt, Milly. They've beaten me up pretty badly. You'll have to come and get me, you and Mother."

"Daddy, where are you?"

"In some kind of boathouse. At least, there's a boat in it, a small sport cruiser up on blocks. I can't tell you where it is; they tied a filthy rag around my eyes and I couldn't see where we were going. But you can find me, I think. If I just keep sending, you can home in on me like a plane to an airport. Try it, Milly."

"You can't get out of there?"

"I'm locked in, child. And hurt besides. Bring something to bash the door open with. That sledge in the furnace room."

"All right, Daddy, I'm coming!"

Mildred got out of her chair and went into the kitchen, where Mama had at last poured some coffee and was trying to drink it. "Mama, listen. We have to go out."

"What?"

"I don't have time to explain now, but Daddy's been communicating with me. Now wait a minute, *please*. You know we can do it sometimes when we try hard. He says he's hurt, Mama. The Trojans beat him up."

Mama had to put her cup on the counter because her hand had begun to shake so uncontrollably. Her eyes grew wide and glassy, almost colorless, as her gaze fastened on Mildred's face. "I don't believe you," she said. "I don't *want* to believe you!"

"Mama, please! Would I tell you such a thing if it wasn't true? He's in a boathouse somewhere, and hurt. We have to go for him."

"What boathouse? Where?"

"Mama," Mildred wailed, "will you please stop asking me questions and come on? Daddy needs us!"

There was really no way Mama could refuse, of course. She hated being told that Mildred and Daddy were able to communicate in ways she didn't understand, but in a situation such as this she could hardly put her hands on her hips and say, "I'm not going!" She had to drive the Olds.

They got into the car, which Mama had left in the driveway, as if she had known they would have to use it. "All right," Mama said, "where is this boathouse?"

Mildred sat with her eyes squeezed shut and her hands clenched in her lap. "Drive out to the Post Road."

Mama didn't speak again until they got there. Then she said, "Which way?"

. "Right."

"How do you know, if you don't know where he is?"

"Mama, I'm hearing him. Don't talk, please." What

she was hearing was her own name endlessly repeated, as if it was being chanted at her by some kind of electronic gadget. "Milly, Milly, Milly, Milly," over and over.

When they reached the junction of West Shore Road, Mama stayed on Post Road, and there was a change in the signal Mildred was receiving. "No!" she said quickly. "The other way! Left!"

"Oh, for heaven's sake," Mama said. But she stopped, made a U-turn, and followed West Shore instead.

Four times more Mildred had to say "Stop!" and then, "Go right," or, "Turn left," and the last turn took them into the driveway of one of the big, handsome homes on Warwick Neck. As they drove in, Mildred waited tensely for floodlights to come on and dogs to begin barking, but nothing happened. The owners must be away, she decided. Maybe that was why the Trojans had picked the place.

"Stop here," she told Mama.

The signal in her head was loud now—"MILLY! MILLY! MILLY!"—and her head was pounding like one of those huge drills they used to break up concrete. She could even taste the pain inside her skull—a sickly sweet taste like some of those gooey drinks for kids. When the car stopped, she got out of it and yanked open the back door and grabbed the sledge off the back seat.

"Come on, Mama."

"Where?" Mama demanded, peering at the big, dark house as if she were afraid it would fall on them and crush them.

"This way." Mildred pointed to the bluestone path which the headlights shone on. It led past the house and down a smooth, sloping lawn toward the sea.

"Milly, we don't have any right to do this! We're trespassing!"

Without bothering to answer, Mildred began running.

The path led to some concrete steps, quite a lot of them, and at their foot was a wooden building painted white. While running down the steps, she gripped the sledge with both hands because it was beginning to feel heavy. Her head was about to explode like a bomb from the force of Daddy's voice inside it. "MILLY! MILLY! MILLY! MILLY!"

At the side of the shed was a door. She ran to it without even pausing.

"Daddy, are you in there?"

"Right here, baby, waiting for you. Did you bring the sledge?" It was really his voice this time, not just something in her head. But it was weak, despite a note of triumph in it. She guessed he was really hurt.

"I have it, Daddy."

"All right. Just wait 'til I get back a little . . ." She sensed he was on the floor dragging himself away from the door. "All right, go ahead. But be careful. Don't hurt yourself."

As she stepped back to take aim, Mama finally reached her and screamed, "No, Milly, you mustn't! We could be arrested!" At the same time, Mildred saw there was a key in the lock.

Lowering the sledge, she stepped forward and tried the key. It turned without any trouble, and the door swung open. The inside of the boathouse was pitch dark.

She had brought a flashlight, but had left it in the car, and, of couse, Mama hadn't thought to pick it up. "Daddy?" she said, stepping through the doorway.

"Here, Milly."

She turned toward the voice and saw him on his hands and knees, crawling toward her. Saw the boat he had mentioned too, or at least a pale shape that looked like a boat. Then Daddy touched her foot and looked up at her, and she began crying. If she had found him on a

highway somewhere, she would have thought he was
some stranger hit by a car.

"Where's Mama?" he asked.

"I'm here, Rog," Mama said and came timidly
through the doorway as if she were walking into a
haunted house. Seeing him, she began to make gasping,
shuddering noises, but almost at once got control of
herself and went down on her knees to look at him more
closely. Then she looked up at Milly and began giving
orders.

"Take his arm on that side, Milly. Lift when I do, but
gently. Don't hurt him, now!"

They got him to his feet, and he held himself erect by
putting his arms around their shoulders. "We must take
him straight to the hospital," Mama said. "Oh God, the
steps. How are we going to get him up those steps?"

By negotiating one step at a time and resting after
each one, they got Daddy to the car and put him on his
back on the rear seat with his knees upthrust. Milly
knelt on the floor to keep him from falling off, and
Mama drove back through Apponaug to the Kent
County Hospital.

It was three weeks before Daddy's face healed enough
for him to return to teaching. During that time, the police found the Falcon in some woods, stripped of its
wheels and everything else that could be removed. When
they were confronted with the fact that their fingerprints
were all over the car, the Trojans finally admitted what
they had done. They had broken into the big house
weeks before and were using the boathouse for a meeting place while the owners were in Europe, they said.
Mildred and Daddy were present at the station when
Captain DiFalco said to them, "When you creeps beat
this man up and left him locked in there, did you actually expect to get away with it? Couldn't you figure out
he'd be found some day, even if he died in there?" The

Trojans only laughed, and Captain DiFalco turned to Daddy and shook his head. "Subhuman, that's what they are," he growled. "Junior monsters. And I'll give you ten to one they don't spend a day behind bars for any of this, because we're going to have a lot of marshmallow peddlers saying they never had a fair shake."

As for Mama, she talked a lot about how the Trojans had beaten Daddy and stripped her car—the missing parts were never recovered—but she discussed the other part of the incident even more.

The first time was a lecture. A kind of a lecture.

The three of them were having dinner the evening Daddy came home from the hospital, and after asking the blessing, Mama took a deep breath and said, "Now, before we start eating, just please let me say something. It's about this *communicating* that you two seem to be able to do by projecting your thoughts to each other. I know other people can do it, too, in varying degrees, and books have been written about it, and all that. I know it's supposed to be all very scientific. But I want you to know I think it's the work of the devil, pure and simple, and if you keep it up, you'll be punished. There. I've said my piece and don't want any discussion, thank you, and I won't be mentioning it again. Roger, I hope your jaw is strong enough to chew this filet mignon. Perhaps I should have bought hamburger, but I wanted something really nice for your first meal at home."

Of course, Mama didn't keep her word about never mentioning her favorite topic again. Until the day she died she found something new to say about it at least once a month. Mama just wasn't going to let the devil put her down.

But Daddy went right on with his experiments, in spite of her opposition.

* * *

On her cot in the lamplit guest room of the Vallière rectory, Mildred stared at the ceiling. *Daddy . . . if you can hear me, please tell me what made me run away from Sam this evening and try to destroy myself at the river. Please, Daddy. I'm frightened.*

Closing her eyes, she tried to concentrate. She didn't have to know where he was, although being able to think of him in specific surroundings usually helped. It was—she looked at her watch—quarter to three in the morning now. He would be in bed somewhere. Somewhere in a village like this one? She formed a mental image of him on a cot like the one she was using, but asleep with his eyes closed.

Daddy . . . Daddy . . . can you hear me?

Something was coming through. Something.

Daddy? Yes, but not Daddy alone. Daddy and someone else. As if she had dialed a telephone number and some kind of mixup had caused two phones to ring.

21

The bustling proprietor
of the Pension Calman,
Victor Vieux,
is standing at his little bar
quietly mixing himself a drink.
To his astonishment,
Dr. Roger Laurence Bell
suddenly walks in
from the street.
It is seven o'clock of a sultry Port-au-Prince evening.

"Dr. Bell!
Then Marie was not mistaken.
She *did* see you here earlier!"
"I could not stay.
I had to go right out again, Victor."
"So you are back.
And did you find your *bocor* in the mountains?"
"I found him."
"Good.
But your daughter was here
with Sam Norman.
They went to Legrun to look for you
and have not returned yet."

* * *

"My daughter? What are you saying, Victor?"

"That she was here with Sam Norman.
They learned you had gone
to visit Margal
and went after you."
"Oh my God," Dr. Bell whispers.

The two men face each other.
Victor searches the other's countenance
for clues.
Dr. Bell seems stricken.
"Oh my God," Bell whispers again,
then turns abruptly and goes stumbling
up the stairs to his room,
where he flings himself on the bed.
He closes his eyes,
concentrates so fiercely on what he is doing
that his teeth draw blood
from his lip.

"Milly," Dr. Bell whispers, "listen to me.
For God's sake hear me.
You must not go to that place.
I am not there.
I am in Port-au-Prince.
Come back, Milly.
Don't go to Legrun!
A devil dwells
in that ghastly place!"

But he is not getting through to her.
He will have to try again,
later tonight,
when conditions may be better.

* * *

He throws a few possessions
into a small suitcase
and hurries downstairs again,
where Victor Vieux still stands at the bar.
"Victor, I cannot stay.
I merely stopped by for some clothes.
I am to be the guest of a friend
for a while."
"Here in the city?"
"Yes, Victor. Here in the city.
I called on him this afternoon
and was invited to stay at his home."
"Perhaps I know him."
"Later, Victor.
I haven't time now."
And Dr. Bell hurries to the door.

Victor calls after him.
"Dr. Bell! Can I drive you?
I am doing nothing just now."
"No, no, Victor.
I will walk."

Strange, Victor thinks
as his guest disappears
along the cobbled driveway.
*Why wouldn't he tell me
where he is going?*

22

Sam awoke with a feeling that something was wrong, then realized what it was and relaxed in bed with a distinct sensation of relief. He had gone to sleep with the lamp burning. The room was now dark. So with the wick turned low, a breath of air from the partly open window had blown the flame out. Or the lamp had run out of oil.

Wondering how his roommate was doing, he listened for the sound of her breathing. Strange. The sound was in the room all right, but not in that part of the room where her cot was.

He sat up, straining to see in the darkness. A pale shape stood near the door—Mildred in white pajamas, with her back to him.

She opened the door, walked out into the front room, and quietly closed the door after her. There was only a faint metallic click from the latch.

Oh no, Sam thought. Not again.

He had gone to bed in his underwear. Why carry pajamas on a wilderness journey such as this? For slippers, he was using the only footgear he had with him: the sneakers he had worn all day. They were on the floor beside his cot. Pulling them on, he reached the door in four long strides.

The front room was dark. Françoise had left no lamp burning there. But again, Mildred's white pajamas revealed her whereabouts. She was at the door that led out to the yard. As he watched her, she stepped out and closed that behind her, too.

Sam crossed the room and silently opened the door again. Stood there watching her go along the walk to the tall wooden gate. In the moonlight he could see her clearly, and she walked like one asleep or drugged. At the gate she halted. It was closed.

She spread its wings far enough for her to slip between them, then turned and swung them together again. Why was she so carefully closing everything behind her? To create a mystery when her absence was discovered? A ghostly figure in the moonglow, she turned to her right and went gliding down the road.

The river again, Sam thought, and somehow was not surprised.

But, damn it, he had no intention of following her down through the village at this hour, just to see what she would try to do at the river. Reaching the gate, he yanked it open and broke into a run. Caught up with her and grabbed her arm.

"Milly! Wake up!"

Her eyes opened and she stood there staring at him, shaking so violently he thought she must be having some kind of seizure. She struggled for breath. He was afraid he was hurting her, yet reluctant to let go for fear she might run away and lead him on a wild chase through the sleeping village.

Then her shuddering subsided and she began to cry.

"Come on," Sam said quietly. "Let's go back."

With an arm around her waist, he led her to the rectory, through the yard and the front room to the bedroom they were sharing. The room was really dark after the moonlight outside. Because his cot was nearer the door than hers, he led her to it and eased her onto it. "Sit still now while I light the lamp."

With the lamp burning and its wick turned up, he saw that her face was wet with tears and stiff with fright. Sitting beside her, he held her hand. "What happened? A dream?"

"Oh, God, Sam, I don't know," she whispered.

"Where were you going? The river?"

She nodded slowly.

"Why? Do you know why?"

"Someone told me to. Told me I had to."

"The same as before, hey? When you left me at the post office?"

"Yes."

"You didn't remember leaving me at the post office. Do you remember leaving this room?"

"Yes, I remember everything."

"Did you blow the lamp out?"

"Yes."

"How do you account for knowing what you did this time, when you didn't before?" he asked gently, trying not to frighten her.

"It—the voice in my head was stronger this time. I was trying—was thinking of Daddy when this other presence interfered, telling me I had to go back to the river. Oh, Sam, I'm scared!" Sobbing, she turned and clung to him, pressing her face against his shoulder.

Sam sat there holding her, saying nothing, waiting for her to exorcise her own demons and regain control of herself. It took a good five minutes.

She said then, "What am I to do, Sam? If it happens again—"

"It isn't going to happen again. Not that way, anyhow. We were lucky. You must have made some sound that woke me up. This time I'm going to have an arm around you."

She looked at him.

"We won't get much sleep, two of us on a cot this narrow," Sam said, "but as far as I'm concerned, it's the only way. What do you say?"

She hesitated only briefly before nodding.

"You get next to the wall," he said. "Then you'll have to crawl over me to get out."

She got into bed, and he squirmed in beside her, drawing the blanket up over them both because the night air was decidedly cool. After some experimenting, they found a position of reasonable comfort, her head on Sam's right shoulder and his right arm around her.

What, Sam wondered, would Daddy say?

Mildred was the first to fall asleep. Sam lay there on his back, eyes open, his right hand gently pressing her against him. She had moved once more just before dozing off, crossing her right arm over his chest and gripping his left shoulder while she burrowed into him. Burrowing for what? he wondered. Protection, or something else? The adjustment had brought *his* right hand in contact with her breast and it was a nice thing to be holding, he decided. His thoughts traveled back to another night in Haiti when he had slept with a woman for the first time. Not of necessity, as now, but for a livelier reason.

After his violent invasion of Kay Gilbert's room at the Jacmel pension, there had been a truce between them, a wait-and-see-how-we-feel kind of thing, for weeks. The friendship had developed in other ways, but not that one. Then, one night, they had driven out to a *tonnelle* near Ganthier, in the Cul de Sac, to attend a service to Zaca.

Ganthier was a miserably poor village surrounded by sand and cactus, and the *hounfor* of Papa Lélio was one seldom visited by tourists. The tourists were taken to voodoo ceremonies in or near the capital where the rituals staged for their benefit were genuine enough in appearance but less so in substance. Like the difference between a Gaugin painting and a photograph of one.

That night at Lélio's, the god of country farmers had come in response to the *houngan's* summons. With the drums throbbing and a dance proceeding in his honor, Zaca walked about the *tonnelle* with great dignity, dressed in his usual blue denim pants and shirt, wearing the traditional tasseled bag over one shoulder and carrying a machete. Every so often, he dug a hole in the earthen floor and planted a seed or two. All very much down Sam's alley, this service with its agricultural symbolism, and he watched it with intense interest.

Because he found it fascinating, so did Kay, she being that kind of woman.

Then, damn it, a tour limousine from the capital had arrived and its driver had ushered half a dozen visitors into the *tonnelle*, and the service ended. A planting ceremony was out of the question for sightseers, Papa Lélio must have thought. They expected something more sensational. And since they were here with money and could not be rudely ordered to leave in any case . . .

Sam and Kay had departed. "Now what'll we do?" Sam grumbled on their way back to Port. "It's too late to go dancing anywhere. Damn. I wanted to see that ceremony, too. My workers in Jacmel have great respect for Zaca."

"Let's just go back to the Calman and talk, Sam."

"You mean it?" The notion that an attractive woman might want just to sit and talk with Sam Norman was not easy for him to accept.

"I mean it."

It was a little after eleven when they arrived at the pension. Normally on a night out together they would have rolled in well after midnight, had a nightcap at Victor's self-service bar, then gone up to their separate rooms. That night, Sam mixed the nightcaps and they sat in the big front room which Victor laughingly called his salon. In bamboo chairs a yard apart, they faced each other.

"Since I wasn't able to learn about Zaca," Kay said, sipping her rum and soda, "suppose you tell me something about you."

"Oh, come on!"

"No, I'm serious. We've been out together half a dozen times now. I even went to Jacmel with you. But I don't know very much about you, Sam. For starters, where were you born?"

"Florida. My dad taught agriculture there. Where were *you* born?"

"Boston. You don't have a southern accent."

"I went to college in Michigan and had to get rid of it in self-defense. You really mean Boston, or a suburb like Brookline or Newton?"

"A Back Bay apartment. Mother was a nurse, Father an intern at the hospital where she worked. They were ahead of their time, living together unmarried. When Mother got pregnant, he wanted an abortion and she didn't. Then he wanted her to marry him, but she wouldn't because he had asked for the abortion. He disappeared before I was born. She never saw him again, and I've never seen him at all." Kay shrugged. "It seems you got into agriculture because of your father and I went into nursing because of my mother. Not very exciting."

"Nothing to talk about," Sam agreed.

"Are your folks still alive?"

"Still in Florida. Dad's in the state department of agriculture now. And your mother?"

"Still nursing. Still in Boston."

Sam finished his drink and looked at her glass, which was also empty. "Another?"

"One more. Only one."

He stood up, frowning at the two glasses in his hands. "You know something, pal? While we've been sitting here discussing our uneventful pasts, we could have been getting that night in Jacmel out of our systems. When I come back with these, let's give it a whirl?"

"All right. I think I have something to tell you."

Sam pivoted to go to the bar, then stopped. A car had rumbled into the driveway outside. "Oh-oh, the Grovers are back." Mr. and Mrs. Grover, from Akron, were a middle-aged, enthusiastic couple to whom Victor Vieux had introduced him. "They went to that tourist voodoo trap in Carrefour tonight and we'll have to hear all about it. Let's head for the loft!" He put the glasses on a nearby table.

Kay quickly stood up and made for the stairs. "I didn't want another drink, anyway," she said over her shoulder as Sam ascended behind her. "Which room?"

"Mine. I want to show you something."

They went into Sam's room and shut the door. There was only one chair, a wobbly reject from the outdoor dining area in the garden, painted pale green. "Show me what?" Kay said as, with a flourish, he led her to it.

"Huh?"

"You want to show me what?"

"Oh, this." He pulled open the top drawer of his bureau and took out a rolled-up sheet of drawing paper. Slipped off the two rubber bands that encircled it. Unrolled it. Handed it to her.

Kay found herself looking at a drawing done with felt-tipped pens of several colors. It depicted a jeep on a country road, the man at the wheel was embracing the woman beside him. The woman's shapely right leg projected from the vehicle and a peasant sandal dangled precariously from the toes of her right foot.

She laughed until tears flowed. Then she said, "But,

hey, I didn't know you were such a talented guy, Sam Norman."

"Wish I were." Sam kicked off his shoes and parked himself on the bed, sitting back against the head board with his hands on his upthrust knees. "What do you have to tell me about Jacmel, pal?"

"We had a man from there at the hospital this week. A man of some standing in the town, I gather. His name was Georges Baptiste. Know him, do you?"

"Big fellow, about fifty?"

"Yes."

"He's a merchant. Nice fellow."

"I asked him if he knew you, and he said yes. He said you're doing a wonderful job out there. But"—she paused, frowning—"I'm not sure I should tell you this, Sam."

"But what?"

"He said you made a big mistake in antagonizing that voodoo man. The one we ran from that night at the street dance."

"Fenelon," Sam said. "And we didn't run. I just didn't want any confrontation while you were with me."

"When I said I was a friend of yours, this Georges Baptiste told me to warn you. He was dead serious about it. He told me to make you realize you're in danger. Fenelon is one of the most powerful *bocors* in all Haiti, he said."

Sam looked at her in silence.

"So," she said, "if you didn't have a bottle in your room that night—and you've already said you didn't—the answer to what happened just might be something Fenelon did after seeing us at the *bamboche* and being reminded how much he hated you. All right?"

"If you believe people like Fenelon have powers."

"Don't you?"

"I'm not convinced."

"Sam," she said, "we've both been in this country a good while. We both came here stone cold to do a job of work, not full of far-out preconceptions. And we've both seen enough to convince us—to convince me, at any rate—that people like Fenelon can be dangerous."

"All right. I'll buy it if you insist."

"What will you do about him?"

"Ease up, I guess. If he's that powerful, my people out there aren't going to stop seeing him. To be truthful, they haven't. He still gets a lot of the money I'm helping them earn."

Silence. Then Kay unrolled the drawing again and restudied it, shaking her head over it with a slowly developing smile on her face. "Sam, this is wonderful. Really. Do me one?"

"That one is for you."

"Thank you. I'm going to have it framed for my room at the hospital." Letting the picture roll itself up again, she rose, put it on the bureau, then walked over to the bed and lay down so that her position approximated the one she had assumed in the jeep that day, her lips under Sam's and one leg outthrust. A little later, Sam reached out to switch off the lamp on the bedside table.

It was their first real sleep-together—you couldn't count that weird night in Jacmel—and they were still in bed at daybreak.

Now the woman in Sam's arms was the daughter of Dr. Roger Bell, and she appeared to be dreaming.

Thinking about Kay Gilbert, Sam had not slept. But Mildred had. With her head on his shoulder and her arm limp on his chest, she had moved only occasionally, and then only to squeeze her belly and thighs hard against him at times, as though responding to some subconscious need. He was sure she didn't know she did it. She made no sound.

Now she was moaning, and her movements were twitchy, jerky, almost violent at times.

Sam raised his left arm and looked at his watch in the lamplight. It would soon be daylight, and they ought to make an early start. "Milly," he said, moving his hand from her breast to give her shoulder a shake. "Hey. Wake up."

She awoke with a prolonged shudder and began to make crying sounds, though she was not really crying.

"What's the matter? Dreaming again?"

"Yes."

Sam turned to face her and looked at her for a moment, then gently shaped his mouth to hers and held it there. It was a quiet kiss, meant to let her know she was not alone with her troubles but had someone to lean on. She surprised him by reading more into it than he intended.

It was a strange kind of lovemaking. Not a word was spoken. Mildred simply pressed her open mouth to his and when the kiss had lasted two or three minutes with her arms around him, she found other uses for her hands than simply to hold him against her. The top of the white pajamas never did come off; only the bottom. What she wanted or needed, Sam suddenly realized, was not the touching, teasing, laughing kind of love-play in which Kay and he had indulged that night at the Calman, but sex plain and simple, quick and sweaty, fierce and frantic. She was under him before he could even get his shorts off.

For a moment he was sure he wouldn't make it to her satisfaction. This kind of lovemaking was so alien to his nature. When he did, and felt her go limp beneath him, he was merely relieved. Getting up, he stood there looking down at her with no idea of what to say. What he finally said was, "Milly, if we're going to make Legrun tonight, we'd better get out of here."

She lay there looking up at him, one foot still tangled

in the kicked-off bottom of the white pajamas. A beautiful woman, blonde where Kay was dark, her body so white that the yellow light from the lamp made it look gilded.

"Sam, I don't think Daddy is in Legrun," she said.

"What?"

"I had a message last night. He's not there."

"You were dreaming. You were moaning in your sleep."

"No, it was more than a dream. He said he isn't in this place we're going to. He's in Port-au-Prince. I had a feeling he is in some kind of trouble or danger. A very strong feeling." For the first time, she seemed aware that she was lying there naked from the waist down while talking to him, and, reaching down, pulled up the blanket that had covered both of them during the night. "Sam, what should we do?"

"He's in the capital?"

"I'm sure that's what he was trying to tell me."

"You and your father really can talk to each other this way?"

"Sometimes."

He thought about it. "Well, look. If we start now, we can be in Legrun tonight, and since we've come this far we ought to see if he's there, don't you think? If he isn't, we can go right back. Did he tell you *where* in Port he is?"

"No."

"Okay," he said, extending a hand to her. "Let's get going."

She used his hand to pull herself up from the cot, and stood there facing him. Suddenly, she put both arms around his neck and pressed herself hard against him, fiercely fastening her mouth to his. Then, just as abruptly and without a word, she let go and began to get dressed.

23

After the first hour, Kay's fear of being alone in such a place was slowly subsiding. It had been real enough earlier, despite the bravado she had feigned for Joseph's benefit. But, after all, she was not really alone. She had Tina. And the trail was not so formidable now. At least, it hadn't produced any more Devil's Leaps.

She and the child talked a lot to push back the stillness. Something had to do that because the silence was immense here. Mile after mile produced no sign of habitation, not even an isolated *caille* such as the one they had slept in last night.

Nothing but forest and mountains and bird song and leaf rustle. And each other.

"Will you be glad to see your mother and father, baby?"

"Oh, yes!"

"What are they like? Tell me about them."

"Maman is pretty, like you."

"Bless you. And your father?"

"He works all the time."

"Doing what?"

"Growing things. Yams, mostly. We have goats and chickens, too."

"What's his name?"

"Metullus Sam."

"And your mother's?"

"Fifine Bonhomme."

Not married, of course. Few peasants ever married. But many living in *plaçage* were more faithful than "civilized" people in other countries who *were* married.

"Will you be glad to see your sister and two brothers too?"

"Yes, Miss Kay."

"Are they older than you?"

"Only Rosemarie. The twins are younger."

"Your brothers are twins? I didn't know that. That must make your family very special." In voodoo, twins played important roles. There were even special services for the spirits of *marassas*. She and Sam Norman had attended one in Léogane.

"Would you like to know about my village, Miss Kay?"

"I certainly would. Tell me about it."

"Well, it's not as big as the one we rode through this morning. Vallière, I mean. But it has a marketplace, and a spring for water . . ."

Just talk, to pass the time. And when they tired of it, Kay let her thoughts drift from Tina Sam, who at this moment was the most important thing in her existence, to the other Sam who had also been important for a time. Riding along in silence, she found herself reliving that last night in Port when he had finally turned up at the Calman.

Nearly midnight. The servants had long since retired to their quarters at the back of the yard. There were no guests other than herself and the missing Sam Norman. She and Victor sat in the kitchen drinking coffee, she still full of a suspicion that something had happened and was being covered up. For the past hour, Victor had voiced only variations on his original theme: "Don't worry. He'll come. He won't spend his last night in Haiti just driving around feeling sorry for himself."

The sound of a jeep in the driveway. Sam had driven a jeep in from Jacmel, Victor had explained, because it needed some repairs. Otherwise, he would have had someone drive him in on this last trip to the city.

She stood up and went to a window. The yard lights were still on. The jeep was the one she had been riding in when her foot had borrowed the sandal.

Sam was walking to the back door.

She opened the door before he reached it. Got a good look at his face as he came toward her. He didn't appear to be drunk. Tired, yes. Wooden with fatigue. But not intoxicated.

"Hi." He reached for her hands. "Sorry I'm late. I got tied up."

She led him to the table where Victor was still seated, pulled back a chair for him and anxiously watched him sag onto it. "Coffee, Sam?"

"I guess so. Thanks."

"Where have you been?"

"Oh, around. Things to do, my last night here."

She brought him coffee. Sat and looked at him.

"How come you brought the jeep back here?" Victor asked. "You said you were going to leave it at the garage."

Sam seemed puzzled. "I said what?"

"You told me it needed rings and you were leaving it at Sylvain's."

"Oh? Well, yes. They don't have the parts." He stopped his cup at his mouth and frowned at Kay. "What time did *you* get here?"

"Just after three." She told him about the bus accident and the pile-up of work at the hospital. "I would have called you, but our phones were dead."

"I know. I tried to call you."

Something was wrong. He wasn't drunk. As far as she could tell, he hadn't even been drinking. But something was wrong.

The cover-up. Victor hiding something. The maids hiding something. Was he in on it too?

Hiding what?

Victor said, "What time do you want me to knock on your door tomorrow, you two?" He knew, of course, that even though they paid for separate rooms they never used more than one anymore—Sam's, because the bed was bigger.

"My plane leaves—"

"I know when the plane leaves, pal. I run a hotel here, remember?"

"*I* have to start back early," Kay said sadly. "Strict orders. If I hadn't promised, I wouldn't be here at all."

"How early?"

"Daybreak."

"Well, then," Victor said, rising, "I think it's time we stopped sitting here wasting the night, don't you?" He looked at them and smiled, but even his smile was not quite right, Kay thought.

She and Sam went upstairs.

While they were undressing, it began. *She* began it.

"Sam, where have you been all afternoon and evening? Didn't you know I'd get here just as soon as I could?"

"You were supposed to be here yesterday."

"But unexpected things happen in a hospital sometimes. You know that."

With everything off but his shorts, he turned to direct a glare at her. Not just a questioning look, but one of sullen anger.

Foolishly, she continued. "No matter what you had to do, you could at least have come by to see if I'd got here. I've been here *nine hours,* Sam."

"I'm sorry."

"Well, what were you doing? You haven't said yet."

"I had to take the jeep to Sylvain's."

The garage. Not more than six blocks away. "Oh, come on. That couldn't have taken more than half an hour."

He didn't answer, and she stopped undressing. She had everything off but her bra and panties, and she stopped. He hadn't even kissed her yet, she realized. She hadn't expected it downstairs in front of Victor, of course. He wasn't that demonstrative, except for the time he had nearly knocked the woman off her donkey. But since coming into this room and closing the door, he hadn't touched her.

Defying the look he was directing at her, she walked up to him, stopped six inches away, and jabbed her fists against her hips. "Sam Norman, are you just a little drunk?"

"Kay, for Christ's sake, this is our last night together!"

"I know it's our last night together. But something's going on here. Something I don't like. First Victor and the girls clammed up on me. Now you're doing it. What's happening?"

"Nothing's happening. You're sore because I had things to do. And it's your own Goddamned fault, because if you'd got here when you were supposed to, we could have done most of them together."

"Most of what?"

"The things I had to do! What the hell's wrong with you? Can't you listen?"

"You're drunk," she said. "I can't smell it, but you're drunk. You have to be."

"Oh, for Christ's sake, knock off the inquisition and come to bed." Wheeling, he yanked back the top sheet and threw himself onto the bed with such force she thought it would collapse. "Come on!" he yelled, pounding the side she slept on.

"No."

"What?" His face took on an ugly, twisted expression of disbelief.

"I'm not getting into that bed until you give me an explanation."

"Well, Goddamn *you!*"

"Don't swear at me, Sam. There's something wrong here, and I want to know what it is. And it isn't just that I got here a day late. You and Victor and the girls are hiding something from me. Now let's have it, huh?" She was trying hard to keep her voice down and her temper under wraps. And was on the verge of tears too, knowing she was on the wrong road to a reconciliation but had passed the point of no return.

Sam was glaring again. "Listen, you," he said. "I'm sick of this shit. Are you coming to bed or not?"

"Not until—"

"Get out, then, Goddamn it!"

With her fists still on her hips, she stood there staring back at him. Sick inside. All twisted up and full of pain inside. But determined not to show it. "What is this? A replay of the night you barged into my room naked in Jacmel?"

He sat up in bed. "You'll never let me forget that, will you?"

"I did let you forget it. I even helped you to forget it!"

"Now you're rubbing my nose in it again."

"Because you're *doing* it again. 'Come to bed.' What am I supposed to do—crawl in there and make love to you after you've left me sitting here the whole day while you've been out doing whatever you've been doing? I'm supposed to *love* you when you haven't even had the decency to say you're sorry and kiss me?" Her eyes filled with tears. "Oh, my God, Sam, what's wrong with you? What's happened?"

"Either get into this Goddamned bed or get out of this room!" he yelled.

"Say that again. I want to be sure I heard you right."

"I said get into this bed or get out of my room!"

"Out of your room. All right. That's what I thought you said." As she backed up to the chair on which she had dropped her clothes, she knew she was shaking all over. Knew she must be as white as the bed sheets. More of the same kind of talk boiled up in her, but she clamped her mouth shut on it. Let him talk that way if he wanted to. She wouldn't.

Knocking the pile of clothes to the floor, she sat on the chair and reached for her stockings and pulled them on. Stockings. She hardly ever wore them but had this weekend because she wanted to look extra nice for him. Grabbing at her dress, she stood up and yanked it down over her head and reached behind her to zip it. Thrust her feet into shoes.

Savagely, she said then, "That's all you ever wanted, isn't it, you bastard? Just someone to sleep with. I should have known."

"What else would anybody want you for?" he snarled back.

She walked to the door. When she turned to look at him, he was still glaring. Her nurse's training would not let her slam the door behind her as she wanted to; she closed it quietly and went down the hall to her own room. Inside, with her door shut, she sprawled on the bed fully dressed and lay there sobbing until sleep came to take her out of her misery.

The rest of that ghastly night was not so vivid in her memory. She recalled waking to a sound of stumbling footfalls in the hall and thinking, *Here we go again. He'll open my door and be standing there to rape me.* But the footfalls went blundering the other way, to the stairs, accompanied by other frightening sounds as he apparently reeled into the corridor walls. Then she heard a whole series of thumps and crashes as he fell down the staircase.

By the time she had her wits together and staggered from her bed to the door and got the door open and at last reached the top of the stairs, herself, it was too late for her to do anything. He lay in a heap at the bottom, face down, and Victor Vieux was kneeling beside him. Unable to utter a sound, she went down the stairs as if walking in her sleep, one slow step at a time, but fully aware of what she was doing, and stood there looking down at him and smelling the rum. If he hadn't been drunk before, he was now. She could have leaned on the rum fumes and they would have held her up.

Victor, on his knees, said, "You'd better look at him, Kay. He may need a doctor."

She knelt at Sam's side. He was still dressed as she had last seen him, in only his shorts. She ran her hands over his familiar body as a doctor would have done, until she could say with authority, "He's all right unless he's hurt inside."

"Can we get him up to bed, then?" Victor asked. "I don't think I can do it alone."

They almost couldn't do it together, but got him upstairs at last and laid him on the bed. She drew the top sheet up over him and nearly, but not quite, succumbed to the temptation to pull it right up over his face. Turning away, she saw the empty bottle of Barbancourt on the chest of drawers. It hadn't been there before.

She looked at her watch. It was twenty past two.

A fifth of rum in two hours?

"Kay," Victor said as he followed her out of the room and shut the door, "I'm sorry about this. Believe me."

"Both of us."

"He hasn't been himself. There's something wrong."

"Another time, Victor. I can't think now."

"Of course. We'll talk in the morning."

"Before you're up in the morning, I'll be on my way back to the hospital. I never should have left there. Forget it, Victor. He's leaving tomorrow, anyway."

When she went downstairs at six in the morning, Victor did not appear. Perhaps he didn't want to. Marie served her a breakfast at the table under the almond tree in the paved garden. Noticing a lump on the girl's cheekbone, Kay said with a frown, "What happened? Did your boyfriend rough you up?"

"Yes, Miss Kay."

"You hit him back?"

"No, M'selle."

"Well, next time slug him," she said bitterly. "Don't let any man push you around. They're no damned good, any of them."

As the afternoon neared its end, the trail ascended to a high plateau and leveled off. It began to widen. Wattle and mud *cailles* appeared on either side, and people stood behind bamboo fences gazing curiously at the strangers.

When, Kay wondered, had they seen a white woman before?

But she was not the main object of their attention, she presently realized. They were staring mostly at the child who sat in front of her.

Tina Sam stared back at them. This was her village.

24

The road divided, and Kay reined the gray mule to a halt. "Which way, Tina?"

"That way!" Pointing left, the child was shrill with excitement.

Kay clucked the mule on again, looked back, and saw the trailing crowd turn with her.

What did they want? And if they recognized the child, why weren't they calling her name and waving to her?

This was not the main road, only a downhill path, a yard or two wide, through a lush but unkempt jungle of broad-leafed plantains and wild mangoes. More wattle and mud *cailles* lined its sides, roofed with thick layers of brown grass. More people stared from yards and doorways, then trooped out to join the procession.

Oh God, don't tell me things are going to go wrong now that I've finally got here! What's the matter with these people?

"There it is! There's my house!" Bouncing up and down on the mule, Tina raised a trembling right arm to point.

Standing by itself near a curve of the path, behind a respectable fence of hand-hewn pickets, it was a little larger than most of the others, with a roof of bright new zinc. "There it is!" the child kept screaming, all but out of her mind with excitement.

"Hey, now. Calm down, baby."

End of the line, Kay thought with relief. In spite of the flash flood, the dragon lizard, the Devil's Leap, here we are. Made it. Be proud, gal.

She turned to look at the crowd behind them and was not proud. Only apprehensive. Worse than apprehensive. Downright scared.

At a gate in the fence she reined in the mule, slid wearily from the saddle and reached up for Tina. A woman came out of the house, a slender, good-looking woman of thirty or so, wearing a dress made of feed bags. RED something. Something MILLS, INC. QUALITY FEED. A walking billboard, she came part way to the gate, staring at Kay. How long since a white woman had stopped at this gate in Bois Sauvage?

Then, her gaze shifted from Kay to Tina, and she stopped as if she had walked into an invisible wall.

The woman began screaming. The sound tore the stillness to shreds and brought a man from the house, stumbling as he ran. He reached the woman in time to catch her under the arms as she sank to her knees, still screaming. Standing there holding her, he too looked at the strangers and began to make noises. Not screaming noises but a guttural "huh huh huh huh" that seemed to burble, not from his mouth alone, but from his whole convulsed face.

A woman on her knees shrieking. A man holding her from falling, going, "Huh huh huh huh." And from the crowd came a response like a storm noise, with words flashing in and out like jabs of lightning.

"Mort! Mort! Li mort!"

Kay clasped the youngster's hand and pushed the gate open. Walked to the kneeling woman. There was nothing she could do to stop the nightmare sounds.

Don't listen to it, Gilbert. Just do what you have to do.

"Is this your mother, Tina?"

The child did not answer. Only hurled herself forward and threw her arms around the kneeling woman's neck and began sobbing, "Maman! Maman!"

The woman wrenched herself free and staggered to her feet, looked at her daughter in horror, and ran. Ran like a blinded, wild animal across the bare-earth yard, past a cluster of graves at its edge, into a field where tall stalks of *piti mi* swallowed her from sight.

Empty handed, the man stood there gazing at Tina as though his eyes would explode like overinflated balloons.

The child looked up at him. "Papa . . ."

"Huh huh huh . . ."

"It's me, Papa. Tina!"

He lurched backward, throwing up his arms. "You're dead!"

"No, Papa!"

"Yes you are! You're dead!"

"Papa, please . . ."

Reaching for him with her arms, the child began to cry. And Kay's reliable temper surged up to take over.

She strode to the man and confronted him, hands on hips and eyes blazing. "This is nonsense. Just because the child has been missing for a while doesn't mean she's dead. You can see she isn't!"

He stared back at her and his heavy-lipped mouth kept working, though soundlessly now. His contorted face oozed sweat.

"Do you hear what I'm saying, M'sieu Sam? Your daughter is all *right*. I'm a nurse, and I know."

"You . . . don't . . . understand . . ."

"What don't I understand? What are you talking about?"

He turned himself slowly to the right, as though his feet were deep in the red-brown earth and he could move

them only with difficulty. Facing in the direction the
child's mother had fled, he brought his right arm up as
though it weighed a ton. With it he pointed.

"What do you mean?" Kay demanded, then looked at
the weeping child, and said, "Don't cry, baby. I'll get to
the bottom of this."

Metellus Sam reached out and touched her on the
arm. "Come." He began walking very slowly across the
yard, his bare feet scraping the earth and leaving drag
marks. Beyond the cluster of graves toward which he
walked was the field of kaffir corn. What could there be
in such a field that would make him afraid of his own
daughter?

Kay began following him, then looked back. Tina
gazed after them with her hands at her face, obviously
all but destroyed by what had happened. The crowd in
the road was silent again. The whole length of the fence
was lined with starers, the road packed solid, but no one
had come into the yard, even though the gate hung
open. She had neglected to tie the mule, she realized.
Should she go back and do it, to make sure the crowd
wouldn't spook the animal? To hell with it.

Metellus Sam reached the edge of the yard and
trudged on through the gravestones—not stones, really,
but crudely crafted concrete shapes resembling small
houses resting on coffin-shaped slabs of the same mate-
rial. Nothing special. You saw the same kind of thing all
over Haiti. Kay looked beyond to the corn field.

Where was the woman?

Suddenly, the leaden feet of her guide stopped and,
preoccupied as she was, Kay bumped into him. He
caught her by the arm to steady her. With his other hand
he pointed to the last of the graves, one that was either
new or had been newly whitewashed.

"Look."

The name was not properly carved. Like those on the

others, it had merely been scratched in with a sharpened stick before the concrete hardened. It was big and bold, though. She had no difficulty reading it:

TINA LOUISE CHRISTINE SAM. 1971–1979.

Fists on her hips again, she studied the inscription, scowling up a storm while her temper boiled to the surface. She turned on the man.

"You shouldn't have done this! Graves are for people you've buried, not for someone you only think might be dead!"

He looked at her now without flinching, and she saw how much he resembled Tina. About thirty, he was taller than most mountain peasants and had good, clean features. "M'selle, you don't understand. My daughter *is* buried here."

"What?"

"She died. I myself made the coffin. Her own mother prepared her for burial. I put her into the coffin and nailed it shut, and when we put it into this grave and shoveled the earth over her, this yard was full of people. All those people you see standing in the road, they were here. They saw it. The whole village!"

Kay got a grip on herself. *Watch it here, Gilbert. Don't, for God's sake, say the wrong thing.* "M'sieu, I can only say you must have made a mistake."

With dignity, he moved his head slowly from side to side. "There was no mistake, M'selle. From the time she was placed in the coffin until the earth covered her, the coffin was never unguarded. Either my wife or I was with her every moment."

We can't stand here talking, Kay thought desperately. Not with that mob in the road watching us. "M'sieu, can we go into the house?"

He nodded.

"And Tina? She is not dead, I assure you. All that happened was that she lost her memory for a time and could not recall who she was."

He hesitated, but nodded again.

They walked back across the yard, to the waiting Tina. Kay put a hand on the child's shoulder. "Come, baby. It's going to be all right." Metellus Sam led the way to the house. She and Tina followed. As she turned to close the door, she saw that the villagers in the road and by the fence were still staring.

If they actually think they buried this child, I don't blame them. I'd probably do the same.

The house was larger than the one Tina and she had slept in last night. Seemed to be, anyway. But before attempting an appraisal, or even sitting down, she said, "M'sieu Sam, will you please see about my mule? He should be unsaddled and given some water, and tied where he can eat something."

He did not seem eager to comply.

"You'll have to put me up for the night or find someone nearby who will," she went on firmly. "So please bring in the saddlebags too."

"You wish to stay the night *here?*"

Kay made a production of peering at her watch, though she knew the time well enough. "I can't be expected to start back to Trou at this hour, can I? That's where my jeep is. I've brought your daughter all the way from the Schweitzer Hospital, M'sieu Sam. Do you know how far that is?"

"All that way?" He peered at her with new respect, then looked again at Tina. What was he thinking? That if the child had been at the Schweitzer, she must be real, after all? No ghost?

"The mule, please," Kay prodded. "Tina and I will just sit here until you return. Believe me, we're tired." As he turned to the door, she spoke again. "And try to find her mother, will you? I want to talk to you both."

While he was gone, she asked Tina to show her

around the house. In addition to the big front room, which was crowded with crude but highly varnished homemade furniture, there were three bedrooms. Despite the zinc roof, which indicated a measure of wealth in such a village, the floors were of earth, hard-packed and shiny from years of being rubbed by bare feet. At least there would be no lizards dropping from overhead thatch.

They sat to wait for the return of Metellus, and Tina began to cry again. Kay said quietly, "Come here, baby."

The child came to her and stepped into the waiting circle of her arm.

"Listen to me, love. We don't know what's going on here, but we're not going to be afraid of it. You hear?"

"Y-yes, Miss Kay."

"You just concentrate on being brave and let me do the talking. For a while, at least. Okay?"

Tina nodded.

Kay patted her on the bottom. "Good girl. Now go sit down and try to relax. The big thing is, we're here. You're home."

It took Metellus Sam a long time to attend to the mule. Or perhaps he spent much of the time trying to locate his woman. Daylight was about finished when at last he came through the door, lugging the saddlebags and followed by Tina's mother.

Having already decided how to handle the situation, Kay promptly rose and offered her hand. "Hello, Fifine Bonhomme, how are you? I'm Nurse Gilbert from the Schweitzer Hospital." Her memory for names was not all that good. She had had to ask Tina again what the mother's name was.

Pretty, like you? Well, maybe. But at close study, it was only a surface prettiness without character. With that baby-doll face, she had probably been pampered

from birth. It was usually so in this country, Kay
thought with a mental sigh. Give these affectionate people a living doll to play with and you could nearly
always be sure of an empty-headed adult who still expected coddling.

Well, the only way to treat such a creature was with
firmness. "Sit down, Fifine. I want to talk to you."

The woman looked fearfully at Tina. She had not
even approached the girl to speak to her, obviously had
no intention of embracing her and speaking words of
welcome.

Bitch, Kay thought. But no. The woman actually
thought she was staring at the daughter she had buried
in that grave outside . . . didn't she?

The door burst open, and three children stormed into
the room: a girl who resembled Tina but was a little
older; two peas-in-a-pod boys a year or two younger.
Rosemarie and the twins, Kay thought. All three were
out of breath but remarkably clean for country kids.
Barefoot, of course, but decently dressed. And handsome.

At sight of Tina, they stopped as though they had
been clubbed. Stared at her with eyes that grew bigger
and bigger. The girl backed up a step. The twins, as if
they were one person, took two steps forward and whispered their sister's name in unison. "Tina!"

Tina lurched from her chair and stumbled to her
knees in front of them, wrapping her arms around their
legs, crying so hard she must have been blinded by her
own tears.

Reassured (when the twins were not destroyed, Kay
supposed), Rosemarie dared to advance again. Dared to
sink to *her* knees and press her face against her sister's.

"Let the children go into another room," Kay said to
their mother. "I want to talk to you and Metellus."

Fifine Bonhomme only gazed at her brood in a silence

of apprehension. It was their father who spoke up, telling them what to do.

"Now, listen, both of you," Kay said. "I'm going to tell you what I know about your daughter, how she was found by Father Turnier." She paused. "Do you know Father Turnier?"

"The priest who used to be in Vallière," Metellus said. "We know of him."

"All right. I'm going to tell you how he found her and what happened afterward. Then *you* are going to tell me why her name is on that grave out there. You understand?"

They nodded their heads in unison.

"After that," Kay said, "we'll decide what's to be done here."

25

"That's how it happened," Kay said.

She had taken her time. Had been forced to take her time because her Creole was not that good. About the only way to be sure she was understood most often was to keep saying the same thing but in a slightly different way each time until it became clear that she was getting it across. But it required patience.

She had repeated the story told to her by the nuns in Cap Haïtien: How Tina was discovered by Father Louis Turnier in a remote *caille* to which, apparently, she had wandered after becoming lost and losing her memory. How the priest had taken her to his residence in Vallière, then to Cap Haïtien. How the sisters there had sent her to the Schweitzer.

The whole story. Because it was terribly important for them to understand that the youngster was perfectly normal. She had even included a brief lecture on amnesia.

In telling of her journey with Tina from the hospital to Bois Sauvage she had been very, very careful not to mention the flash flood, the dragon lizard, or the strange occurrence at Devil's Leap. Oh, very.

"Now then," she said firmly, "*you* do the talking, please. Explain that grave to me." Expecting little from the child's baby-faced mother, she directed her request at Metellus.

"Tina took sick and died," he said.

"What made her sick?"

"We don't know. We asked her if she had eaten anything the rest of us had not. Only a mango, she said. A boy named Luc Etienne gave her two of them when she was passing his yard on her way home from a friend's house. One was for her, one for the twins. But nobody was home when she got here, so she ate hers and when we returned an hour or so later, she was not well."

"How do you mean, not well?"

"Her stomach hurt and she had *la fièv*. A really high fever. I went at once for the *houngan*."

"And?"

"He came and did things. Brewed a tea for her and used his hands on her, things like that. He is a good man. He stayed the whole night trying to make her well. But in the morning she died."

"Who said she was dead? This *houngan*?"

"All of us." Metellus returned her gaze without flinching. "It is not in dispute that she was dead when we buried her, M'selle. When someone dies, the people we call in may not be as learned as your doctors at the hospital, but they know how to determine if life has ended. Tina was dead."

"And you think this mango that was given her by—by whom?—"

"Luc Etienne."

"—might have caused her death? Poisoned her, you mean?"

"Perhaps. *Something* made her ill. She had not been sick before."

"There were two mangoes, you said."

"Yes."

"Did anyone eat the other?"

He shook his head.

"What became of it?"

"After the funeral, we opened it up, I and some others, to see if it had been tampered with. It seemed to be all right, but, of course, you can't always be sure. Some people are wickedly clever with poisons. Anyway, we buried it."

"Did you talk to this Luc Etienne?"

"Yes, M'selle."

"What did he say?"

"Only that the mangoes were from a tree in his yard, perfectly innocent, and he gave them to Tina for herself and the twins because he was fond of children. Especially of them."

Speaking for the first time, Tina's mother said, "Our children liked him, too. He was a nice young man."

"What do you mean, *was?*"

"He is not here now."

"Oh? When did he leave?"

"Soon after the funeral, didn't he, Metellus? Just a few days?"

Metellus nodded.

"Where did he go?"

Metellus shrugged and said, "We heard, to Cap Haïtien, where he makes a lot of money betting on cockfights. But who knows for sure?"

Feeling she had sat long enough, Kay rose stiffly and walked to the door. It was open, but would soon have to be closed because the yard was turning dark. There were still people in the road and at the fence. But most had departed. She looked across the yard toward the cluster of graves.

Turning back into the room, she frowned at Tina's father. "And you personally put Tina into a coffin and nailed it shut and buried it, Metellus?"

"Yes, M'selle. Personally."

"There is no doubt in your mind that she was *in* the coffin when you buried it?"

"None at all."

"Are you saying, then, that the child I've brought back to you is not your daughter, but someone else?"

He looked at his woman, and she at him. He turned to meet Kay's demanding gaze again. "M'selle, what can we say?"

With her fists against her hips for perhaps the fourth time that day, Kay faced them in a resurgence of anger. "You can admit there's been a mistake, that's what you can say! Because, look. When the name Bois Sauvage was read to this child by a doctor reading a map, she clapped her hands and cried out, 'That's where I live!' For weeks she hadn't been able to remember anything of her past, but the name Bois Sauvage changed all that. Then she remembered her name—her full name, mind you, just as you've got it inscribed on that grave out there. Tina Louise Christine Sam. And she remembered *your* names and her sister's and the twins'. So if she isn't your Tina, who in the world do you think she is?"

The woman whispered something.

"What?" Kay said.

"She is a zombie."

"Oh, for God's sake! Zombies are dead people, if there *are* such things. Tina is a normal, healthy child!"

"Li sé zombie," the woman stubbornly repeated, then rose from her chair and went into a bedroom. Returning with a lamp, she placed it on a table and beckoned her man to come and light it. "I must prepare some food. M'selle, do you eat our kind of food? Chicken? Yams? Peas and rice left over from noon?"

"Thank you, yes. But wait. We ought to settle this before we think of eating. What do you intend to *do* about Tina?"

"That is up to Metellus." She opened the door of the

room where the children where. "Rosemarie! Come and help with supper!"

Both girls responded, but she held up a hand when Tina tried to follow the older one from the room.

"Not you."

"But, Maman, I can help too."

"No."

Her tears glistening in the lamplight, the child retreated and shut the door. The woman turned to direct a silent command at Metellus.

Rising, the man exhaled heavily and said, "I will make a light in the kitchen and get a fire going." Then, to Kay, he said, "Excuse me, M'selle," and walked out the front door.

Later that evening Kay tried to break down the woman's resistance, but failed. She probably could have convinced Metellus, she told herself, had the child's mother been a different kind of person. It was a pathetic situation. Tragic. The father was strong and intelligent but unwilling, obviously, to make trouble for himself by challenging this baby-faced feather-brain he slept with.

I need sleep myself. We can pick this up again tomorrow.

It had been decided that she and Tina would share a bedroom, though the other children had told their mother Tina could sleep with them. Only with the greatest reluctance had Fifine allowed the child to sit at the supper table, and not once during the meal had she looked at or spoken to her "zombie" daughter.

Kay's temper had more than once surged up like lava. She was exhausted now from having expended so much energy controlling it.

Go to bed, Gilbert. Maybe during the night Metellus will find himself some guts.

She lay with her right arm around Tina, the child's

head on her breast. A lamp burned low on a chest of drawers made mostly of woven sisal.

"Miss Kay?"

"What, baby?"

"My mother doesn't want me. What will I do?"

"It's all a big mistake, *ti-fi*."

"They think I'm dead. Did I die, Miss Kay?"

"Of course not."

"Why do they say I did, then? Even Rosemarie and the twins."

"Because they . . ." *Oh, Christ, baby, I don't know why! I'm way out of my depth here and don't know what to say or do about it. I'm out of my depth the way Sam Norman was, and he didn't have any answers, either.*

The child was silent. Fell asleep. Kay moved her arm and lay there in the lampglow staring at the roof and thinking. *What am I doing in this place? I don't understand these people. What am I doing in Haiti, anyway, for God's sake? None of us who come here really know what we're doing. All we can do is kid ourselves into thinking we have superior intellects while we muddle along and make mistakes and foul everything up.*

But she knew she was tired. That, she was sure of. All day long on a mule, most of the day scared because Joseph had left her alone with the child. Her knees ached, her thighs burned, her arches must be permanently warped from the stupid stirrups, even her fingers were cramped from holding the reins, and nothing but sleep would change anything.

She listened to Tina's breathing and it helped, it was soothing. After a while, she dozed off.

There was a tapping sound at the room's only window. A window with no glass in it, and she had decided not to close the shutters lest the smell of the kerosene lamp give her more of a headache than she already had.

The tapping was on one of the open shutters, and she sat up in bed and turned her head in that direction, still half asleep, and heard the voice of Metellus Sam whispering to her from the opening.

"M'selle . . ."

"What is it?" she said to the face peering in at her. Still a strong, good-looking face, it was warped with some kind of fear now. The lampglow created yellow highlights in the white of his eyes.

"I have to show you something!"

She looked at the watch on her wrist. Why, on this crazy pilgrimage, was she always trying to find out the time in the middle of the night?

Three-ten. Well, at least she'd been sleeping. Would be rested tomorrow.

"What do you want, Metellus?"

"Come out here, please. Be careful not to wake anyone!"

"All right. Just give me a minute."

She had worn pajamas to bed. Was damned if she would get dressed at this idiot hour just to go into the yard to see what he wanted. A glance at Tina. The child was sound asleep. Starting for the door barefoot, she remembered what *chigres* could do to the toes of the careless and went back to put on her sneaks. Then left the bedroom, walked silently across the dim front room with its clutter of chairs, opened the door, stepped outside, and found him waiting.

He took her by the arm and whispered, "Come!"

He led her across the yard, through moonlight bright enough to paint the ground with dark shadows of house, fence, trees, graves. He walked her to the graves. Next to the one with Tina's name on it was a hole now, with dirt piled at its edge and a spade thrust upright in the dirt.

"Look, M'selle."

She approached the edge and peered into the excava-

tion. Saw what he had done. Unable to move the concrete slab that covered the grave, he had dug down
beside it, then tunneled under. Far enough under, at
least, to find out what he wanted to know.

"You see? The coffin is gone!"

She nodded. There was nothing to argue about. He
had dug enough dirt out to prove his point. Not enough
to risk having the slab sag into his excavation, but he
had certainly discovered there was no wooden box under it. She stood there staring and heard all the usual
night sounds in the silence. Crickets. Tree toads. Croak-
ing lizards. Insects.

"How could anyone have stolen it without moving the
slab?" she asked, but knew the answer before finishing
the question. Let him say it anyway.

"M'selle, we don't do the tombing right away. Not
until the earth has settled. In this case it was more than
six weeks before I could go to Trou for the cement."

Which you brought back on a mule, she thought,
walking the whole way back yourself so the mule could
carry it. And then you built this elaborate concrete thing
over the grave to show your love for a daughter whose
body had already been stolen.

Gilbert, what the hell are you saying?

"Metellus, I don't understand this."

Let him explain it, even though she guessed how he
would do so.

"There can be only one answer, M'selle. I know my
daughter died. I know I put her into a coffin and buried
her here. The coffin is not here now. So . . . she is a
zombie."

"She was not really dead, you mean."

"Well, there are two kinds of zombies, as perhaps you
know. Those who truly die and are restored to life by
sorcery; that is one kind. Others are poisoned in various
ways so they only seem to die, then are taken from their
graves and restored."

Still gazing into the hole, Kay nodded. The second kind of zombie was the one believed in by most Haitian peasants, of course. And it was hard to censure them. You heard some strangely convincing tales.

"You think Tina was poisoned?"

"Now I do, yes."

"With that mango you told me about?"

Metellus reached for the spade and, holding it in both hands, turned to frown at her. "Luc Etienne gave her two mangoes. One for herself, one for the twins to share. You know what I think? I think on the way home she got them mixed up, and when she found no one at home and ate her mango, the one she ate was the one she had been told to give to the twins."

"I don't understand." This time she really did not.

"He wanted the twins for some special purpose. Twins are different."

"Who? This fellow Etienne?"

He shook his head. With a glance toward the house, he began quietly putting the earth back into the hole. "Not Etienne, M'selle. At least, not for himself. He was friendly with a much more important person at that time. With a *bocor* in Legrun, named Margal. There are people here who say Luc Etienne was that man's pupil."

"The legless one," Kay said.

He stopped the spade in mid stroke. "You know of him?"

"I think he tried to stop me from coming here."

"Very likely. Because you know what I think happened after he stole the coffin from the grave? I think he brought Tina back to life the way they do—with leaves or herbs or whatever—and then sold her to someone in some distant place where she would not be known. He wanted the twins, yes, but still would have stolen Tina to sell her. Someone who needed a willing servant would have paid him well."

"And she wandered away."

"And the priest found her."

"How did Margal know I was bringing her back here?"

"That man would know, M'selle. He probably knows we are standing here discussing him right this minute." Metellus plied the spade faster now, obviously anxious to get the job finished. But again he stopped and faced her. "M'selle, Tina cannot stay here. Next time, he will surely kill her."

"I think you're probably right." *Gilbert, what in God's name are you saying? Has this spooky grave-dig in the moonlight got your mind? You were trained to be a nurse!*

"I love my daughter. You must know that by now."

"I'm sure you do."

"Fifine loved her too, but she can never feel the same again. You must know *that.*"

Kay nodded.

More earth fell into the hole, adding its lumpy sound to the noise of the night things. In the moonlight Metellus was a strange figure working there by his daughter's grave: a man deserving of respect, Kay thought. Many of the country people were like that. Solid, sincere, polite. *And,* of course, beset with superstitions as burdensome as Sindbad's Old Man of the Sea.

He finished refilling the hole. Turned to her with the spade over his shoulder. "M'selle, I have a brother in Port-au-Prince."

"Oh?"

"He is two years younger than I and has only two children. He would give Tina a home, even send her to school there. She can't say here. All of Bois Sauvage knows she died and was buried in this yard and must now be a zombie. She would be shunned, even if Margal did not destroy her."

"You want me to take her to your brother?"

"Will you? I will ride out with you to where your jeep is."

She thought about it while he gazed at her, awaiting her reply. A white owl flew across the yard from the road to the field of *piti-mi*. "I'll sleep on it, Metellus. Tell you tomorrow."

"M'selle, you must love the child or you would not have done so much for her already."

"Tomorrow, Metellus," she said and, deep in thought, walked slowly back to the house.

26

"We are going to destroy your president, Dr.
   Molicoeur."
"Why?"
"Because Margal wishes it."
"Who is Margal?"
"A man with no legs."
"I do not understand."
"A man who lost his legs
as a result of a beating
administered by thugs
sent to kill him
because he refused to assist
some member of your government.
That is what he told me.
He wants revenge
and you have been selected
to obtain it for him."
"But why me?"
"Because—it is simple—
you have access to the president.
You see him almost daily.
He trusts you."
"I will not do it!"
"I wish I could hope so,

Dr. Molicoeur.
But you will."

They sit in the study
of Dr. Molicoeur.
Their conversation is interrupted by a light,
polite knock
on the closed door.
Glancing at Dr. Bell
and receiving a nod of permission,
the Haitian rises
and goes to the door
and opens it.
His beautiful young wife,
a light-skinned girl who once rode a Mardi Gras float
as Haiti's beauty queen,
smiles at her husband and Dr. Bell
and says with a smile,
"Dinner is ready."

At dinner,
in the presence of this charming woman
and her delightful, small daughter,
Dr. Bell is sad,
knowing that the success of his mission
will destroy them.
His mind screams yet another challenge:
"Margal, I will not do this!
You cannot force me to do this!
I refuse!"
And, as before,
his hands begin to shake,
his face pales,
and his pores spurt sweat.

Madame Molicoeur,

in sudden alarm and compassion,
abruptly leans toward him.
"What is wrong, Dr. Bell?
Are you ill?"

"Forgive me. It will pass."

And it passes.
But only when his mind abandons the challenge
and bows again
to the will of the legless man
in the mountains.

In his room,
Dr. Bell lies awake for hours,
waiting.
In the deep stillness of the night,
he calls again to his daughter,
who is on her way to the terrible place
she must not be allowed to reach.

"Milly, Milly,"
do not go!
I am not there.
I am in the capital.
Turn back, child,
please,
for God's sake.
That man is a devil
who finds it all too easy
to have his way with people like you and me."

27

Vallière was behind them. The trail snaked on and on through shades of green and sounds of silence. Had Daddy really reached her last night?

He could have. He had sounded most anxious to, in order to tell her he was not where she thought but in the capital, in trouble, and needed her. When it was that important for him to make contact, he usually was able to.

Like the day when Mama . . .

She had been home alone that day in the house on Gorton Pond in Warwick, Rhode Island. Daddy was in Vermont, finding out whether he would or would not be teaching philosophy there in September. Mama had gone to New York with her friend Edna Vaughan to do some shopping.

Seven P.M. She was standing at the kitchen sink with an opened can of spinach in her hand, wondering whether to heat it or just put some dressing on it and have it cold. Along with the lamb chop she was broiling, of course. Absolutely no other thought but what to do with the spinach. And Daddy had reached her.

"Milly?"

She was startled, but managed to answer him. At least to acknowledge the contact.

"Milly, do you know what hotel your mother and Edna Vaughan planned on staying at?"

"They weren't going to a hotel, Daddy. They were invited to stay with a friend of Edna's on Riverside Drive."

"Do you have a phone number?" Daddy had drilled it into them never to go anywhere without leaving a number where you could be reached in case of trouble.

"I'm sure she left one on the telephone table. But, Daddy, why aren't you phoning me instead of this? You know how I suffer from headaches afterward!"

"I can't get to a phone, Milly. I'm out in the middle of the lake here in a sailboat. Got the job, came out here to relax, and then suddenly got this feeling. Call your mother, Milly. Tell her she mustn't drive home with Edna. It's terribly important! She must not drive home with Edna!"

But when she called the number Mama had left by the phone, no one answered. Ring, ring, ring for ten minutes —no answer. For the next hour she dialed again every five minutes, and still got nothing. It was too late, anyway. Mama and Edna wouldn't have left New York as late as this. Edna hated driving at night.

Months later, when Edna recovered enough to go into details, she got the story of what happened. "We were just going along there in Connecticut, not even fast, Milly, I'm sure not even fifty, and just as we came to one of those overpass roads with the big abutments—you know, those big stone abutments that scare you anyway—well, just then a dog ran into the road. It was only a mutt, but I tried not to hit it, and I guess I sideswiped the abutment."

The accident had occurred fully half an hour before Daddy contacted her, if you could believe Edna's story that she had looked at the dashboard clock only just before it happened, so by the time Daddy got the message out there in his borrowed sailboat on the lake in Vermont, Mama was already dead.

But the important thing was that Daddy had been able to get through to her at that terrible time.

Had he done so again last night? Was he really in Port-au-Prince, in danger, or had she just dreamed it while she was asleep in Sam's bed with Sam's arm around her?

How could she know?

She rode on through the forest silence, their guide ahead of her and Sam behind. Sam was right, of course. It would be stupid to turn back now, when they were so close to their destination. Still, she had the feeling they were wasting time and should be going the other way. Twice this morning she had closed her eyes, let her mule just follow their guide's, and strained to establish another contact with her father. *Daddy, please, where are you? Can you hear me?*

She tried again. It still didn't work.

When she opened her eyes, the mule ahead had disappeared. Probably, she had let her own animal slow down; it was a bit lazy at times. Stick to business or we'll never get there, she told herself with a touch of annoyance. Turning in the saddle, she was relieved to see that Sam Norman was still behind her.

Alfred Oriol had looked back to be sure he was unobserved before nudging his animal with both feet to make it quicken its stride. He knew where he was and what he was approaching. Knew, too, that he was receiving instructions.

All yesterday he had expected to receive a message of some kind, but none had come. After his promptness in letting the legless one know they were coming, he had felt let down. But Margal had only been waiting for the proper place, he knew now. This was it.

In haste, but still with great care, he urged his animal down the slippery, steep-sided trench, lifting his feet from the stirrups lest they be crushed. Near the bottom, he reined the mule to a halt before letting it make that treacherous right-angle turn onto the Devil's Leap. Ten yards farther on, he slid off the beast's rump and ran back to the turn, stripping off his shirt as he went.

The shirt was white. Not very clean now, but still mostly white. Holding it by its tail, he flattened himself against the cliff wall and waited.

A thought occurred to him, and he asked the question. *What will I do, Margal, if the woman alone goes over? The man will tell the police who did it!*

You can frighten his animal, too, before he can turn it around in that place.

Yes, of course. He will be too startled to defend himself.

Mildred stopped. Looked down. Waited for Sam Norman to ride up behind her.

"Sam, I don't think I like this. Is it safe?"

Sam, too, looked down the trench. Frowned at its steep clay walls. Saw how slippery it seemed to be. "Hold on a minute." Dismounting, he walked on down the chute a few yards, peering ahead at its shadowy convolutions, then, with difficulty, made his way back up. "We'd better walk."

With his help, she dismounted.

"Better let me go first," Sam said. "Lead your mule by the reins, but let them hang loose and keep an eye on him. If he should lose his footing and start to come down on top of you, drop the reins and get out of his way."

She nodded, but her face was lined with apprehension.

Sam led his mule around hers and started down, following his own advice. Tricky. That night dew had been heavy here and the sun hadn't yet penetrated enough to dry it even a little. He tried to look up past his own lurching animal to see how Mildred was managing, but she was well behind, descending even more slowly than he. Damn Oriol, where was he when he was needed? He was paid to be a guide, not to go waltzing off ahead at a pace to suit himself.

A turn at the bottom? It seemed so. A chunk of sky was visible there so there must be a sharp drop into space, and the trail had to go to the right or the left. Should he call to warn Mildred? No. Better get himself past the place first, then walk back to help her if it was as nasty as it appeared to be.

Emerging from the chute, he saw where he was, saw the valley below him, how far down it was, and took in a breath that sounded like a mule sucking up water. Looking left, he saw nothing. He turned right and saw that the trail wound along a sheer cliff face. He would have to lead the mule away from the bottom of the trench to clear the turn for Mildred.

At that moment, a figure leaped out at him from a niche in the cliff wall. A howling, gone-crazy figure naked from the waist up, brandishing a white shirt. The mule shied, ripped the reins from Sam's hand, and reared in terror, slashing the air with its hind legs, then went over the edge with a noise like a prolonged human scream of terror.

Supposed to be Mildred's mule with Mildred on it, Sam thought, recognizing Oriol. "You bastard!" He dropped to one knee and took the fellow around the thighs as Oriol lurched in, unable to overcome his momentum. Dumped him with force enough to stun him. Then dropped him hard, both knees in the fellow's gut, and slammed a fist into his face.

"You murdering son of a bitch!"

But there was no time now. Remembering Mildred,

he staggered up and ran back to the trench. Reached it just as she came in sight above, gingerly stepping down the last couple of yards with her animal sliding behind her.

"Easy now," he warned, with no time to tell her more.

Rounding the right angle, she saw Oriol sprawled in the trail ahead. Froze. Caught her breath but made no outcry, only turned her head to look in alarm at Sam as he came up behind her, leading the mule.

"Take your animal now," Sam said, putting the reins back into her hand. "I have to talk to this louse."

He went forward. Stood over Oriol and looked down and saw the man's eyes flicker open. Frightened eyes, their whites dirty and flecked with red.

"All right, Mister." *Keep it conversational, Sam, if you want any information.* "You tried to kill Miss Bell. Why?"

Flat on his back, staring up, Oriol rolled his head from side to side.

"Don't give me that." Sam picked up the shirt. "You took this off and came out waving it, yelling your damned head off, to scare my mule into going over the edge here. Which he did. But you were expecting Miss Bell's mule with her on it, not me leading mine."

Silence.

"Come on. Who put you up to it?"

No answer.

"*You* don't have any reason to want her dead, for Christ's sake. But you listened with both ears when I was telling Pàul Lafontant about Dr. Bell, didn't you? Then you sneaked out of the shop, didn't you? What for? To send a message to Legrun that we were coming?"

Again, silence.

Sam turned his head to glance at Mildred, who stood

there, wide-eyed. He looked at the man on the ground again.

"Why doesn't Margal want us to visit him?"

No reply.

"He doesn't, does he? He's so anxious for us *not* to get there that you would even commit murder to prevent it. Are you going to talk, Oriol, or just lie there until I get mad enough to kick you over the edge here?"

The man with the canteloupe-rind face rolled his head again and looked fearfully at the rim of the trail. "I know nothing, M'sieu."

"What do you mean, you know nothing! You killed my mule!"

"Someone made me do it."

"Who made you do it?"

"I don't know, M'sieu. I swear! My mind was possessed. Voodoo!"

Sam was quiet for a moment. Then he said, "Get over against the cliff, Oriol. No, don't get up"—as the fellow began to struggle to his knees—"just slide over there."

Oriol obeyed, still staring at him with those red-flecked eyes.

"Milly, lead your mule on by."

She did, stopping when she reached the guide's animal a few yards beyond.

"All right, Oriol. If we were going the other way, I'd take you to Trou and hand you over to the police," Sam said, glaring down at him. "Consider yourself lucky we're not. I'm taking your mule. You can walk home, damn you, and I'll be glad if you never get there." He looked at the man for another few seconds in silence, then turned away.

Oriol watched the two of them continue along the trail, leading their animals. Watched them disappear. He pulled himself to his feet by grabbing at the cliff wall.

Stood there rubbing his jaw. It was beginning to swell. Maybe it was broken.

"No," he said suddenly. "No, Margal!"

A look of terror took possession of his face. Jerking himself around, he stared along the cliff passage in the direction his companions had gone. He was alone. There was no one he could call to for help.

He began feeling his way along the ledge, back toward the right-angle turn at the foot of the trench, as though the ledge had suddenly become only inches wide.

"No . . . no . . . I didn't! I didn't tell them anything!" he whimpered aloud.

You did. But worse than that, you stupidly failed me!

"I didn't know, Margal! How could I know they would not be riding their animals? Or that he would be the first to reach me?"

Very well. Go home.

Relief wiped the terror from his face as he groped along the wall to get off Saut Diable before the legless one could change his mind. Ah, good, he was around the right angle and in the trench now, with a wall on his right side, too, instead of that awesome drop into space. A rest, just a short rest leaning against the wall, not even sitting down, and he would climb the trench and go on.

The right-hand wall looked better for resting than the left. Not so mucky. Almost inviting, in fact. With a sigh of weariness, he planted his feet at its base and leaned back against it.

Only when he was falling, did he realize that the legless one had tricked him and he had still been on the cliff trail, not in the trench at all. And there was no wall on that side of the cliff trail to lean against.

His screams lived on in echoes for quite a while.

28

You've been wrong about Sam, Daddy. Yes, you have. Very.

She was not really talking to her father this time. Not that way. Just thinking what she might say to him when she found him. Riding along behind Sam, studying the breadth of his shoulders, she thought of how he had handled their guide back there where the trail crossed the cliff, and then thought of other things he had done since their departure from Port-au-Prince. The friction between Sam and her father was a thing she would have to eliminate. Because—face it—she wanted Sam Norman, and Daddy would have to accept him.

You hear, Daddy? I want this man. Now, be quiet, please, and listen to me once without interrupting. I know you think you dislike him, but that's unfair. Totally unfair. You liked him well enough in the beginning and were pleased when he asked me out. Oh, I know. What you really wanted was for me to keep him coming around so you could absorb his first-hand knowledge of Haiti. But you liked him, too, and only stopped liking him—don't deny it—when he refused to spend the summer with you in Haiti, helping you with your research. That was when you turned on him. Only then, and for no other reason. You don't like to be said no to.

217

Not trying to project her thoughts at this time, she expected no reply and received none. In fact, having mentally had her say, she was quite content to forget her father altogether and concentrate on other things.

Why, back there in Vallière, had she tried twice to go to the river?

Why had Alfred Oriol, who didn't even know her, tried to kill her at the cliff?

What was happening?

Her thoughts returned to her father, and this time she tried to get through to him. *Daddy, do you know what's going on? Is that why you tried to reach me last night?*

No answer.

If he really had reached her, had he known that she and Sam were sleeping together? No, it didn't work that way. It never had for her, at any rate. The day he was on the lake in Vermont, she hadn't known where he was until he told her.

The mule ahead had slowed. Sam was looking back over his shoulder. "We're coming to a village," he said when she was close enough.

"Bois Sauvage?"

"Must be." He looked at his watch. "Two-twenty. We'll have to stop here and ask the way to Legrun. I have no idea whether it's on this trail or on some little side track."

"All right."

A frown reshaped his mouth as he looked at her. "Something else I have no idea about is where we'll sleep tonight, Milly. A dirt-floored peasant hut, more than likely. Perhaps not even a bed."

She nodded.

She looked tired, Sam thought. Ought to be tired, after so much steady riding. Since the clash with Oriol at the cliff, they had stopped only twice, and then only briefly. "Want to rest before we ride into this place?"

"No. I'm okay."

He rode on. The trail had widened and there were thatch-roofed *cailles* on both sides now. People in the yards stared. So did the occasional peasant walking the road. Sam kept an eye out for someone to question about the route.

They were nearing the center of the village. The houses were closer together and the starers more numerous. He spotted a gray-haired oldster standing at a gate in a bamboo fence. Halting his mule beside the fellow, he raised a hand in salute. *"Bon soir, compère. Honneur."*

"Respect, M'sieu."

"I wonder if you can help us. We're on our way to Legrun and are not familiar with the road."

"Legrun?"

"Yes. How far is it from here?"

"Perhaps four miles. But the road is difficult."

Sam turned to Mildred. "Only four miles, he says."

"Good."

"And how do we get there, *compère*?"

Opening his gate, the villager stepped out and pointed in the direction they were traveling. "Go straight on, M'sieu, paying no attention to a small road that goes downhill to the left. Just beyond the marketplace, which is closed today, you will see a path on the right marked with a cross to Baron Samedi. That is the way to where you are going, and it might be well to ask the baron's protection."

Sam had heard almost none of it.

"M'sieu?" The old fellow frowned at his lack of attention.

"Yes . . . thanks," Sam muttered, and swung himself out of the saddle. His gaze was glued to a spot forty yards distant, where a young woman and a child, holding hands, had stepped from a yard and were walking along the road's edge toward him. The child was Haitian, about nine years old. The woman wore a khaki shirt and pants, and was white.

Sam broke into a sprint.

The woman and child saw him coming and stopped. With a trail of red dust rising behind him, he skidded to a halt before them and stood there staring at the woman's familiar face with its dark, wide eyes and crown of near-black hair.

Her sensuous mouth was open in pure astonishment. She had not known he was even in Haiti.

Extending his hands, he slowly let them fall when she failed to respond.

Inside him the sudden bright light dimmed and went out. *She still hates your guts, Norman. Why shouldn't she?*

"Kay . . . how are you?" An inane question, but what else to say?

Recovering from shock, she let her pent-up breath out and said, "Sam Norman, what in the world are you doing here?"

"Looking for you, for one thing."

"For me?"

"Since I learned you were headed for here. I'm also taking someone to Legrun." He nodded toward Mildred, still seated on her mule at the gate. "Her father's a big man at the college where I teach now. He came here weeks ago and hasn't been heard from." Sam found he could not stop staring at her—her eyes, her mouth, all the remembered things about her—even though it was obvious she didn't care anymore. Just looking at her restored feelings he hadn't had about a woman since those days now long past. Finally, he said, "Is this the little girl from the hospital?"

"Yes. We've been visiting her friends. People who

used to be her friends. Tina, this is an old friend of *mine*, M'sieu Norman."

"*Bon soir,* M'sieu." The child seemed strangely subdued, even sad, as she offered her hand.

Sam held the hand and said, "How are you, Tina?" Then to Kay, with a frown, "*Used* to be her friends? What gives?"

"It's a long story." Too long, Kay thought. This morning, in spite of that empty grave in the yard, she had said fiercely to Metellus, 'No, I won't take her to your brother in Port-au-Prince. At least, not until I'm convinced you're right about the people here. Today I'm going to take her visiting and see how people react. I just can't believe they'll reject such a lovely child!"

Now she had to admit that Metellus had been right, and there was only one solution to the problem. Thank God he *had* a brother who might give the youngster a home.

Sam said, "You must have got here yesterday."

"Yes."

"Are you staying long?"

"I plan to start back tomorrow, with her." She nodded toward Tina, who still clung to her hand.

"Taking her *back*?"

"That's part of the story. A long one, as I said. Look," she said, glancing past him toward Mildred. "Hadn't you better introduce me to your friend? Two white women in a place like this . . . If we don't speak, the whole village will explode with curiosity."

He led her to the gate and made the introductions. Mildred leaned from the saddle to accept Kay's hand. "I certainly never expected to find someone like you here."

"Your father is in Legrun, Sam tells me."

"We hope so. I'm almost afraid to find out."

Kay looked at Sam. "Have you ever been there?"

"No. Our friend here"—indicating the man at the gate—"was just telling me how to get there when I saw you." Sam at last felt he might touch her without triggering memories of their last God-awful night together, and lightly laid a hand on her arm. "Look, if you're starting back tomorrow, why can't we all ride together? That is, if Milly and I can get to Legrun this afternoon and find out about her father. If he's there and okay, we'll be taking him back at once. If he isn't there, we'll be leaving anyway."

"Come, talk to Tina's father. Perhaps he can help you."

Mildred frowned at her watch.

"It won't take long," Kay said.

She led the way, and Sam walked beside her, leading his mule. Mildred rode. At the house, Kay talked to Metellus while he watered the animals. "How long will it take these people to get to Legrun?" she asked him.

"About an hour and a half, M'selle, after the rains we have had."

"Why don't you go along to guide them? I've decided to take Tina to your brother, as you asked. If Miss Bell and Mr. Norman accomplish their mission in time, they'll ride to Trou with me tomorrow and you won't have to go."

Looking hard and long at Sam and Mildred, Metellus hesitated, then with obvious reluctance said, "Well, M'selle . . . all right."

"Don't you want to?"

"I will take them."

He's afraid of Margal, Kay thought. *Well, I don't blame him. If a daughter of mine turned up alive after I'd buried her months ago—or thought I had—I'd be queasy, too*. One thing she was sure of: The people of Bois Sauvage were afraid of Tina. On seeing the child today, most had refused even to look the youngster in the face and speak her name.

Metellus excused himself and returned in a few moments, astride a mule. To Sam and Mildred, as they prepared to ride out with him, Kay said, "I don't suppose you two have had much to eat today . . . ?"

"Some stale bread and a can of corned beef," Sam replied wryly. *You would think of that, Kay baby. Bless you.*

"I'll try to buy a couple of chickens and have a meal ready when you return, then." She frowned. "That is, if you *will* be returning tonight. What do you think, Metellus?"

"They have to, M'selle. Strangers cannot stay in Legrun. They will have to sleep here in Bois Sauvage somewhere."

"I'll try to find beds for you, then," Kay said. "Good luck, Miss Bell. I hope you find your father."

29

Along one of the few stretches of trail where they could attempt a conversation, Mildred said, "I like your nurse, Sam. Have you known her long?"

"Met her when I worked here, is all."

"And you've kept in touch?"

"No. She planned on working here a long time, and I never expected to come back."

As the old fellow in Bois Sauvage had warned, the trail was difficult. Their guide, Metellus, seemed bent on making it even more so by setting a furious pace. *Damn the man*, Sam thought. *If he'd been in the saddle since daybreak as we have, he wouldn't be so eager.* Had he been next in line he would have yelled at the fellow to slow down, but Mildred was following Metellus.

"Sam," she called back, "if we don't find Daddy in Legrun, what can we do?"

"Well, you said he was in Port."

"But we don't know where in Port."

"Maybe you can talk to him again and find out."

"Sam, don't be sarcastic."

"Who's being sarcastic? You say you can talk to him. I believe you." *At least, I believe you think you can. Which isn't exactly the same thing, is it?*

The trail grew rougher and their brief dialogue came

to an end. The mules toiled up a ladder of boulders now, straining with every step. It must get dark early here, Sam thought, unhappily eyeing the high mountain forest hemming them in. At times, even the sky was hidden by massed tree limbs. Was that the answer to their guide's haste? His knowing they would have to leave Legrun early or spend the night there even if strangers were not welcome?

The path broke out of the forest, straggled over a grassy plateau painted pure gold by the afternoon sun, then plunged down again. Here, Metellus had to abandon his haste or risk a broken neck. The animals gingerly felt their way down a boulder-strewn trench. The trench gradually widened into another grassy clearing, this one dotted with thatch-roofed huts. Sam counted five of them, plus one substantial, metal-roofed house. From a vertical cliff on the right tumbled a forty-foot waterfall that filled the vale with sound.

Reining his mule to a halt ten yards from the largest house, Metellus raised an arm to point. "Margal lives there. I will take the mules and wait for you by the waterfall. Remember, please, we must leave here well before dark. That road at night is too dangerous."

"Don't worry, friend," Sam said.

He and Mildred dismounted, turned their animals over to their guide, and walked side by side to the house. He was looking, he realized, at the first painted house he had seen all day. Margal apparently believed in being different and was wealthy enough to indulge his whims. His abode was bright red.

The front door swung open. A massive, moon-faced woman wearing a flaming red dress stood waiting for them.

Sam went through the formalities. "*Honneur*, Madame."

"*Respect*, M'sieu."

"We would like to speak with M'sieu Margal. We have come all the way from the capital to see him."

She took her own good time to look them over, then nodded and stepped back to clear the doorway. "Please, come in."

Putting caution before politeness, Sam led the way and found himself in a room that surprised him, and not only for its great size. Its floor was of tavernon, the close-grained cabinet wood that was now even rarer and more expensive than Haitian mahogany. Tables and chairs, even one oddly shaped chair near the door, were of the same exquisite wood. Did it grow here? It probably did, but must have cost Margal a small fortune all the same, if only for the sawing. The walls were of clay but painted like the outside of the house, and intricately decorated as well. In this unusual room each was a different color: aquamarine, rose, black, green. The effect was startling.

"Be seated, please," the woman said. "I will ask if the master wishes to see you. This is his time for resting." She watched Mildred sit and waited for Sam to do the same. "Not there, M'sieu," she added quickly when he moved toward the odd-shaped chair. "That is the master's."

"Sorry." Sam veered away, but not before noticing what a really remarkable chair it was. Its back was vertical, its seat a flat platform littered with varicolored cushions. It had wide, flat, slotted arms. Fit a board across those arms, using the slots to anchor it, and the chair could be a desk, a work table, even a dining table.

He sat elsewhere, and the fat woman disappeared into a connecting room, leaving the door open behind her.

Sam looked at Mildred. She was peering at a small table beside the forbidden chair. "Sam," she said, rising. "Look!"

She went to the table and Sam saw she was gazing at

a display of photographs in cardboard stand-up frames. When he reached her side, she pointed to a photo of her father.

"So he *is* here," Sam said. "Or was."

"I've never seen this picture of him before, Sam. In fact, I haven't seen *any* new ones in recent years. He dislikes having them taken."

"Maybe Margal took it with a Polaroid." Sam peered at the others. "This one seems to be the same sort." He indicated a head-and-shoulders snap of a youngish-looking white man with close-cropped blond hair, then saw the same man in another picture next to it—a group picture much larger than the other two—in which the same fellow stood on a platform under a huge portrait of Adolph Hitler and appeared to be addressing a gathering of carbon copies of himself, all in uniforms adorned with swastikas. As Sam stooped to examine all three pictures more closely, the woman in red spoke from the doorway behind him.

"If you will be seated again, the master will speak with you."

He and Mildred returned to their chairs, Sam saying with a shrug, "Sorry. Miss Bell just noticed the photo of her father." *And I'll bet you already know she's Dr. Bell's daughter, don't you, Big Bertha?*

The woman went back into the other room and reappeared in a moment with a strange figure in her arms. As she walked to the chair with it, Sam took a quick look and felt himself become rigid.

Had the fellow been whole, he would have weighed about a hundred fifty pounds and been perhaps five foot six. His legs ended above the knees, however, and Big Bertha held him against her mountainous bosom simply by looping one strong arm under his buttocks. With both of his arms encircling her neck, his face was partly hidden by the folds of flesh under her chin.

Seemingly without effort, she carried him to his special chair and set him down. His hands rested on its arms and his spine was supported by its vertical back. The colored cushions softened the contact. While she was arranging him thus, he paid absolutely no attention to her, but kept his head slumped on his chest.

Then, when she had finished and stepped back, he raised his head, and Sam saw his face—his whole face—for the first time. He caught another breath that was little more than a gasp. His heartbeat quickened wildly. A wave of cold coursed through him, chilling the sweat on his body.

On at least three previous occasions he had looked into those eyes. They were the most piercing of any he had ever seen in a living creature. The face in which they glittered had seemed younger then; perhaps the ordeal of losing both legs had aged it. The body, too, had certainly been less frail than it was now. But despite certain deliberate alterations, there could be no doubt about the man's identity.

The changes had been cunningly contrived, Sam had to admit. A previously hairy face now was clean-shaven, surprisingly thin-lipped and angular in its nakedness. The formerly close-cropped head was now awrithe with a thick, stringy mass that resembled the dreadlocks of Jamaican Rastafarians.

Incongruously, the fellow wore an expensive purple sport shirt and cream-hued slacks, the legs of which had been shortened and sewn up to hide his stumps. And even more incongruously, he returned Sam's stare of recognition with a totally innocent, "I bid you welcome, M'sieu. My name is Margal. Please tell me who you are and why you have come here."

Sam told him.

Margal gazed at the fat woman, who had retreated a few steps and stood with her arms crossed over her bulging breasts. "Ah, yes—Dr. Bell. He was here for a week a long while ago, was he not, Clarisse? *Did* he stay a week?"

"Six days."

The gaze flicked back to Sam. "And you have come all this long way expecting to find him still here? I am so sorry." Changing targets again, he shook his head sadly at Mildred. "And you, M'selle. You must be most anxious."

"Miss Bell doesn't speak Creole," Sam said.

"Oh? A pity. Then I must address myself to you, M'sieu, no? But what exactly can I say to you?"

"Tell us what Dr. Bell did while he was here."

"He asked questions."

"About you? Your work?" Sam glanced meaningfully at the walls to let the man know he understood the import of the many symbols painted on them. There were serpents, bulls, boats, and other designs employed in vèvès drawn at voodoo ceremonies. There were even gaudy lithographs of Roman Catholic saints and one of Christ with a bleeding heart. As a *bocor*, Margal used these icons in ways not intended by those who revered them.

"Dr. Bell asked about my work, yes," the legless one said, and the piercing eyes again impaled Sam.

"We understand he came here with a guide," Sam said. "A man named Ti Pierre Bastien."

"That is so."

"Did he leave with that man?"

"He did."

"Did he say where he was going?"

"We naturally assumed he was returning to Port-au-Prince."

"I see. Do you mind telling me exactly when he left?"

The man on the chair turned again to his plump companion. "Do you remember, Clarisse?"

"It was weeks ago, Margal. Who knows how many?"

"Yes, who knows. We have many callers, M'sieu. It is hard to keep track."

Mildred said, "Sam, ask him if Daddy gave him that picture, will you?"

Sam put the question in Creole.

"No. I have my own camera, M'sieu." The *bocor* pivoted to his woman again. "Bring it, please, Clarisse."

Clumping from the room, Clarisse returned with a Polaroid of fairly recent vintage. "A marvelous instrument!" Margal exclaimed, motioning her to hand it to Sam. "Of course, obtaining film is sometimes a problem, but my people go out to Cap Haïtien now and then." He smiled at them, a picture of innocence. "M'sieu, M'selle, I should like to have photographs of you."

The look on Mildred's face said no, but Sam ignored it. "If we may have one also, *compère*—of the two of us with you, that is."

"But of course. Clarisse, you hear? You are to take three pictures. One of Dr. Bell's daughter, one of M'sieu Norman, and then one of the three of us together. You understand?"

"I understand." With no small effort, the fat woman positioned herself in front of Mildred, clicked the shutter, handed the picture to Margal, and awaited his nod of approval. Repeating the procedure with Sam, she received another nod, then stood on widespread feet at a proper distance from the *bocor's* chair and motioned Sam and Mildred to take their places at Margal's side.

Mildred was reluctant to do so, Sam saw. Perhaps she had heard or read some of those silly tales about photos and pins. Quietly, in English, he said to her, "This could be important, pal. Let's not louse it up." With a glance at the false smile on his face, she obeyed.

They stood one on each side of the man, and Clarisse

took a picture, lumbering forward to hand it to Margal
when the camera produced it. He clapped his hands over
it like a child before passing it to Sam, who grinned and
tucked it into his shirt pocket, then looked at his watch.

"Well, *compère*, it seems we have come a long way for
nothing. Dr. Bell is evidently back in Port-au-Prince."

"It would seem so."

"Thanks for your hospitality, anyway."

"It is nothing. And you will begin your return trip
when? Tomorrow?"

Sam thought of Mildred's mindless walks to the river
in Vallière. Of Alfred Oriol's attempt to send her plunging over the cliff later. "I guess not." He shrugged.
"We're both pretty tired. We'll rest in Bois Sauvage for
a couple of days."

"I wish you a safe and pleasant journey, my friends."

I'll bet you do, Sam thought, but solemnly shook the
man's hand, then the woman's, before motioning
Mildred to precede him to the door. When he turned to
look back and nod farewell, that strange figure on the
chair lifted a hand and smiled at him. Such an innocent
smile, Sam thought; but something in the intensity of the
bocor's gaze sent shivers along his spine and robbed his
mouth of moisture.

Metellus was waiting at the foot of the waterfall as
promised, anxiously glancing up at the sky as he paced
back and forth through the cascade's exhalation of mist.
Sam looked up, too, wondering whether they had taken
more time than they should have. It didn't seem so. The
sun was still high enough to insure their return to Bois
Sauvage before nightfall.

Why the panic, then? Or was it just a normal dread of
this unsavory place?

Shrugging it off, he helped Mildred to mount, then
did so himself and signaled their guide that they were
ready to depart. "But take it easy, Metellus, will you?

Stop once in a while. Don't be so eager to break our necks."

"I will try to go more slowly, M'sieu."

Metellus clucked to his mule and it moved out. Mildred's animal followed. Sam was just about to bring up the rear when he found himself stiff as wood in the saddle, staring wide-eyed at an approaching apparition.

The man had emerged from the gloom of the forest ten yards distant and was truding along the path toward them. Man? Somewhere between thirty and forty years of age—it was impossible to estimate more closely —he wore pants and a shirt of khaki reduced to filthy strings. His feet were wrapped in rotting banana leaves loosely held on with bits of rope-vine. Hair that must have been blond once hung shaggy to his shoulders. His skin was fishbelly white. His mouth hung open as though the muscles had become useless. With unblinking blue eyes as dull as cloudy marbles, he stared straight ahead while plodding past Metellus, then Mildred, finally past Sam, as though walking in his sleep and totally unaware of their presence.

On his right shoulder, this apparition clutched a thick bundle of dead branches chopped to firewood length. From his left hand dangled the machete that must have done the chopping. The reek of him lingered long after he had passed.

Sam turned in the saddle to watch him. Saw him trudge across the compound to the big red house of Margal. Saw him plod through the yard to a smaller building that, with its upthrust chimney pipe, was surely a kitchen.

He disappeared into the kitchen with his load of firewood.

Turning again, Sam saw that Mildred had been watching the creature too. "Milly," he said, "did you see who that *was*?"

She slowly nodded. "The one in the picture. The Nazi. Sam . . . what's *wrong* with him?"

He hesitated. Should he tell her what he thought? No. If he did, she might decide the same thing could have happened to her father.

And what if her father *was* still here in the compound, reduced to the status of servant or slave? What if he had never been allowed to leave?

With an exaggerated shrug Sam said lightly, "It looks as though Hitler's little admirer decided to live here a while and learn a few things from friend Margal . . . and is finding the going a bit rougher than he expected." To forestall any further questions, he flapped a hand at Metellus. "Let's go, *compère,* hey?"

They did not stop until they reached the place where Mildred and Sam had talked before. Since it was still daylight and there was no further need for haste, Metellus agreed to rest.

Mildred and Sam dismounted and sat on an outcrop of black rock, rubbing the aches from their thighs.

"Sam," she said, "it seems I was right, don't you think? I did get a message from Daddy, telling me he wasn't at Legrun."

"It seems so."

"Now we have to look for him at Port-au-Prince."

Which will be about as easy as trying to find the old needle in the hay, Sam thought, but nodded.

"Why were you so determined to have a picture of Margal, Sam? That *was* what you wanted, wasn't it?"

He took the print from his shirt pocket and held it so they could both examine it. "You see what we've got here? Not just you, me, and Margal. Just before she snapped it, I moved a step to the left. See the table beside Margal's chair? The photos on it?"

"Well . . . yes."

"They could be important. Anyway, I wanted a picture of our sorcerer, because unless I've got a faulty memory, Margal isn't his name."

"What?"

"His real name is Fenelon," Sam said grimly, "and I knew him all too well in Jacmel before he lost his legs. He hates my guts with a passion."

30

Kay Gilbert was leaning from a chair and reaching to the floor for her sneakers, when she saw them turn in at the gate. She had just come in from the backyard after bathing. In this house the water for drinking and cooking was carried from the village spring, but that for other uses fell from heaven. Bamboo gutters caught rain from the zinc roof and conducted it into a pair of old oil drums.

It must have been a job to lug those two heavy drums to this remote place, she had thought while standing naked in the yard, washing herself.

The sneakers on, she called to Tina in another room, "Hey, baby, your father's home!" then walked out to greet the arrivals. Only three of them, she noticed. No Dr. Bell. "You didn't find your father?" she asked, holding Mildred's mule while the woman dismounted.

The daughter of Dr. Bell shook her head. Sam and Metellus dismounted, too, and Metellus nodded to Tina, who had followed Kay from the house. Peering at the door, the Haitian said in a tone of annoyance, "Where's your mother? Can't she even come with some water for us?"

Kay looked at him, hesitated, and decided there was no way she could avoid telling him. "Fifine and the chil-

237

dren have gone to her sister's, Metellus."

"What?"

"I'm sorry. She asked me to tell you she won't be coming back while Tina is here."

As he stripped the mules, dropping their gear on the ground, Metellus looked more frustrated and bewildered than angry. He kept glancing at his daughter and shaking his head. "You'd better come with me," he said to her as he led the mules away.

Tina trotted along at his side. Kay, Mildred, and Sam watched in silence until they disappeared behind the house.

"What happened at Legrun?" Kay asked then.

Sam told her some of it. Now was not the time, he decided, to discuss Margal's past.

"Well, at least you know there's nothing wrong," she said. "Dr. Bell must be back in the capital somewhere, no? Or maybe off in some other part of the country, trying to interview other Margal types. I found you a place to sleep."

Looking more than just physically tired, Mildred said, "Thank you. Is it far?"

"Just down the road. Supper will be ready for us when we show up. You two must want a bath first."

"God, yes," Mildred said with a forced laugh.

"It's an open-air bathroom. I'll show you." Touching her on the arm, Kay indicated the pile of gear on the ground. "You'll need a change of clothes, won't you?"

"What? Oh, yes . . ." Wearily, Mildred sank to her knees to fumble in a saddlebag.

Kay watched her with compassion. They had a nearly exhausted woman on their hands, she decided. One who needed not only a bath, but food and rest. Lots of rest. You had to admire her, though, for attempting a journey like this on her first visit to the Caribbean's most primitive country.

Finding what she wanted, Mildred struggled to her feet. Kay led her around to the water drums. Returning, she found Sam in the house, sprawled on a chair in the front room.

"So you found us a hotel," he said.

"It wasn't easy, Buster."

"I'll bet. How long did it take you? The whole time we were gone?"

She nodded. "The house is small and nearby. I didn't think to ask there at first, then someone suggested I try it because the woman lives alone." Moving to a chair from which she could really look at him, she seated herself. *Sam Norman, louse,* she thought. *Sam Norman, drunken lout. Sam Norman . . . question mark.* It *had* taken her a long time to find a house where he and his Mildred could spend the night. And an even longer time to locate someone willing to sell a pair of chickens. This remote village was not geared to accommodate strangers.

Of course, if she had known that Fifine and the children would be leaving, Sam and Mildred could probably have stayed right here. But it was too late now, and, besides, Fifine might return.

"You know," she said after a silence, "it's a little fantastic, our meeting again like this."

Sam thought about it and moved his head negatively. "Not really. You're here with the youngster because of Margal. He's almost certainly responsible for what happened to her. I'm here because Mildred's old man heard about him and came here to see him."

"Well . . ."

"The only real coincidence is that we arrived at the same time." Rising, he went to the open front door and looked out. "Now, where did Metellus get to? I want to ask him something."

"He's probably gone after his family."

Sam turned to frown at her. "They're convinced, are they? That the girl's a zombie?"

"Fifine is convinced. Without her, I don't think the children would be too big a problem. But it doesn't matter. The village won't accept Tina anyway."

Sam continued to frown. "Tell me something. Did strange things happen to you on your way here?"

"I'm not sure."

"What do you mean, you're not sure?"

"Well, certain things *seemed* to happen. I can't make up my mind if they were real or not. Why?"

Sam took the photograph from his pocket. "This is Margal. Do you know him?"

She studied it. Shook her head. "No, I don't think so. Should I?"

"You saw him once. The night I barged into your room in Jacmel. It's Fenelon."

"What?" She peered at the picture more closely.

"You wouldn't know, I guess. You only saw him at night under a street lamp. But I'm positive. My old friend, Fenelon. Maybe his real name *is* Margal. Maybe he came from here in the first place, and only returned here because he lost his legs. The important thing, it seems to me—"

"The important thing, Sam," she interrupted in a whisper, gazing fearfully at his face, "is that he hates you. Oh, my God, you've got to get out of here! Does he know you recognized him?"

"I'm not sure. I think so."

"It doesn't matter. *He* must have recognized *you*."

"Hell, I told him my name before I realized who he was."

"Oh, Sam—" She fell silent as Mildred, now wearing clean pants and shirt, stepped through the doorway with a wad of dripping clothes in her hands. Dr. Bell's daughter looked a lot better, Kay decided. Refreshed. Even relaxed. "You did your laundry, huh?"

"There was a wash pan out there and some soap, so I helped myself. But I can't find a clothesline."

"You don't hang; you drape. Here, let me." Rising, Kay took the wet clothes and stepped out the door, heading across the front yard toward the fence.

With a nod to Mildred, Sam pushed himself up and went to wash off the day's grime.

The house down the road was smaller than Tina's home, with a sitting room scarcely large enough to accommodate the three of them for supper. Before serving the meal, its owner, a tiny, solemn-faced woman named Resia, showed Sam and Mildred the bedrooms they would use. Each was barely big enough to hold its cot-size wooden bed. She herself would use the front room, she said.

"She'll sleep on the floor?" Mildred asked, ill at ease.

Sam relayed the query in Creole.

"My child, until I was your age I never slept anywhere else but on a floor."

Her man was dead, Resia explained. Had chopped his foot with a machete and let it become infected. He was a good man. They had seven children, all of them grown up and gone away now. Again, Sam translated.

Where, Mildred wondered, had seven children slept in a house this size?

Resia's cooking leaned heavily on hot peppers, but that did not reduce their appetites; it merely slowed their attack a little. And while the birds were lean and tough, even Mildred agreed they were tastier than the pampered ones sold in Stateside supermarkets.

The ache in his belly somewhat attended to, Sam slowed his rate of intake even more and gazed at Kay, seated opposite him. "You were going to tell me of certain things that happened on your way here. Let's get

back to that, shall we?" Answering the question on
Mildred's face, he added, "It's a thing we were working
on while you took your bath."

"Oh."

"I didn't say things *happened*," Kay reminded him. "I
said they *seemed* to happen."

"Okay. What seemed to happen?"

She told of the flash flood at the fording and how she
had fallen from her mule. "The more I think about it,
the more I feel it may have been all in my mind. Not the
fall, of course. That was real. But I may have got scared
and frightened the mule into throwing me."

Sam looked at Mildred, who made no comment.

"That night, my mind played tricks again," Kay continued, and told about the lizard. "I might blame my
imagination for that, too, but Tina said she saw the
same thing and was just as scared as I was. Then, the
next day, at that shuddery place called Devil's Leap . . ."

She told of the midday darkness and the fire that was
not a fire. Of how her guide, Joseph, had refused to go
on afterward. "So on that occasion all *three* of us
thought we saw the same thing, and I just don't know
what to believe."

"Margal," Mildred said quietly.

"You think so?"

"I do."

"Putting thoughts into our heads?"

"If conditions are right. And we're the kind of people
he can do it to." Mildred told how she had slipped away
from Sam at the Vallière post office and been compelled
to go to the river. How she had tried again to go there
in the middle of the night. "I know *I'm* susceptible to
mental suggestion," she said, "because for years I've
been able to talk to my father by mental telepathy.
Nothing happened to Sam on this mission to Margal,
you'll notice. Only to me."

"And to Oriol," Sam reminded her.

"Yes. Our guide. He was told to kill me."

Startled, Kay said, "He what?"

Mildred told of the guide's attempt to frighten her mule into plunging off the cliff trail. "Like me," she said to Kay, "you must be one of those Margal can influence. I'm not surprised he could sway Tina and our two guides. He knows them."

"He knows Sam, too," Kay pointed out.

"But evidently wasn't told Sam was coming."

They had finished eating while they were talking, and now the woman of the house came to take away their plates. They waited in silence until she departed. Then Mildred said, "Now can we get to the *why* of it? Assuming we're right, and really into some kind of witchcraft here—for what reason is Margal doing these things?"

Kay said, "I think we can guess why he tried to stop me from bringing Tina here."

"Why?"

"Because that grave with the child's name on it is no fake. She died and was buried there. Except, of course, she wasn't dead—she'd been poisoned and only seemed to die—and Margal stole her from the grave and revived her." Gazing at Mildred, she added with a shrug, "You're new to Haiti, so I don't suppose you believe that."

"You mean Tina is what they call a zombie?"

Resia, appearing suddenly with coffee, must have caught the words "Tina" and "zombie." In Creole she muttered, *"Tina sé youn zombie, oui!"* Then she continued to mutter while transferring three small cups of steaming black coffee and a bowl of brown sugar from a rusty tray to the table, and was still talking to herself when she hurried away. Not once had she looked at any of them.

Kay frowned at Sam. "Did you hear what she said?"

"That it was the twins Margal really wanted. What was that about?"

"The mango that poisoned Tina was one of two, given her by someone in the village. One was supposed to be for her, the other for her twin brothers."

"And she mixed them up?"

"Resia thinks so, obviously. Metellus does too."

"Twins," Sam said. "*Marassas*. She could be right, you know. They're special. But when Tina ate the mango, he took her anyway. Probably sold her to someone for a servant girl."

"And because she hadn't suffered brain damage, as most of them do, she recovered enough to run away. Then the priest found her."

"And when Margal got the word that you were bringing her back here, he did his damnedest to stop you. If someone from this district had been bringing her, he probably wouldn't have bothered, but a nurse from the Schweitzer—"

"Might ask questions. Might find out what happened and report him."

"Correct. And send him to prison." All at once they had a dialogue going, Sam realized. In the past, they had done it often, sometimes batting ideas back and forth for miles as they jeeped over Haiti's fantastic roads. He would gladly have kept it up, but now there were three of them.

Mildred, her cup at her lips, said, "Why did he try to stop *us* from getting here, Sam?"

"I can't think of a reason."

She lowered the cup to the table, spilling a little as her hand trembled. "Has something happened to my father? Something Margal doesn't want us to find out about?"

Sam thought of the man with the firewood, and lifted from his shirt pocket the photograph taken in the *bocor's* multicolored living room. He called the woman of the house. When she appeared, he beckoned to her and showed her the picture, pointing to the photo of Dr. Bell on Margal's chairside table.

"Resia, do you know this man?"

She stepped back, her glance darting in horror from him to Mildred. "You two should never have had your picture taken with Margal! Are you mad?"

"Never mind that. Do you—"

"Don't you know the things he might do with a picture like this?"

"Please, Resia, do you *know* this man?"

She made herself calm down. "All I know is that he came through here some weeks ago with a guide, on his way to Margal's."

"Have you seen him since?"

"No."

"You don't know if he came *back* from there?"

"I saw him only the once."

"All right. Thank you." Sam put the photo away and looked at Mildred, whose face was white. "Now, don't jump to conclusions," he said gently. "He could have come through here early in the morning before most people were up and around. Probably did, in fact. I'll question Metellus. I was going to, anyway."

Tonelessly, Mildred said, "Something has happened to him. Why else would Margal have tried to keep us from coming here?"

"You said your father told you he was in the capital."

She only stared at him.

"Look," Sam said then, "we've got a long, hard day ahead of us tomorrow. Why don't you just relax now? I'm going to walk Kay home."

She nodded.

It was dark now. Had been for a long while. Side by side, he and Kay walked up the all but blacked-out road through the gentle tree-toad whistles and insect hummings. A scent of jasmine, almost too sweet, floated on the night air.

"Well, hey," Sam said softly.

Kay turned her head. Her dark eyes searched his face. "Hey what?"

"Here we are again."

"Here we are where?"

"Alone together. You still at war with me, pal?"

"Why didn't you write?"

"How could I, after our last night at Victor's?"

"You could have. A piece of paper. An envelope. A stamp. Just a 'Dear Kay, let's scratch that one off, shall we?' would at least have helped. It wouldn't have killed you to try."

Sam trudged on. To stop could be fatal. So long as they were climbing the path together, with the uneven ground tricking them into touching now and then, there was progress. If he stopped, he'd be back at square one.

"Kay . . . how could I write? My God, I don't even know what I *did* that night. Even what I *said* to you."

"You said plenty. Believe me."

"I was drunk."

"Not then, you weren't. But you were leaving the country, you expected me for the weekend, I didn't show up, and you felt cheated. You still could have written to say you were sorry.

"I *am* sorry."

"Now you tell me."

He stopped in spite of himself. Turned to face her. Reached for her. "Kay, believe me . . ."

She stepped back, shaking her head. "Sam, I need time."

"Of course you do. But—"

"No. I need time to get used to the idea that you're here at all. You knew you might run into me. You had a chance to examine your feelings and brace yourself. I didn't. Until a few hours ago, I thought you were in the States, out of my life forever. I didn't even know *where* in the States. All I knew was that in two years I hadn't heard from you. Not even a card at Christmas. After all we did together . . . not a line, Sam. Not a single word." She backed away again as he tried to close the gap between them. She shook her head. "No, Sam. I'm not ready for this. I'm not sure I can ever be ready again."

Sam stopped himself, not knowing what to do. This was a new Kay, one he didn't know and was in no way prepared for. He knew the one with the temper, the adventurous one, the clowning one. He knew the one who would give a peasant woman a new pair of sneakers in exchange for a worn-out sandal which she also returned to the woman. He couldn't cope with this new maturity. "All right," he said at last, "I'll wait. I'll wait a long time if I have to. You'll see."

They walked the rest of the way in silence, still touching occasionally when the dark and lumpy path nudged them together as if trying to tell them something. On reaching the fence where the crowd had gathered when Kay first arrived, they found Metellus leaning on it, a lonely figure gazing vacant-eyed up the empty road to the village.

"Did you find Fifine and the children?" Kay asked him.

"They would not come back. Tina alone is here."

"I'm sorry." She touched his hand and went past him to the house.

Sam said, "Come inside a minute, will you, Metellus? I want to ask you something."

The Haitian followed him in.

Sam produced the photo and asked the same question he had put to the woman in the house below. Holding it under a lamp, Metellus peered at the face of Dr. Bell.

"Yes, I saw this man. Ti Pierre Bastien, who used to

live in this district, brought him. They were going to Legrun."

"Did you see him come back out?"

"They both came out—let me see—five days ago."

"Only *five days ago?* You're sure?"

"My eyes saw them, M'sieu."

"Why didn't you tell us this before taking us to Legrun this afternoon?"

"You didn't say you were looking for someone. Only that you wished to visit Margal."

Sam studied him. Was that all they had said? There had been talk about Dr. Bell, he was sure, but perhaps it had been in English. "Well, all right. Just one thing more, Metellus. About Margal. I used to know that man in Jacmel, when I worked there. I always thought he belonged there. When he came here two years ago, was he a stranger to you people?"

"Far from it, M'sieu. He was born here in Bois Sauvage."

"Thanks. That helps to explain his presence here. Did you ever hear the name Fenelon?"

"Fenelon? No."

"He was always Margal?"

"Always Margal. Born here, as I say. And when he lost his legs and feared he might lose his life, he came back here and built that house of colors in Legrun. The sorcerer's house, we call it. Everyone here would be happier had the politicians taken his life instead of only his legs."

Sam nodded and turned to say good-night to Kay.

As she stood there returning his gaze, the lamplight did something to her face, transforming it into the softer, mistier face he had seen so often on the pillow beside his own. This, not the other, was the face his mind had conjured and tormented him with for the past two years when, despite himself, he had thought about her. Keeping his hands at his sides took a lot of self control.

"Think about it, pal, will you?" he said.

She moved her head slowly up and down.

"Tomorrow, then, early," Sam said, and departed.

31

At last,
thank God,
he and Mildred are communicating.
After hours of struggle
he is getting through to her.

But Margal is reaching him, too.

With all his will
Dr. Bell resists the voice in his head,
clenching his hands,
tensing his body,
trying to pray.
But in the end, the voice triumphs
as it always has,
and his own,
now filled with guile,
projects a different message.

"Milly, no . . .
I am not in Port-au-Prince.
Don't look for me in Port-au-Prince.
If you just heard someone telling you
to do that,

ignore it.
Hear me, Milly.
I am at home in Vermont.
I became ill in Haiti
and had to fly back here.
So come to Vermont, child . . .
Don't waste any time
looking for me in Port-au-Prince.
Come straight home!"

Is that his daughter projecting a reply
the way she did
when she found him in the boathouse
that day?
The way she did
the day her mother died?
Yes,
but she is confused now.
All she seems able to say is,
"Daddy I don't understand.
Where *are* you, Daddy?"

And that other voice
from the evil red house in Legrun
keeps interrupting,
saying fiercely,
"I am not a patient man, Dr. Bell!
You test me at your own risk!"

32

Sam awoke in the night and heard Mildred talking.

His room was dark. Lifting himself on his elbows, he peered into the darkness and saw it was also empty. She was not there with him. Her voice was coming through the thin wall of wattle and clay that separated her bedchamber from his.

"But I don't understand. Please, Daddy . . . I don't understand."

He had placed a flashlight on the floor beside his bed on retiring. Now he groped for it and switched it on. He had slept in shorts and undershirt. Pulling on his sneaks, he stepped to the wall and pressed an ear against it.

Just outside the room's single window an owl softly screeched. A bad omen, the peasants would have said.

"Daddy, I'm wholly confused," Mildred was saying. "Where *are* you? One minute you say you're in Port-au-Prince and I must find you; the next minute you're back in Vermont and I should go home. If you're at home, when did you leave Haiti? Why?" A pause. "Now *you* sound confused, Daddy. Please . . . what's happening to us?"

Sam turned to the door. Opened it silently and stepped into the room where they had eaten supper. The table had been moved to one side, and the lady of the house slept on a mat in the space it had occupied. He

253

had to step over her to reach Mildred's door.

At the door, he paused, listening again.

"Daddy, I don't know what to believe," Mildred was saying. "None of this makes sense. You can't be at home waiting for me and in Port-au-Prince wanting me to find you at the same time." There were tears in her voice. Tears of frustration, Sam sensed.

He opened the door.

Odd. He had expected to find her out of bed, probably standing beside it in a kind of trance-state as she conversed with her father. His flashlight revealed her lying in bed on her back, half covered with a blanket, her eyes wide and her gaze directed at the thatch overhead. He wondered what she saw or thought she saw. Could she sometimes actually see her father when they established contact like this, or did she only hear him?

"Well, I don't know what I'm supposed to do." A note of annoyance sharpened her voice now. "To leave the country, I have to return to Port-au-Prince anyway, so I suppose I'll look for you there. But where am I to look? Where? I can't make you out, Daddy. *Vergeau?* Is that what you're saying: *Vergeau?* Or are you trying to say Vermont again?"

Silence. Then, suddenly, she voiced a cry of alarm or pain and sat bolt upright in bed, the blanket falling from her to show Sam she had gone to bed in her clothes. She was staring at his flashlight, apparently terrified. He spoke her name as he approached her.

As he sank onto the edge of the bed and reached for her to quiet her, she grabbed at him, pressed her face against his chest, and began sobbing.

He let her sob it out. The kind of long-range conversation he had just listened to must play hell with one's nervous system, he thought. When she seemed to be herself again, he said quietly, "Want to tell me about it, in case I can help?"

"I . . . was talking to my father."

"So I gathered."

"But he had two voices." The flashlight, lying on the bed now, lit the confusion on her face as she let him go and leaned away from him. "He was two *persons*, Sam, each telling me something different. Where is Vergeau?"

He shook his head. "I don't know any Vergeau in Port. Could he have said Turgeau? That's one of the residential neighborhoods."

"Perhaps that's what he said. He wasn't coming through well. He sounded as if he were struggling, like a man tied up and desperately trying to free himself. All through the conversation he was like that. Just when I'd think I was really talking with him, this other side of him would take over and I'd get the feeling he was . . . well, being *told* what to say to me."

Sam said, "And when he was told what to say, where was he?"

"He said he was in Vermont then, and I should come straight home."

"But the voice you think was really your father said he was in Vergeau?"

"I think so, Sam. Oh, God, I'm just confused."

Sam looked at his watch. The time was four-fifteen. "It'll be daylight soon. Do you want me to stay here with you till then?"

Later, he wondered what she would have said had there been no sound from the sleeper in the adjoining room. There was a fair-sized commotion, however, as the woman awoke and got up, clearing her throat in the process. Apparently, her day began now—at least, when she had to prepare breakfast for guests making an early departure.

Sam patted Mildred's arm. "Just try to unwind for a little while. We'll soon be on our way."

33

They left Bois Sauvage at daybreak, the village emerging from the morning mist as they rode through. Sam led, with Tina perched proudly in front of him and constantly turning her head to smile up at him. Mildred was next, deeply worried about her father. Where was he: Port-au-Prince or Vermont? Kay, on her gray mule, brought up the rear, gravely pondering the relationship —was there one?—between the man and woman ahead.

Birds filled the eerie grayness with twitterings. Squatting women waved from charcoal breakfast fires, and naked children stared big-eyed from doorways that were still dark. A sleepy cock wandered under the gray mule's forefeet and, indignant, flew squawking into a cactus bush that injured his dignity still more.

What a country, Sam thought. I never should have left.

With Bois Sauvage behind, they rode on in silence, except for Sam's quiet exchange of chatter with the child leaning back against him. No problems, no decisions to make, until, long later, they approached the place called Saut Diable. In sight of that fearsome stretch along the cliff face, Sam reined in his mount and slid from the saddle, reaching up to swing Tina down beside him.

"If Margal is going to try stopping us, this is where

he'll do it, don't you think?"

"What can we do?" Kay asked.

He pulled a coil of sisal rope from his saddlebag. "I bought this from Tina's father with some vague notion of letting that gray mule of yours lead us through here."

"Letting a *mule* lead us?" Mildred said.

"Well, it's our *minds* Margal has been using to create his illusions, Milly. I doubt he can use a mule's mind. And this big gray is steady and reliable."

Mildred looked doubtful but Sam quietly proceeded to tie the rope to the gray mule's reins while she and Kay dismounted. He then ran the rope along the animal's back and said, "I'll give him his head and walk close behind him. He's not a kicker. Tina, you'd better be next."

Tina reached for his free hand. Kay and Mildred fell in behind.

"What if the other animals don't follow?" Kay asked.

"Let's hope they do."

Sam clucked the big gray into motion, and it stepped out with no hint of nervousness. Gripping the rope, he followed. The others, holding hands, moved onto the ledge after him.

Almost at once, the magic began.

It was a little different this time. Margal's supply of illusions was unlimited, it seemed. There was no darkness. No towers of flame leaped up from the valley floor, nor was there the reek of smoke, to make them think they were treading a ledge above some weird hell. This time, the sheer wall of rock on his left slowly dissolved into a field of green grass. The stone path under his feet and the yawning depths to his right became part of it. With no rope to cling to and no gray mule to lead him, he never could have followed the trail's many convolutions. Sooner or later, he would have blundered off its outer edge and gone hurtling into the valley, or crashed into the rock wall on the other side. If the latter, he perhaps could have clung to the wall and worked his way along it to safety like a man walking a narrow ledge on a skyscraper, high above a city street, but he doubted he had any such composure. In any case, what about the others?

Briefly, he looked back. They were close behind him, in single file and holding hands, but, like him, they appeared to be walking through a limitless field of grass. Strange. In the short time he dared to keep his head turned, the two trailing mules came into view as though rounding a turn on the cliff trail, yet there was neither cliff nor trail. They simply materialized bit by bit until they were wholly in view. But, thank God, they did not seem to be confused.

Nor did the big gray. *He* certainly saw no puzzling field of grass, only that stone ledge along the face of the cliff. He clop-clopped on with consummate calm and Sam walked on behind him, looking straight ahead now, hanging onto the rope and finding enormous comfort in the warmth and smell of the animal's broad rump. Faintly, he could hear the thumping of the other two mules behind him.

"Kay?" he called.

"Yes, Sam?"

"Are you getting the picture I'm getting? A field of grass—sort of a meadow—extending for miles?"

"Yes, and no trail to follow through it. Just a feeling I could safely stroll off in any direction."

"You, too, Milly?"

"The same, and I'm scared."

"Just keep close to me. This mule isn't seeing any meadow. He knows what he's doing. Tina, baby"—Sam squeezed the small hand he was holding behind him—"are you all right?"

"Oh, yes, I'm fine."

Suddenly, Kay's voice, almost a scream, ripped through the stillness. "Mildred, for God's sake, what are you doing? Let me go!"

Sam froze, yanking on the rope to stop the big gray. Lurching around, he looked back. "My God," he breathed.

There was the trail again. The old familiar sliver of track snaked along the face of the cliff, flanked on its outer edge by that sheer drop into the valley. On it, the two women faced each other in combat. With her feet braced only a few inches from the edge of space, her breast and shoulders heaving wildly, Mildred had hold of Kay's hands and was doing her utmost to drag Kay to her. But they were nearly the same size, same weight, and Kay was resisting with all her might.

"Milly, stop it!" Sam thundered.

She heard him and flashed him a look of fury, her contorted face that of a creature only part human. Spitting like a maddened cat, she doubled her efforts.

It was more than Kay could handle. Inch by inch, she was pulled toward the brink despite a desperate struggle to grip the stone with her sneakers.

Sam let go the rope and went stumbling past Tina toward the combatants, yelling at the child as he went, "Don't move, Tina! Don't move a step!" Kay, thank God, had released the child's hand when Mildred turned on her. Otherwise, Tina might have been dragged into the struggle.

Suddenly, Kay's feet found a projection in the ledge of stone and she put everything she had into one fierce effort. *Her* breast heaved. *Her* shoulders strained backward, cording her arms. Caught by surprise and jerked off balance, Mildred lost the initiative. Kay hauled her within reach and swiftly freed one hand for a chopping stroke to the side of the neck.

With a wail of pain Mildred went to her knees, but

furiously struggled to stagger up again. Kay bent an arm
and smashed it against her upturned face, halting the
effort. Just as Sam reached them, Kay followed that
with a downward lunge that pinned the other to the
trail, flat on her back with her feet beating a feeble tat-
too on the stone.

Sam, not needed, nevertheless went to his knees
beside them and peered into Mildred's upturned face.
Slowly, it emptied itself of madness and became only a
chalk-white, stupid mask with vacant eyes. The eyes
sought his and seemed to beg for understanding.

Before he spoke, he looked at Kay. Her expression
had changed, too. Where there had been bewilderment,
then desperation approaching terror, there was now
only the slackness of relief. Her hands had been at
Mildred's neck, holding Mildred down. She let go now
and leaned back.

Satisfied that she was unhurt, Sam returned his attention to the woman on her back. "What the hell were you
trying to do, Milly?" he demanded.

Her eyes needed time to focus. Dully, she shifted her
gaze from his face to Kay's. "*He* told me to kill you,"
she whispered. "Oh, my God, Kay, I'm sorry."

No one spoke for a moment. Then Sam, still on his
knees and still staring, said in a low voice, "He could see
his thing with the meadow wasn't working. He had to
try something else."

"I'm sorry," Mildred said. "Believe me, Kay, I'm
sorry." Weakly, she reached for Kay's hand and clung
to it.

After a while Kay said, "It's all right. We all know
what he's capable of."

"But I almost did kill you!"

"Are you all right now?" Sam asked, peering closely
at Mildred's face again.

"I think so. He doesn't . . . he isn't talking to me now.

It was just for a minute or two. We were walking through that strange meadow . . . all that grass where I knew there couldn't be grass. I pictured him working on our minds . . . that awful face of his with its terrible eyes and hideous mop of hair . . . and suddenly he had control of me. Then . . . oh God, he screamed at me to kill her."

Weakly sitting up, Mildred now gazed at both of them with eyes that seemed to focus better. "I suppose . . . I suppose I opened a door for him by thinking of him that way. Kay, I'm so sorry."

"It's all right, Mildred." Kay stood up and turned away. Suddenly stiffened. "Sam! My mule!"

The big gray had gone on without them. It was nearly at the end of the cliff track. As it went plodding around the sharp turn there, little Tina stood motionless on the trail where he had left her, gazing after it.

"No problem," he said, "unless the track becomes a meadow again. Let's get out of here before it does."

Reaching Tina, he clasped the child's hand and led the way along the cliff face, with Kay and Mildred following closely. The other two mules clopped along behind as though nothing had happened. The strange sea of grass did not return. Beyond the Devil's Leap, at the top of the long, steep trench, they found the big gray waiting quietly for them.

There were other bad moments on the way out to the coast, but none as potentially fatal as the one at Saut Diable. Fully aware of the danger now, they were on guard every moment. Especially Mildred, who freely acknowledged her special susceptibility and even seemed eager to discuss it.

"All those experiments with Daddy," she said during a rest stop, "I never thought they were doing things to me, making me vulnerable to people like Margal, but they were, weren't they? I wonder if Daddy was easy for him too."

They were still short of their destination when darkness forced them to stop. Alongside the trail, a small stream gurgled cheerfully through massive boulders, and Sam built a fire at its edge. Supper consisted of cassava cakes from Bois Sauvage and sardines provided by Paul Lafontant in Trou. After bathing, they retired to a mossy ledge and talked while waiting for sleep to come.

At first, the talk was of Mildred's father—where he might be and what the sorcerer of Legrun might have done to him during his stay there. He was in Port-au-Prince, Mildred insisted. Doing what? "I can't imagine, but I feel certain the voice telling me he had left Haiti was not *his* voice. I'm beginning to think Margal may have some awful power over him."

"It won't be easy to find him in the capital," Kay warned. "That's no small city."

"We'll start in Turgeau and hope for luck," Sam said.

Tina fell asleep then, snuggled against Kay for warmth and comfort, and the talk changed to a discussion of her chances for a decent future. She would be better off in the capital than in primitive Bois Sauvage, Sam insisted. "If, that is, this uncle sends her to school and doesn't make an unpaid servant of her." Mildred disagreed, sleepily insisting the child needed her mother.

"Not that mother," Kay countered with a flash of anger.

Then the weariness of the day took over, the talk died, and the only sound in the forest silence was the quiet chatter of the stream.

A little after eleven the following day, they reached the coast at Trou and returned the rented mules to Alcibiade. Sam paid for the animal that had been lost at Saut Diable. The shopkeeper, Paul Lafontant, reported that Alfred Oriol had not returned.

"More than likely, he fears you will tell the police about his attempt to kill you. We may never see him again."

At the police post, Dr. Bell's jeep was still in the yard. "He obviously didn't come out of the mountains here," Sam said to the corporal, "so where *did* he come out? We know he left Legrun."

"There are other roads he could have traveled. He could have gone all the way to Port-au-Prince by mule, had he wished, M'sieu. For me, the more important question is why he wished to go to Legrun in the first place. No sensible man would visit that place."

"He's not the only one to go there. We saw another white man in there—a German-looking fellow. Do you know who *he* is?"

"Did he speak our Creole with an odd accent?"

"We didn't talk to him."

"Too bad. But it must be the same man. About thirty? Blond hair?"

Sam nodded.

"He came here about six months ago, by camion from the capital, asking where he might find the *bocor* Margal. We told him, and he went into the mountains on foot. A strange fellow. We ask for people's names, as you know, and he showed us papers that said his name was Hans Hauser, but we think now the papers were counterfeit. He sought Margal, who is a black man, yet I think he was unhappy talking to blacks, even to us when he asked directions. He felt himself superior."

Sam nodded.

"When is friend Hauser, or whatever his name is, likely to return from that place?" the corporal said. "Can you tell me?"

"Don't hold you breath."

"It is like that?"

"It seems to be. Maybe you should investigate."

"Maybe." The corporal's shrug conveyed total indifference. "But we are short-handed here, as you have seen. I seem to remember we wrote to the immigration people, telling them of our suspicions concerning the man's papers, and they haven't replied yet. Of course, if they ask us to go to Legrun and bring him out, we will do so. Or try to."

Leaving the police post, Sam had a chance for the first time in hours to talk to Kay alone. Mildred had lingered to sign some papers concerning her father's jeep, and to use the bathroom. "When am I going to see you again?" he asked, reaching for Kay's hand as he walked with her across the station yard. She and Tina would be returning to the hospital now in her jeep while Mildred and he drove on to the capital.

She turned her head to study his face. "Do you want to see me again, Sam?"

"You know I do."

"It's been a long time. You didn't write. You didn't phone . . ."

"Pal, we've been over that before. How *could* I, after what happened?"

She was silent for a moment, then nodded. "All right. There *were* better times than our last one. What are your plans now?"

"I agree with Mildred that her father must be in the capital. We'll be trying to find him."

"And I'll be taking Tina there to her uncle. It will mean an overnight for me, at least."

"The Calman?"

"Will you be there?"

He nodded.

"Then I'll go there, too. Let's leave it at that for now, Sam."

He took the keys from her hand and started the jeep

for her, to be sure it felt and sounded right. Then he lifted Tina in, pressing his face to the child's while she had her arms around his neck. After watching Kay slide in behind the wheel, he leaned forward to try a kiss he was not sure would be welcomed.

Surprisingly, it was. But then, as if angry with herself, she ground the vehicle into gear and drove off so fast that he barely had time to step back out of the way.

34

The book-lined study of the house in Turgeau.
Dr. Bell sits facing his host,
gazing at the man
the way Margal taught him to.
"Why?"

"But I have told you why, Dr. Molicoeur.
Is it so very hard for you to understand
that Margal wishes revenge
for the loss of his legs?"

"But why are *you* so involved?"

"Because I went to Legrun
to talk to him.
And because a young neo-Nazi
all the way from Schleswig-Holstein
had arrived there before me,
begging to be taught the powers
that might make him another Hitler.
But he offended Margal with his arrogance
and mysteriously became something else."

"Leaving Margal with an idea, I presume."

*   *   *

"Leaving Margal with something
that became an idea,
then a vast ambition
when I turned up in the Nazi's footsteps.
'You wish to learn from me, Dr. Bell?' he asked.
'Whatever you can teach me,' I replied.
But the pupil became the servant,
though without quite dying first as the Nazi did.
Now I serve Margal
but am your master, my friend."

"Dr. Bell, I do not wish to murder my president!"

"But you will."

In the privacy of the study.
The door is locked.
Dr. Bell lifts from his pocket a small glass bottle full of
colorless liquid.
"Margal called this 'the three deadly drops.'
You talk with the president frequently."

"I do."

"Then in due course I will give you this
and you will know what to do with it.
But first you must make preparations.
You will form a government
with yourself at its head.
You can do this.
You have important friends."

"Why must I form a government?"

"Because Margal wishes you, Dr. Molicoeur,

to succeed the man you will kill.
At the proper time,
he will go on to the larger powers
envisioned by the Nazi."

"And if I refuse?"

Dr. Bell's gaze fastens on the other's eyes.
His own eyes acquire a luminosity
strangely intense.
"I am at this moment commanding you
to do something, Dr. Molicoeur.
What is it, please?"

"You are commanding me to kneel before you."

"Why are you not kneeling, then?"

The Haitian scholor hesitates but a moment,
then slides forward on his chair
and sinks to his knees,
his head bowed,
his eyes closed.

"When will you begin
the task assigned you, Dr. Molicoeur?"

"As soon as I can."

"Be warned.
Margal is not a patient man."

The eyes slowly open.
The Haitian whispers, "Dr. Bell?
This monster you call Margal is a peasant
and we are men of learning.

Is there not some way we can fight him together?"

Dr. Bell returns the other's pleading gaze
and his hands clench.
"I wish to God there were."
A convulsion grips his body.
Agony leaps into his face.
Hoarsely, he cries out,
"No, no!
I am not defying you!
I will do as you say!
Margal, do not torment me."

35

"He was here," Victor Vieux said, "but he is not here now."

Sam stood with Mildred at the Calman's little bar, sipping a rum and soda which the proprietor had just handed him. "And you don't know where he is?"

In his familiar white shirt and black bow tie, Victor Vieux resembled a penguin as he solemnly wagged his head. "He came here first about noon—let's see—three days ago."

The day Milly and I reached Vallière and she first talked to him.

"Marie thought she saw him and told me," Victor said, "and when he returned in the evening he admitted he'd been here. He had just returned from Legrun, he told me, and stopped by to change his clothes and have a bath before calling on a friend. 'Now I am here to pack a suitcase and leave again,' he said, 'because the friend has invited me to be his house guest for a few days.' "

"He didn't tell you his friend's name?"

"No, Sam."

"Suppose we go upstairs and have a look in his room," Mildred suggested. "He may have left a note for us. You did tell him we're here in Haiti, didn't you, Victor?"

"Of course."

Sam finished his drink and, putting the glass on the bar, turned to look at her. She was tired after their long journey from Trou. The road had been rough, the day hot, and the hour was now nearly midnight. Neither of them had yet been upstairs for a bath or a change. Woodenly extracting themselves from the jeep in the driveway and walking into the pension on legs that ached from every pothole, they had found Victor at the bar, waiting for guests to return from a folkdance performance so he could lock the doors.

Victor handed Sam a key now. "This will open his door. Return it in the morning, eh?"

Sam led Mildred to the stairs.

They climbed in silence, Sam remembering the many times he had ascended these same stairs, at about this hour, with the girl who now, if all had gone well for her, should be asleep in her room at the Schweitzer. Opening the door of Dr. Bell's room at the end of the upstairs hall, he stepped in and switched on a light.

Following him in, Mildred looked around and said, "He must have been in a hurry."

Sam frowned at the bed. It was strewn with clean things her father had apparently removed from bureau drawers, then decided not to take with him after all. Tossed on a chair were soiled, sweat-darkened khaki clothes which he must have worn on his return journey from Legrun.

Sam walked over to the bureau, looking for the note Mildred had hoped they might find. As he stood there with his back to her, he heard her take in a quick breath, then became aware of another sound in the room's stillness.

It was one he had heard before in this room: the faint but rhythmic beat of a voodoo drum. Turning, he peered at the drum beside the bureau. Was it moving? Could he be certain its goatskin head was actually vibrating? As he tried to make up his mind, still another sound demanded his attention. This one was a quick, soft tapping on the bureau top.

His gaze went to the two earthenware jars there. Were *they* doing what they seemed to be? Swaying? Quivering? He recalled what Victor had said on leading him into this room days ago: Victor seated on the bed, watching him while the drum seemed to whisper and the *govis* appeared to dance.

"Put your ear to them."

He leaned forward now and did so again, first to the black and white jar, then to the rose, red, and green one. Both were softly singing. He could not be mistaken.

Behind him, Mildred suddenly cried out, "No! I can't!"

He spun around to face her.

She was ghastly white as she walked backward, staring into space and sobbing, "No, no, I can't . . . I won't . . ." Violently trembling, she sank onto the edge of the bed.

Sam strode to her and took her hands. "Easy, now. Take it easy, Milly. What's going on?"

"It's this room. Oh, God, Sam, get me out of here!"

He lifted her by the elbows and put an arm around her, but she could not stop shaking. "No, no!" she kept whimpering. "I won't!" He led her to the door and over the threshold into the hall. All the way along the hall to her room she kept moaning, "I won't . . . I can't . . ."

The master key opened her door and he walked her to the bed. Helped her to lie down. Then closed the door and lay beside her and talked to her in whispers until her trembling finally subsided.

"Who was it?" he said then. "Margal?"

She nodded.

"Telling you to do what?" At Saut Diable, Margal

had told her to kill Kay, no? What was it this time?
Something about her father?

"I don't know, Sam."

Lying. She had to be, or why had she kept saying she
wouldn't do it? But this was no time to question her.
"Go to sleep," he told her gently. "I'll be right here with
you. We can talk about it later."

Go to sleep, she thought. He doesn't know. Oh, my
God, if he knew! But the warmth of him beside her, even
though they were both fully clothed this time, was com-
forting, was what she needed. Maybe, knowing he was
here, she really could go to sleep and shut out the memory of what had happened just now. The drum . . . those
things on the bureau . . . Margal's voice reaching her
through the drumming and chanting . . .

I won't do it! I won't! I love him!

But could she resist? At that awful place called the
Devil's Leap, she had not been able to resist him when
he ordered her to turn on Kay Gilbert and drag her over
the edge.

But she was tired now. So tired after the long jeep ride
and what had happened in Daddy's room. Her eyes
closed. With Sam's arm around her, giving her a feeling
of security, she at last fell asleep.

Later, much later, she heard her father's voice and
realized she was awake, alone on the bed. Sam was no
longer beside her.

There was torment in the voice, an agony, as though
Daddy were being forced to use all his strength in his
effort to reach her. As though he were hanging by his
fingertips from the cliff trail at Saut Diable, knowing he
must fall but scratching to hold on just a little longer.

"Turgeau, Milly . . . I am in Turgeau. Please try to
find me, but be careful . . . oh, God, be careful. He is a

fiend, that man. Don't let him into your mind or he will own you. . ."

The word "Turgeau" was repeated several times. Then the voice faded away to nothing, and she fell asleep again.

Downstairs, Sam Norman was on the telephone. He had been there for half an hour, trying to get through to Jacmel despite the late hour. At last, a voice answered, and it was the one he wanted—the proprietor of the pension at which he had lived while working there.

"Leon? Sam Norman. Sorry if I got you out of bed, old boy, but—"

"*Who* is speaking?"

"Sam Norman. So soon you forget, hey?"

"*My* Sam Norman? It can't be! Sam! What are you doing back in Haiti? When did you arrive? How long will you be staying? When are you coming to see me?"

"Whoa, Leon, whoa. One thing at a time."

"But I am overwhelmed. I never dreamed—"

"At the moment, I need some information, Leon, and it's late. We can talk about other things later, hey? Just tell me one thing. You remember that fellow Fenelon— the sorcerer, *bocor*, witch doctor, whatever he ought to be called? The one I fought with because he was taking so much money away from my farmers?"

"Of course, *mon ami*."

"Just tell me one thing. Is he still there in Jacmel?"

"Is he still here? No. Not since just after you left."

"Where is he?"

"Nobody seems to know, Sam. He had an accident. Some strong-arm fellows from the capital came out here and beat him half to death. Broke his legs so badly they had to be amputated. When he recovered, he left, but I can't tell you where to. Some say he feared another attack and went to hide himself in the mountains. Others say he was born in the mountains anyway and just went home. Why? What do you want with such a man?"

"Nothing, Leon, believe me. It's a long story, one I'll have to tell you later when we have more time."

"Come and see me!"

"I hope I can. I want to very much."

"With that lovely woman of yours. That nurse. Have you married her yet?"

"Not yet, Leon."

"You're an idiot. Anyway, come see me and bring her with you. I'll kill a pig in your honor."

"Thanks. In any case, I won't leave Haiti without calling you again."

Sam hung up and made himself a short drink, then stood at the bar sipping it while remembering his long-ago war with the man now known as Margal.

36

The narrow blacktop streets had been fairly crowded earlier with cooks, maids, houseboys, and yardboys going to work in the area's elegant homes. With *marchandes*, too, singing out the virtues of their wares as they trudged along under head-loads of laden baskets. *"Min bel pois! Min bel café"*

But now, at ten A.M., with most servants at work and the automobile traffic thinned to a trickle, the district seemed all but deserted. The blacktop glistened under a blazing sun and sent up shimmering waves in front of Sam's prowling jeep.

"Nothing?" he asked wearily—just as he had asked all day yesterday and the day before. They had concentrated so fiercely on finding Mildred's father that he had scarcely spoken to Victor yet, for God's sake.

Beside him, looking desperate, Mildred opened her eyes and shook her head.

"But he did reach you again last night. You're sure of that?"

"Yes, Sam." *And so did Margal, interfering with what Daddy was trying so hard to tell me. I'm sure of that too, God help me.*

Sam scowled. "I can't think of any other place-name that sounds like Turgeau." In his mind he toured the

277

city, naming the parts in which a man like Dr. Bell might be invited to stay at a friend's house. It was no help. If Milly had heard the name "Turgeau" they were in the right place.

But, though for more than two hours she had concentrated fiercely on establishing contact with her father, they had drawn only a blank so far.

"Shall we call it quits for now, Milly?" He could use a drink back at the Calman. Some breakfast, too. They had been in such a hurry to get started, they had had only coffee. Good Haitian coffee, but still not much to build a morning on.

"Please . . . just a little longer, Sam. He *wants* us to find him. He said so. And he sounded so . . . so much in need of us."

"Okay."

Quiet streets, mostly up or down hill. Handsome houses with walled yards and lots of trees. Frangipani. Jacarandas. Mangos. Breadfruit. Congo-pea hedges and gaudy yellow-red flame vines. Now and then a marvelous, uplifting aroma of coffee beans being roasted over a charcoal fire in someone's yard. But nothing from Daddy.

Not a word.

Not a whisper.

"Let's go back and see what Victor has for lunch," Sam said at ten minutes to twelve by his oft-looked-at watch. "We can come here again this afternoon."

"Well . . . all right." Daddy had said, "Find me, Milly" as if his life depended on it. Why was he silent now?

With a sigh of relief, Sam turned the jeep down Avenue de Turgeau to Rue Capois and around the Champ de Mars to the pension. When he pulled into the Calman's driveway he found himself stopping behind a jeep from the Schweitzer Hospital and knew that Kay Gilbert had kept her word.

Suddenly, nothing else mattered very much.

They lunched on crab soup at the back-yard table under the almond tree, and Kay said she had delivered little Tina to her uncle an hour earlier.

"She'll be all right. He's a lot like her father, warm and decent, without the father's peasant ignorance. In the long run, it will be even better for her than if she had been accepted in Bois Sauvage."

"Good," Sam said. "She's a nice girl." He told how Mildred and he had spent the morning—and yesterday, and the day before that—unsuccessfully trying to locate Dr. Bell.

Lunch over, Mildred said she would like to go to her room for a while. "It doesn't make sense for us just to go back there and continue driving around, Sam. Perhaps if I lie down and concentrate, I can reach him again." *Just once, please God, without interference.* She stood up. "Can I look for you in about an hour, say?"

"I'll be here."

She nodded to both of them and turned away, walking slowly across the red-brick yard to the rear door of the pension. Kay looked at Sam and frowned.

"Can she do that? Get through to her father whenever she tries?"

"Not whenever. Sometimes."

"I wish I knew more about that kind of thing, Sam."

"I wish I knew more, too. I'd sure like to know how a man like Margal does what he does."

"Well, you used to say there were things in voodoo that defied explanation. And there are. Things have happened at the hospital that certainly can't be explained away as if—"

Sam stopped her by reaching across the table, over a fallen red almond leaf, to touch her hand. "Kay," he said, "shut up, will you?"

Her gaze found his eyes and she understood what she saw there. "All right."

"Tell me what I did that night."

"You know what you did."

"Only dimly. The way I might recall a bad dream."

"You . . . well . . ." Her hand turned in his, her fingers curling to interlace with his fingers, and her dark eyes continued to gaze unblinking across the table at his face. "We got into an argument. I'd been waiting for you for hours, and you hadn't even come by to see if I had arrived from the hospital yet. When I asked you why, you told me to make love to you or get the hell out."

"Make love or get out?"

"Yes."

Still holding her hand, Sam stood up. "Come on."

"Where? To your room again?" She seemed about to refuse.

"I want to talk to Victor."

"All he knows is that after I left your room, you killed a bottle of rum in a couple of hours and fell down the stairs. The two of us carried you back up and put you to bed."

"I want to know what I did before that. You told me . . . I think I remember you told me there was some kind of conspiracy of silence about what I did while I was waiting for you to show up." Still holding her hand, he circled the table and waited for her to rise. "Talk to him with me, will you?"

They walked across the waves of red brick together and found Victor Vieux at a table in his kitchen, eating a bowl of his crab soup. He rose when they entered.

"Victor, may we sit with you for a minute?" Sam asked.

Victor's wise eyes scrutinized their faces for a few seconds and his sharp mind interpreted what they saw. He silently held a chair for Kay. "You want to know whether you should be back together again," he said after re-seating himself and gently pushing the bowl of soup away. "*Mes amis,* I can't tell you how happy I am. Ever since you, Sam, telephoned me from Vermont to say you were returning to Haiti, I have been hoping for this moment. Now, how can I help?"

Sam put his elbows on the table and propped his chin on the backs of his hands. "What happened that night, Victor?"

"Where should I start?"

"With me. It began even before Kay got here, didn't it?"

"Yes, Sam. You arrived from Jacmel in a jeep that needed repairs. You were to take it over to Sylvain's, you said, and somebody would come from Jacmel in a few days to pick it up. Do you remember what you did here at the Calman?"

Sam shook his head.

"I told you Kay was not here yet, and you flew into a rage. You accused me of trying to win her away from you—all kinds of crazy things—don't ask me to repeat them, please. When I tried to remonstrate, you struck me. Knocked me down. My girls came screaming from the kitchen, and you struck them, too, but at least they stopped you from kicking me when I was on the floor. Then you stormed off again in your jeep."

Kay looked at Sam and saw his face go white as the kitchen wall behind him.

"My God," he whispered. "Victor . . . I'm so sorry."

"We know now that you drove to Sylvain's garage," Victor went on quietly. "Do you remember that?"

Again, Sam shook his head.

"Sylvain and one of his mechanics—young Pierre, the lad with whom you hunted guinea fowl so often in the Cul de Sac—disagreed with you a little about what ought to be done to the vehicle. Only a little, mind you.

But you flew into a rage and struck them both, and when Sylvain fell to the garage floor with a broken jaw, you tried to kick him senseless, but Pierre and a helper stopped you. Then you stormed out of *there*, cursing *them*."

Sam shut his eyes, then whispered, "Go on. What did I do next?"

"What you did after that, we don't know," Victor said gently. "Perhaps you just drove around the city. The girls and I talked about what you had done. We decided you must be ill. Marie even wanted to make a bush-tea drink for you, I remember—an infusion of cor-ossol leaves which is sometimes helpful in such situations. Oh, we were worried. I telephoned several places where you might be. But the hours passed with no sign of you, and then Kay arrived." He looked at Kay. "You asked Marie about her bruised face, if you remember."

Kay nodded.

Sam's face went even whiter.

"You returned. Kay was here and we talked a while, and then the two of you went up to your room, to bed. You were not drunk then, I am positive. I remember asking you why you had not left the jeep at Sylvain's and you said they hadn't the parts. Or is that what you said? Something, anyway. You were acting strangely, very strangely, but you were not intoxicated. Do you know what I think?"

"What do you think, Victor?" Kay said.

"First let me tell you why I think it. Two of your peo-ple from Jacmel—your AID people, Sam—came in for the jeep a few days later and told me something about your last day in Jacmel. It seems you sought out that fellow Fenelon there, the *bocor* who had been giving you so much trouble for so long. You went to his place and told him again to stop taking money from your farmers or you would come back for an accounting and he would regret it. Is that true?"

"I suppose so," Sam admitted. "I felt I had to do something about him before leaving, or he'd move right in."

"That was your mistake. Fenelon is no ordinary country *bocor*, I have since found out. He is nearly as famous as this Margal you went to see."

"Fenelon and Margal are the same person. I've been meaning to tell you."

"What?"

Sam explained, adding, "I phoned my old friend Leon, in Jacmel, to make sure."

Victor did not seem too startled. "My first thought," he said with a shrug, "was that the two of them probably knew each other. That they were master and pupil, perhaps. For while we have many so-called sorcerers in Haiti, few have the powers those two are said to possess."

"And you think Fenelon was responsible for what I did that day, Victor?"

"I think he accepted your challenge, *mon ami*. Yes. What you did when you arrived here in Port, turning on Sylvain at the garage, on me, on my girls, was not of your own volition. Especially not of your own doing was what you may have said or done to this woman who loves you, though what happened I don't know, of course, because I was not a fly on the wall of your room and she has never hated you enough to tell me." Victor gazed at them both for a moment, smiling now, and then stood up. "Why don't the two of you go upstairs and talk about this, eh? You don't need me anymore."

Kay frowned at him. "Wait just a minute, please. Why didn't you *tell* me this?"

"My dear, you never came around after Sam left the country. You started staying with a nurse in Petionville whenever you visited the city. Or so I've heard."

"You could have called me. Or written."

He shook his head. "How could I know there was still something between you? The wish didn't father the fact. In truth, when you stopped coming here, I was sure it was finished."

Sam stood up. His hand on Victor's shoulder, squeezing hard, conveyed his feelings. He turned to Kay, took her hand, would have walked her out of the kitchen had she not held back for a moment.

"What about Mildred?" she asked.

"Daddy can wait," Sam said firmly. "You and I have some catching up to do."

37

Dr. Roger Laurence Bell of Vermont,
once more seated in the book-lined study
of Dr. Decatus Molicoeur of Haiti,
is listening to a recital of plans by Molicoeur
for the imminent removal
of Haiti's president
and the takeover
of the country's government.
But Dr. Bell is not able to give the Haitian
his undivided attention.

Dr. Bell has been hearing the voice of Margal,
not weakly as from a great distance
but so strongly that he feels
the *bocor* must now be somewhere close by.
In truth,
the voice now thunders in his head
the way it did
when he sat in the room of many colors
hour by hour and day by day
as Margal's pupil.

Has the legless one followed him here
to witness the death of his enemy

and the fall of the government?

The *bocor* is surely not far from this house.
And his message is clear.
And Dr. Bell is fully aware now
of the futility
of trying to resist.

Dr. Molicoeur
mechanically continues his recital.
Though desperately unwilling
to do what he has been ordered to do,
he has been remarkably efficient.
The president may be dead as early as tomorrow.

But now, unexpectedly,
a voice from the Pension Calman
breaks into Molicoeur's dissertation,
interrupting the voice of Margal as well.
Dr. Bell finds himself
holding up a hand for silence.
Fiercely, he concentrates on a message
from his daughter Mildred.

"My dear Milly," he replies
without moving his lips.
"It is not necessary for you to find me.
I will meet you instead.
Leave your hotel.
Walk through the Champ de Mars
to the statue of Henri Christophe.
I will talk to you there.

"Yes, Daddy."

Dr. Bell once more fastens his gaze

on the face of Dr. Molicoeur.
"I must go to my room for a moment.
Then I wish to be driven to the Champ de Mars.
Wait for me in the driveway with your car."

Upstairs,
he takes a small bottle of aspirin tablets
from a cabinet in his private bathroom,
empties it,
and pours into it three drops
of the colorless liquid from that other bottle
given him days ago by Margal.
Descending the stairs,
he walks out of the house.
The car is waiting in the driveway.
Dr. Molicoeur is at the wheel.

"Where in the Champ de Mars, Dr. Bell?"
"To the statue of Christophe, please."
With only a nod,
Molicoeur puts the machine in motion.
They reach the road round the park.
They stop near the statue.

Between rows of shrubbery,
along a path,
Dr. Bell proceeds briskly,
to a handsome pedestal.
A heroic figure rides a muscled horse.
There he waits,
a fragile, unassuming figure
under the relentless midday sun.
And to this spot a little later
comes his daughter Mildred.
At sight of him
she breaks into a run

and completes her journey
with arms outflung
and a cry on her lips.

Dr. Bell sternly lifts a hand
to halt her.
"You are late."

She looks at him in bewilderment,
sudden despair.
"But Daddy . . ."
His eyes silence her.
She stares back at him,
terrified.

In a low, mechanical voice,
he tells her exactly what she must do.

Then, handing her the aspirin bottle,
Dr. Bell walks back to the waiting car.
To the sad-faced man at the wheel he says,
"We can return to your house now, my friend,
and finish our discussion."

In his head, the voice of Margal,
surely traveling no great distance now,
triumphantly purrs.

38

"We ought to go back downstairs, darling," Kay Gilbert whispered to Sam Norman. "Mildred does want to find her father, you know."

Naked and in a head-to-toe embrace, they lay in each other's arms on Sam's bed, spent now but still entwined and clinging. It was like it had been before, Sam thought, a little awesome in its intensity. But better in some ways, too, because all the doubts were gone now, all the questions answered.

"Are you going to tell Mildred about us?" Kay asked.

"Of course."

"Let me go down with you, then. And, Sam . . ."

"What, baby?"

"Find her father soon, will you? Put the two of them on a plane as quick as you can. When do you have to be back in Vermont yourself?"

"I don't have to be back at all. I don't have to teach at the blasted college. There are jobs open in forestry; I'm already approved for a good one. I could even land something here until your Schweitzer commitment runs out."

"Darling, that's great."

Sam folded her against him for a last kiss, and it was a long one with his free hand straying over all the parts of her it could reach. The feeling returned that there was something total about loving this woman, and always had been. After two long, empty years he now felt they had never been apart.

Dressed again, they descended the stairs and found Mildred waiting at one of the small tables in the bar, with two drinks in front of her. Looking annoyed, she pushed one of the glasses toward Sam as he and Kay sat down.

"I was beginning to think I'd have to go without you."

Sam said, "Sorry," and reached for Kay's hand. Holding it, he gazed solemnly across the table and said, "I've got something to tell you, Milly. When we've found your father, I won't be going back to the States with you. Kay and I are getting married."

"Well . . . congratulations."

Sam searched her face for an emotion but found none. Strange. He had thought she was fond of him—a little, at least.

She was oddly pale, he noticed. Had been even before Kay and he sat down. Her eyes were peculiarly lack-lustre, as though she were not entirely aware of what she was doing.

"Drink your drink," she said, indicating the rum and soda she had pushed in front of him. "Time is precious. Let's not waste any."

Sam said with a shrug, "Why repeat the morning's mistake, Milly? There's time enough to be sensible. Did you get through to your father?" He handed his drink to Kay. "Take this, Kay. I'll make another." Rising, he turned to the bar.

Mildred's sudden gasp caused him to turn again and stare at her in astonishment. Kay was staring, too. The pale face had gone so white it seemed splashed with milk. Her mouth was open and quivering, and her clenched hands made a drumming sound on the table top.

Automatically lifting her glass to her lips as she leaned forward, Kay said through an anxious frown, "What's wrong? Mildred, what's the *matter* with you?"

"Oh, my God!" Mildred lurched to her feet and stood there swaying, gazing hypnotically at the glass in Kay's hand. Sam saw her face change from stark white to a ghastly dark red as blood rushed back into it. Saw her eyes fill with a sudden rush of horror. "Oh, my God!" she shrieked. "No, Kay! Don't!" Then her arm slashed across the table, and the glass passed from Kay's hand into her own, just as the sandal that day had passed from Kay's foot to the foot of the woman on the donkey. Only a little of the amber liquid splashed out.

Mildred stood there clutching the glass and screaming, "My God, I can't live like this any more! I can't! I won't! That awful man owns both of us! It's impossible!" Turning her gaze wildly on Kay, then on Sam, she walked backward from the table, screamed again and jabbed the glass at her mouth.

Her head went back. Before Sam could even move to stop her, the amber liquid was down her throat, the glass falling from her hand to the floor, where it bounced on the wood without breaking, then struck a metal lamp base and burst into fragments.

Struggling for breath, with both hands gripping her throat, Mildred sank to the floor while Sam stumbled toward her and Kay stood frozen, staring in horror.

39

"Everything is in readiness,"
Dr. Molicoeur says sadly.
"I am to breakfast with him tomorrow.
Before his coffee is finished
he will be dead.
At that hour,
our people will be in the palace
ready to step in and take over.
Nothing will go wrong.
I wish to God something might,
but it will not.
Dr. Bell,
for what you have done to my mind
I despise you even while obeying you."

"We are two of a kind, then, my friend,
because I despise my master
while obeying *him*."

A gentle knock on the door interrupts them.
Dr. Molicoeur looks questioningly at Dr. Bell.
Bell nods.
"Come in," Molicoeur calls out.
The door opens.

His lovely young wife enters.

"Will you be ready for lunch soon, you two?"
She smiles in her innocence.
"I think so, darling. Yes."
She departs, closing the door.

Dr. Bell rises, gently sighing.
A change takes place in his face.
The sadness becomes bewilderment.
Then shock.
And then horror.
"No, Mildred, no!
Oh, my poor child . . ."
He turns wildly to his host.
"I must leave you!"
He rushes across the study,
claws the door open and races down the hall.
He wrenches the front door open.
He descends the veranda steps to the driveway.
He gasps down the road
toward the Champ de Mars.

Dr. Molicoeur follows, unnoticed behind.
He prays, for the sake of his wife and child,
that something may have happened
to postpone the morrow.

Dr. Bell is entering a whirlpool
likely to suck him down.
Someone is telling him to halt,
to go back,
to cease his rebellion,
return to blind obedience,
or suffer the consequences.
With every step he takes,

the voice grows more threatening.

He races down Rue Magny
to the park where he spoke to his daughter.
He runs through the park,
along a path lined with shrubs and beds of bright
flowers.
The voice is stronger with every stride.
He struggles to reach the Pension Calman,
knowing that he is nearing also
the man with no legs.
Margal has indeed come from his place of iniquity
in the mountains.

He gasps for breath.
He looks wildly about him.
Which of the many houses
harbors the fiend?
The many different kinds of houses:
old and new ones,
large and small,
fragile coops of the very poor.
Everywhere in this land
the peasant shack stands next to the mansion.

Where is Margal?
Close by, without a doubt.
His raging voice is almost too loud to be defied.
But Mildred is dying.

At the Calman.
Dr. Bell stumbles on the red-brick driveway.
Limp with weariness,
he staggers into the pension.
His daughter lies on a sofa in the big front room.

A strange man, on his knees beside her,
a stethoscope over her heart.
Sam Norman, a young woman Dr. Bell does not know
stand hand in hand, intently watching.

Tears flow down his cheeks.
Dr. Bell approaches the sofa.
He gazes down at his daughter.
The voice of Margal,
fearsomely close by,
thunders death, destruction in his head . . .

40

"Dr. Bell!"

The name burst from Sam Norman in a muffled explosion as he turned from the couch and saw Mildred's father lurching toward him. Bell's face told of his torment and the conflict raging within him.

Grabbing at Sam's arm, the older man stood there swaying. "Will she . . . Sam, will she die?"

The doctor answered that, rising from his knees and facing them. "I am sorry," he said in French. "There is nothing I can do."

Releasing Sam's arm, Bell sank to his knees to peer into his daughter's face. The face seemed strangely peaceful now, though only a few moments ago it had been a battleground of emotions.

Sam looked at Kay but said nothing.

Bell rose to his feet.

A change had come over him with the realization that his daughter was beyond rescue. A cold fury had replaced the conflict there. Sam stepped away, half expecting to be blamed and attacked for what had happened. But the fury was not directed at him. Without even a glance at him, the man from Vermont strode briskly across the room to the door.

Letting go Kay's hand, Sam said under his breath,

"Wait here for me, baby. Okay?"

She nodded. "But be careful!"

He followed Bell out of the pension.

At the big open gate, Bell hesitated, but only for a few seconds while turning his head left and right as if to home in on a signal he was receiving. Turning to his right, he went quickly along the sidewalk, past the pension's ornate fence, with Sam twenty paces behind him. When he turned right again, it was to enter the unpaved driveway of one of the smaller, older houses fronting the Champ de Mars, almost directly opposite the Palais National.

Warily, Sam followed.

Dr. Bell walked quickly up the driveway and into a small rear yard fenced with rusty sheets of zinc. Under an aged soursop tree grazed a mule that he had seen at Margal's compound in Legrun: a big, dark-brown beast capable of bearing a heavy burden. Bell paused to frown at a strange device lying on the ground nearby amid saddle-mats of woven banana trash.

It was a chair of bamboo, obviously designed to be placed on a mule's back. Was it the chair in which the legless *bocor* had been conveyed here from his mountain retreat, with some of his servitors leading the animal over those difficult mountain trails and attending to his physical comfort during the journey?

I am right, Bell thought, clenching his hands in fury. *He is here, this monster who caused my daughter's death.*

At the back of the house, a flight of rickety wooden steps angled up to a second-floor veranda that looked as though it might collapse under the weight of any man who dared tread on it. Bell put a trembling hand on the railing and gingerly ascended. They would be in an up-stairs room from which they could watch the palace, would they not? He thought so.

As he reached the top of the stairs, Sam Norman en-

tered the yard below and looked up. Saw Bell go gingerly along the rotting veranda and halt before a closed
door. The door was red, or had been once, and bore on
its upper half a voodoo symbol containing three black
circles in a row.

Bell cautiously opened it and stepped inside, out of
Sam's line of vision.

Sam approached the stairs and climbed them slowly,
testing each before trusting it with his weight. Reaching
the veranda, he looked along it at the termite-eaten
boards and winced with apprehension, reminding himself that Dr. Roger Bell of Vermont weighted con-
siderably less than he did. Then he grasped the veranda
rail and made his way carefully toward the red door,
which was now open.

When he had left the veranda, Dr. Bell found himself
in a narrow corridor that ran from the back of the house
to the front. For this time of day it was surprisingly
dark, perhaps because the four doors it contained, two
on each side, were closed and there were no windows. A
door at the front was half open, however, allowing a
shaft of sunlight from some window in the room facing
the Champ de Mars to slant into the hall. It was toward
this that Bell slowly made his way, fully aware of his
peril.

The voice in his head was a hiss now, and he well
knew what that could mean. During his apprenticeship
in Legrun, Margal had been hissingly angry with him a
number of times. Twice he had been made to crawl back
to his quarters, across the compound, on his hands and
knees. On a third, more terrible occasion he had been
forced to make the journey on his belly, like a
salamander, pausing every few yards to scrape up
donkey droppings in his path and eat them. "To teach
you to obey me," the legless one had hissed. "For until

you have learned to obey *me*, you cannot know how to make others obey *you*!"

There were voices in the room he was approaching, and he slowed his pace to a silent shuffle, barely moving his feet. Had he turned back when he neared the source of the voices, he would have seen Sam Norman at the red door behind him, but he did not turn.

Reaching the doorway in front, he flattened himself against the wall beside it and tried to hear what was being said. And heard, but it was in Creole and therefore incomprehensible to him. Had Margal always spoken to him in English? He did not know. Mostly, the cripple had talked to him through his mind, reaching him with thoughts alone. Perhaps thoughts needed no language.

I never should have begun this study. A man needs a stronger mind than mine, a mind able to resist the hellish forces it may encounter. From the very beginning—from those first innocent experiments with Mildred—I've been stupidly playing with demons . . .

The sounds in the room had ceased. He inched closer to the open doorway and dared to look in. The room held four persons.

Margal sat on a wooden lawn chair that had wide, flat arms and a mound of pillows to keep his crippled body comfortable.

The tall, wasp-waisted man lounging on an ordinary kitchen chair near the window was Ti Pierre Bastien, the Haitian who had taken Bell to Legrun.

On the floor, beside Margal's chair, sat a second Haitian named Volny, equally strong but mindless, capable only of following the *bocor's* orders. A zombie? Perhaps. At the compound he had performed only menial tasks.

The fourth man was the blond Nazi who, after traveling all the way from Schleswig-Holstein to beg the *bocor's* help, had stupidly offended him and ended up with nothing. Less than nothing. Seeing him there, Bell vividly remembered the morning of the man's downfall.

"What command am I directing into your mind, M'sieu Hauser?"

"You are telling me to kneel before you."

"But you are not kneeling."

"This is nonsense! I am receiving the command. Be satisfied with that. Only to my Führer would I kneel, and he is dead."

"M'sieu Hauser, I warn you—I am not a patient man."

"You speak to a future ruler of the world, Margal, not to some stupid Haitian peasant! I have already told you who I am! I warn *you* not to think I can be—"

What had happened then, in that room of many colors, was a thing that might happen again here in this house on the Champ de Mars, Bell knew, if he dared to step into Margal's presence and challenge the man. One moment, the German had been standing there before the sorcerer's chair, glaring in defiance. Next moment, he had been gasping for breath with his hands clutching his neck while his knees went limp, his body sagged, and slowly, writhing in agony, he had collapsed on the floor. In the two or three awful minutes before his struggles ceased, he uttered no sound louder than a gasp or moan, certainly nothing like a scream, although his blue eyes, hideously wide, had once looked at the legless creature on the chair and surely begged for mercy.

Fat Clarisse, Margal's woman, had come then, in response to the sorcerer's summons, and picked the Nazi up and carried him to another room. And when Bell saw him the following day, he had been as he was now, a man whose mind and will—both remarkably strong before—had apparently been taken from him, leaving only an empty shell to obey Margal's orders with never a murmur of protest.

If I face Margal now, I could end up like that, God help

me. But he killed Mildred! He killed Mildred!

He looked down at his hands. They were all he had. The cripple had given him no weapon when sending him on this mission to the capital; had told him he would need none if he had learned his lessons well.

The hands curled now, aching to fasten on Margal's throat. Sucking in a deep breath to steady his thudding heart, Dr. Bell stepped from the corridor wall and strode into the room.

On the big wooden lawn chair, Margal stiffened at sight of him. The seemingly frail body became rigid, and the powerful hands gripped the chair arms like metal claws.

By the window, Ti Pierre Bastien stared at Bell in mild astonishment, letting his lower jaw drop so that his mouth resembled a frog's.

The two zombies seemed unaware that anything had happened.

Bell strode forward, arms extended, fingers twitching. His hands had never closed on any man's neck before, but they would do so now. Were they strong enough to squeeze the life from the creature facing him? He was not sure, but he could try.

Propelled by his fury, he covered half the distance. Then the sorcerer's gaze met his.

Margal seemed not to move—not even his lips. But his eyes were lasers and the voice in Bell's head was a shriek commanding him to halt.

He shuffled to a stop.

Now the legless body did move a little, leaning slightly toward him. One hand rose from the chair-arm, and a bony forefinger pointed. Though yards from Bell's chest, it felt like an arrow shot into him.

"Kneel, Dr. Bell!"

"No! I will not!"

"Kneel!"

The agony in Bell's chest climbed into his throat and

cut off his breathing. His hands fluttered to his neck and squeezed, trying in vain to drive the pain out. Slowly, he sank to his knees.

A weapon . . . he should have brought a weapon . . . but where could he have obtained one? Never in his life had he used a firearm, anyway . . .

The room began to spin, and the figure on the chair, triumphantly holding him with his gaze, began to blur and fade in a turbulent fog of redness. No one else had moved; that was the astonishing thing. No one but Margal, and Margal, only slightly.

From the doorway Sam Norman saw it happen and brashly rushed into it.

Voicing a kind of kamikaze yell, surely an involuntary bellow, Sam reached the groveling figure of Dr. Bell and hurdled it. Not for him the hypnotic gaze of the figure on the chair; he had seen its effect on Bell and kept his eyes averted.

His headlong rush carried him to the chair itself. His groping hands found its big flat arms and heaved upward. The chair went over backward, and the legless man rolled out of it onto the floor, frothing at the mouth in his fury.

Sam dived over the chair and landed on top of him. Got him under the arms. Reared back and stood up, lifting him high. Hurled him into the wall.

Margal fell. A splash of scarlet marked the wall where some part of him had struck it. Hitting the floor on his stumps of legs, he drove his knuckles against the ancient boards to hold himself erect.

A hideous, shattered figure, he nevertheless still had a gaze that could drill into Sam's eyes and cause a bolt of lightning to explode in his head. The lightning was followed by a voice so terrible, it threatened to crack Sam's skull.

Will yourself dead, white man! Die!

Sam shook it off and strove to attack again. Managed two steps and felt himself no longer in this rotting house in the heart of Port-au-Prince but on a vast, empty plain, battling a hurricane of fiery wind. Floating in space before him, the face of Margal took on a leer of triumph while the wind turned into a rushing wall of flame that seemed certain to burn the clothes from his body and sear the flesh from his bones.

He knew what was happening. It had happened before, hadn't it?—not only to him but to the others. The sudden flash flood at the river. The monstrous lizard on the bed. Mildred's attempts to drown herself at Vallière. The terrifying illusions at Devil's Leap.

Damn you, Fenelon, you can't do this to me!

He took a step forward and the flames closed around him, blinding him with their crimson fury.

Will yourself dead, white man!

"To hell with you, Fenelon!"

In the midst of the flames, barring his way, loomed a figure he dimly recognized as the tall, thin-waisted man who had been sitting by the window. A horizontal forearm came at him like a fence rail, aimed to shatter his throat and stop his breathing.

Sam jerked himself aside and slammed a fist into the confident face above it. The fist jolted the face aside. The fence-rail arm wilted as the man fell. But against the wall Margal continued to scream.

"Die, white man, die! Do you not hear me?"

Floating in flames there, the face of the legless sorcerer was that of a devil in a fiery furnace. To reach him, Sam had to enter the furnace. With arms outflung, he went in, ignoring the reek of smoke in his nostrils and the feeling he was being burned alive.

It won't work this time, Fenelon. We're not at Saut Diable. This is just a room in a house on the Champ de

Mars, and the house is not on fire. You're through anyway, damn you. Can't you feel your voice growing weaker?

True, the voice shrieking its monstrous commands inside his head was less shrill. Being slammed into the wall must have taken more from the *bocor* than the smear of blood left on the cracked plaster. But was the fire wholly an illusion? A searing pain in his left leg caused Sam to stop and look down. His pants were ablaze in a way the rest of the room was not. He dropped on one knee to slap at the flaming cloth, and the pain leaped to his hands.

Was it possible? Had Margal this time created an illusion so powerful it had bridged the gap and become reality? He looked up—straight into the sorcerer's crimson face, now only five or six feet away. It wore an unholy leer of triumph, and the voice in Sam's head, too, was obscene with triumph.

Burn, white man, burn! No one defies Margal!

Sam straightened again, snarled "Damn you!" and attempted another step forward. Made it and was about to try another when a voice stopped him. It came from the hall doorway and was a real voice this time, not one in his tortured mind.

"Step aside, M'sieu!"

He lurched about. Into the room strode two men in Khaki army uniforms, each with an M-1 rifle at the hip. Sam dived out of their line of fire and the weapons jerked into action, filling the room with chatter.

Against the wall, the legless body of Margal danced weirdly for a few seconds on the rigid arms that held it erect and then, riddled, collapsed to the floor.

The rifles swept to other targets. To the broad-shouldered man, now on his feet again, whom Sam had felled with a fist to the face. To the blond, vacant-faced German and his fellow zombie. Then to the sprawled figure of Dr. Bell, but Sam's yell ripped through the room to stop that.

"No!" he bellowed in Creole. "That one's an American—not one of them!"

The guns were silent. Advancing, the two soldiers walked past Sam with scarcely a glance at him and frowned down at Margal. Into the room after them came a man Sam did not know: a handsome Haitian who hurried over to Dr. Bell, now struggling to rise, and with obvious compassion helped the older man to his feet.

The smoke in the room was thickening. Alive with crackling sounds and streaks of scarlet now, it rose from parts of the old wooden floor to swirl darkly to the ceiling. Sam's pant leg burst into flames again. He knelt to slap the flames out.

"This man is still alive, Dr. Molicoeur," one of the soldiers said, peering down at Margal.

Molicoeur left Dr. Bell and walked over to the sorcerer. Sam followed. The legless body lay in a spreading pool of blood, but the eyes were wide behind a thickening film, and the mouth was moving.

But the voice was not the one Sam had heard in the room of many colors at Legrun. Nor was it the one he had just been hearing in his head, screaming at him to die.

It was that of little Tina, saying defiantly in Creole, "I won't, I won't! I'll run away, you'll see. The very first time you send me for water or firewood I'll just run away because you're a wicked man."

The voice changed. Deepening, it became that of Dr. Bell, speaking English. On hearing it above the sputter and crackle of the flames from the blazing floor, Bell came limping over to stare, astonished, at the twisted lips from which it issued.

"I wish only to learn from you. No, no, I will not do

this terrible thing you ask of me. I wish only to learn! I know nothing of your president or your country's politics. You must not force me to do this thing."

Suddenly, the voice caused Sam to stiffen as though an electric current had shot through him. It was his own voice now—distorted, unnatural, snarling, but his nevertheless.

"Listen you . . . I'm sick of this shit. Are you coming to bed or not? Either get into this Goddamned bed or get out of this room!"

Then the sorcerer's mutterings drifted into another tongue, slowly and brokenly now as he became weaker.

"*Ich bin der Sohn von Adolph Hitler . . .*"

"Dr. Bell!" Sam reached for the man at his side. "You speak German. What is he saying?"

"I am the son of Adolph Hitler . . ."

"*. . . und muss meines Vaters Arbeit weiter ausueben . . .*"

"And must continue my father's work . . ."

"*Du musst den dummen Wunsch . . .*"

"You must abandon your stupid desire for revenge . . . you ignorant black fool . . . it is childish. Help me and I offer you a share of the world . . . the whole world . . ."

Margal's mouth stopped moving. The eyes still stared up at those watching, but saw nothing. One of the soldiers said anxiously, "Dr. Molicoeur, if we don't get out of here—"

"What shall we do with these people?" Molicoeur asked, frowning at those on the floor. "Is there time, do you think, to—"

"No, no! It is better to leave them! Who knows what life may be left in them to rise again? Let them burn!"

Molicoeur led the way, holding the arm of his fellow doctor of philosophy. Sam, trailing the two soldiers from the room, had to pick his way through spurts of flame and hold his breath to keep the smoke from filling his lungs.

When he turned in the doorway for a last look back, the bodies on the floor were ablaze in a room swiftly becoming the fiery furnace it had earlier only seemed to be.

"Dr. Bell, good-bye. I'm sorry it had to end this way for you." Sam put out his hand.

With his flight ready for boarding, the man from Vermont had time only to press the hand, then turn to Kay and wish her happiness again. He had not been able to attend the wedding at the Calman yesterday; it had been the fourth and final day of his interrogation by the authorities.

He was perspiring now, and Sam guessed it was only partly because of the heat. Inside the airport, something to do with the climate control apparently wasn't working. Outside, the sun beat fiercely on roofs and runways.

"You've no idea when I shall be seeing you again?" Bell directed the question and his gaze at them both.

Sam shrugged. "A year or so, maybe."

"Can you be happy that long in this strange country?"

"We were before," Kay said, smiling.

"Ah, yes. Well . . . thank you for your help. And good-bye."

Bell's step was heavy as he turned away. The plane taking him to New York would also be carrying the body of his only daughter.

Sam reached for the hand of the woman beside him. They would be staying a few days more at the Calman; then Sam would begin his job, overseeing a farming operation in the Artibonite, only a few miles from the hospital. Except when Mrs. Sam Norman had night duty, they would spend their nights together.

Dr. Bell turned for a final wave, and they waved back. Sam put an arm around his wife.

"Shall we have a drink at the bar here or go back to Victor's for something more interesting, Madame?"

"Let's go back, M'sieu," she said. "Who needs a drink?"

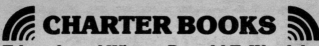

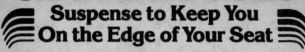